She closed her eyes and enjoyed every stroke of his hands, thinking how nice it was to be with him. Her breathing deepened as she felt his lips softly kissing her on the back of her neck and shoulders. Spinning her around on the stool, he continued on the front with Shante giving in to every kiss. She felt his hands slowly go down her back and brace her buttocks. She wanted to pull back, but couldn't. He lifted her body up onto the granite countertop of the island and stood between her legs, passionately kissing her. She felt the hardness of her nipples as they pressed against his chest.

She wanted to stop herself but couldn't. Fornication was against everything she believed in, everything she represented, but this was different. It wasn't mere lust; it was love. She wanted to express it. How could she without crossing the line? She was never a tease. However, she wanted to feel his hard body against hers. Maybe she could touch his body without allowing him to enter hers. So, she pulled his neatly tucked-in shirt out of his pants, slipped her hands underneath and slowly moved her hand up and down his muscular back.

∽⧉∾

LADY PREACHER

K. T. RICHEY

Genesis Press, Inc.

INDIGO

An imprint of Genesis Press, Inc.
Publishing Company

Genesis Press, Inc.
P.O. Box 101
Columbus, MS 39703

ISBN: 13 DIGIT : 978-1-58571-333-2
ISBN: 10 DIGIT : 1-58571-333-3
Manufactured in the United States of America

First Edition

Visit us at www.genesis-press.com
or call at 1-888-Indigo-1-4-0

DEDICATION

First, I must give all praise and honor to God who has been my all—Comforter, Peace, Joy, Healer, Provider, and more than I could ever express. Without Him, I would not be here today.

I must thank my family: my daughter, Andrea, who has been the light of my life. Thank you for your support and for being such a wonderful person. My parents: L.C. and Juanita and my siblings: Charles, Russell, Michael, and Rodney; my brother-in-law, Stanley and my sister-in-law, Lola, I thank you for everything you have done for me and Andrea throughout the years. Even when you did not understand my vision, you supported me and I will never forget your help. To my niece and nephews: Charvis, Jewell, Johnathan and Aaron, thanks for keeping me entertained. Charvis, keep your head up!

Everyone should have anointed friends like mine. First to Sandra Allen, the loving, motherly friend, thank you for allowing me to cry on your shoulders and having a listening ear when times were tough. Thank you, Thomas, Mama Rose, Lucky, Ariel and the children for allowing me time at your home to rest and vent.

To Ruby Harmon, the keep-it-real, matter-of-fact friend. Thank you for your encouragement and your diary and all the times you reminded me of what God said. See the manifestation! Keep the faith. It's not over. Girl, go get that money.

To Melisa Strong, a tiny woman with a big voice, the cheerleader. No one can out-yell you. Thank you for being so upbeat every time I talked with you and reminding me of the goodness of God. God has great work for you. Keep on praising.

To Pastor Ronald D. Barton, the comedian and classmate from Morris College. Thank you for keeping laughter in my life during the good and the bad.

To Victoria Christopher Murray, I thank you so much for your integrity and your help. Thank you for guiding me in the right direction and encouraging me along the way.

To Chandra Sparks Taylor, I could not have done it without you. Thank you for your firm hand and clear direction.

To the Genesis family, Deborah Schumaker and all that help me through this process, I thank you for all you have taught me and allowing me to minister through print.

I have much love for the pastors and ministries that have supported my ministry throughout the years: Rev. C.S. Sanders, the late First Lady Margaret Sanders and the Pilgrim Rest Baptist Church family; Pastor Curtis Johnson, First Lady Charla Johnson, and the Valley Brook Baptist Church family; Pastor Ronnie Williams, First Lady Helen Williams and the Generostee Baptist Church family; Pastor Jerry Greene, Elder Agnes Greene and the Perfecting The Heart Ministries family and

Pastor Mary Nance and the St. James Pentecostal Holiness Church family. To the Ananias Christian Center crew in South Carolina, Philadelphia, New York, New Jersey, the Caribbean and Europe, pastor loves you. You hold a special place in my heart. You are the best group of people in the world. I have nothing but love for you.

Finally, I dedicate this book to a great Southern writer, Eudora Welty, who told me when I was eighteen years old that I was going to be a writer and I laughed. Almost thirty years have gone by and now that, which she had spoken, has come to pass.

CHAPTER 1

Shante Dogan hated these conferences. "Seems like every preacher on the East Coast is here," she griped to herself as she surveyed the room at the opening day reception of the Seventy-sixth Annual Convocation of the East Coast Ministerial Association and listened to the steady buzz of ministers loudly greeting one another. Last year, almost five thousand had been in attendance; this year, it looked like many more than that seemed to be crammed into this small reception area.

Despite her distaste, she had attended many of these conferences in the past. To her, it was always the same old thing: a bunch of preachers trying to out-preach or out-sing each other hoping to fill their calendars with speaking invitations for the next year. It was always a diverse gathering—Baptist, Methodist, Pentecostal, male, female, black, white, Asian, Hispanic. Year in, year out, the overall mix was basically the same. In fact, the only notable change year-to-year has been in the names of the churches. Traditional names like Mt. Calvary, St. Paul, and King David had morphed into names like Worship and Praise Cathedral, Morning Glory Christian Centers International, and Jehovah Jireh Street Ministries. Some had names so far from the mainstream Shante had to wonder what name-changing process they'd gone through.

Everyone had a business card. Preachers love to show off their titles: bishop, elder, right reverend, or prophet. *This is definitely the year of the apostle. I have twenty-three cards, and sixteen of them are apostles,* Shante reflected, flipping through what she'd collected thus far.

"Hello, Pastor Dogan," a deep voice said, "I see you made it back this year." A light-skinned, morbidly overweight man in a bright yellow suit stood in front of her wearing a big, countrified grin.

"Oh yeah." One look at his suit and Shante found it hard to keep a straight face. *Where does he find his clothes,* she wondered. "You know I can't miss one of these meetings. How are you doing, Bishop Thompson?"

"Oh, I'm blessed and highly favored. How are you?"

"I'm quite well. How is Mother? Is she feeling better now?"

"She's doing much better. You know she got out of the hospital. The doctor thinks they got all the cancer during the surgery. She'll be starting chemotherapy next week. I wanted to stay with her, but she encouraged me to come here. Thank you so much for the flowers. Yellow roses are her favorite," Bishop Thompson said as he moved closer to her and lowered his voice. "So, have you found that husband yet?"

"Bishop, don't start that again." She smiled, taking a sip from her cup of juice. It was her protection from the flesh-pressing horde. As long as she held on to it no one would get too close. But Bishop was a different story. He had taken it as his mission to get her married and was always telling her God was sending her a husband.

Getting married was the last thing on Shante's mind. There were times when she had thought about it, but she was much too busy to get into a serious relationship. Besides, many men seemed intimidated by her success and the fact that she was a preacher.

"Well, you know I told you what the Lord revealed to me," he said, moving closer still and practically whispering. "He's probably here at this conference. Mingle a little. He just might find you."

"Bishop, leave me alone," she said, smiling affectionately. "I'm getting away from you. Tell Mother I'll continue to pray for her. I'll call her when I get back home."

She left the bishop and walked quickly toward the refreshments table. Midway there, she heard a voice that made her shiver: her ex-husband, Kevin Bryson.

"Hey, Doobie. Where are you going so quickly?"

"I would appreciate it if you didn't call me that," she responded. "Excuse me. I have to go speak to someone," she said and kept walking. She dreaded running into him. Their marriage had not been a happy one, and she had gone to considerable length to distance herself from him. The mere sight of him caused memories from a deep part of her heart to surface, followed by emotions she had fought hard to repress. She had to keep thoughts of him at bay and tried to stay focused on her sermon and on her purpose for being at the conference.

The room reeked with clashing colognes. She hated shaking the hands of many of the male attendees, as their scents would transfer to her hands. God forbid they hug her. Then the foul mix would be all over and she would smell as if she had bathed in something concocted by aliens. She tried hard not to touch too many people, but touching was almost an art form at a conference like this and almost impossible to avoid. The smell was beginning to sicken her. She dug into her purse for a mint to calm her stomach.

"Look a here, look a here," a hoarse voice said from behind her.

Shante sighed, knowing what was coming next. At that moment, she thought about how hard it was for a lady preacher to attend these meetings and remain untouched by random acts of lechery. There always seemed to be a piranha in the midst trying to hit on you.

In this setting where it didn't matter how many degrees a woman had or how long she had been a preacher, she was bound to encounter someone trying to test her faith. She thought it troubling people saw women preachers as temple whores and felt free to make suggestive remarks in their presence or even touch their bodies at will. She felt the reason for this kind of behavior was fairly simple: Some men didn't take a woman's ministry seriously.

Shante had earned her master's degree in counseling. She had been in the ministry nine years and had been a pastor for the last seven at the New Pilgrim Baptist Church. She was proud to have been unanimously elected pastor after serving under Reverend Claude Anderson until his death.

She was recognized as an astute businesswoman, a dedicated community leader, and a dynamic minister of the gospel. She had taken New Pilgrim from 250 members at the time of Reverend Anderson's death to more than two thousand members today. Her leadership had put New Pilgrim in the forefront of community improvements, educational reform, and economic development.

She was highly respected and loved by young and old; the young for her honest, straightforward talk and sense of humor and the old because she continued to incorporate the old songs and sayings into her sermons. Everyone loved her for her teaching, preaching, and bright personality. She was a much sought-after speaker for conferences, revivals, and other events, but none of that mattered to this man, and she knew it.

She knew he was looking at her butt. She was forty-five years old and she knew she looked good. She worked out daily to remain fit and physically able to meet all the pastoral demands of a busy metropolitan church.

"Hey, pretty lady."

She turned and was face to face with a short, elderly man who was openly leering at her. He looked old enough to be her grandfather. "Hello, Apostle Jenkins," she said, looking at his conference badge.

"I was checking you out across the room. You know you're a classy piece of ass," he said, subtlety not being one of his finer virtues.

That he tried to come on to her did not surprise Shante. However, she was stunned he was bold enough as to say something like that to her in a roomful of ministers. Staring at the old man dressed in a shiny gray suit with a jacket ending below his knees she said, "Excuse me?"

"You're a classy piece of ass. As I always say, ass without class don't do anything for me. So what are you doing later on tonight? Maybe we can . . ." Taking no note of her expression, he continued his clumsy come-on. She was insulted. Here she was at a conference of ministers—one of the keynote speakers—and this man didn't care. He was only looking at her as a female and, therefore, easy prey. *Well, today he picked the wrong sister.*

"If you think I'm one of those temple whores you meet at these meetings, you better think again. I'm a woman of God. I'm not interested," she whispered in a tone that left no doubt she wasn't playing with him. But the man had the sensibilities of a rhino and the finesse of a charging bull.

"That's what they all say until they find out I drive a Bentley," Jenkins boasted.

Shante's heart began beating faster as she tried to keep her voice low. She wished she could attend one of these conferences without someone insulting her and treating her like a piece of meat. Tensed and exasperated, she strained to keep her cool so as not to draw attention to her flushed and furious face. In a low but firm voice, she spat out, "Let me tell you—"

"Hello, Apostle Jenkins," someone said, interrupting their exchange. Turning, Shante was relieved to see her friend Maxwell Patrick standing behind them.

"Hi, young man," Jenkins said, giving him a big smile. Trying to look innocent, he stepped back from Shante and began sipping his coffee.

"It's good to see you again. You're looking mighty sharp in that suit. Is that your Bentley I saw them parking outside?" Max asked as they shook hands and embraced.

"You know I'm the only one around here who drives that car. Of course, it's mine," Jenkins replied, sounding aggrieved.

"You're trying to make it hard for us young men. We can't keep up with you."

"Well, you know I do what I do."

"And you do it well." They both laughed. Shante was glad someone had interrupted them. She was sure she could not take much more of this man's insults. She took slow, even breaths and felt her calm slowly returning.

"Pastor Dogan, how are you today?" Max asked, turning to Shante.

Her body relaxed as she tried to keep relief out of her smile. "I'm well. How are you, Reverend Patrick?" she asked, shaking his hand and fighting the urge to throw thankful arms around him.

"I'm blessed. I wanted to talk with you about speaking at a conference coming up at the church," he said, putting a hand on her shoulder. She could feel peace, like a refreshing breeze, pass from his hand to her body.

"I see you two have business to talk about. I'll see you later," Apostle Jenkins said and began making his way through the crowded room.

"My knight in shining Armani. Thanks for rescuing me, Max." Again, she was tempted to hug him but did not for fear people would assume something was going on between them.

"I saw him walking toward you. I tried to get to you as soon as I could," Max said.

"Do you know what he said to me?" Shante asked, trying to pretend she was focusing on the table rather than on him.

"He gave you that classy ass speech, didn't he?"

"So you're familiar with that ignorant pickup line?"

"Yeah. He's used that line all over the place. Did he tell you about his car? He thinks his car will help him get anyone he wants. Shake him off." Max looked around the crowded room. "There are a lot of people in here. Have you eaten?"

"No, I was going to eat here tonight, but the food looks less than appetizing."

"I know. As much as we pay to attend this thing, you would think they would have better food. Hey, meet me at the restaurant around the corner."

"I don't know . . ." she said, hesitating. "There are too many people here."

"Come on, you said you were hungry."

"I can order room service."

"I'll tell you what. There's a little Japanese restaurant a couple of miles from here across from the beach. You can get there in a few minutes. Why don't we meet there?" Max persisted. "I'll call you with the directions."

"A couple of miles from here? Okay. Can we meet in thirty minutes? I want to go to my room and change clothes," she added, gladly seizing the opportunity to get away from the assembly.

"Thirty minutes is fine. I'll see you there," Max said as he walked.

Shante greeted a few people and then made her escape, casually strolling to the elevator. She ran to the bathroom as soon as she entered her room; she had been waiting all day to get out of her clothes. Ready to relax, she was glad she had requested a room facing the ocean. Being in Hilton Head in March before the summer heat had taken over always relaxed her. The sound of the waves had already begun to strip away her tensions. She had arranged her schedule to arrive there a day early to pray, work on her sermon, and unwind. She slipped into her favorite pair of jeans and her Delta Sigma Theta sweatshirt and removed her makeup. Looking in the mirror, fixing her hair, she saw the scars on her face—the remnant of her marriage to Kevin. The half-moon-shaped scar under her right eye where he had hit her with his fist and the ring he wore cut her; the long scar that ran from her left ear to the corner of her top lip that came from hitting the edge of a sofa table after Kevin hit her; the small keloid that formed after he slammed her against the doorframe and cut her chin. They brought back unpleasant memories for her. She wore heavy makeup to cover them up and most people could not tell she had them. But, having known Max many years, she felt no need to get dressed up for him. She could relax and be herself. Having a few minutes left before she had to leave, Shante went out on her balcony to savor the cool ocean air.

The moon beamed down on the Atlantic Ocean, its light shimmering on the dark water. She watched the white waves move to and away from the shoreline. The tranquil scene and the coolness of the March air soon took her into a spirit of worship. She closed her eyes and listened to the roar of the ocean.

"God, you are awesome. You are mighty. You are the one who created the heavens and Earth. All the Earth proclaims your glory. I love you. Each and every day you have shown your grace and mercy. I thank you."

The sound of her cellphone ringing interrupted her meditation. The caller ID showed it was Camille, her daughter, who was away at college. She wondered why she was calling. She knew Shante would be at the conference and would have a busy schedule. Sighing, she answered the phone.

"Hi, Mom," Camille said.

"Is everything all right?"

"Yeah, I just called to see how you were doing," Camille said, laughing.

"How much?"

"What? You act like the only time I call you is when I need money."

"No, Camille, you call me all the time. We have great conversations, but I know your 'Mom, I need some money' tone. What's up?" She always seemed to know when her daughter wanted money and when she only wanted to talk. She was thankful she had a beautiful and successful daughter and thankful they had a good relationship. They talked to each other about everything. Many of her friends envied their relationship and often asked how she was able to raise an independent twenty-year-old woman by herself.

"You know me too well. I'm going to have to change up my stuff," Camille said.

"Remember, you came from me, and I know the game."

They both laughed loudly.

"Are you still coming down next Thursday?"

"I know you didn't ask me that. You know I am. Gwen is coming with me."

"Well, I need fifty dollars. Can you put it in my account?"

"Camille, you should have fifty dollars. I just put five hundred dollars into your account last week."

"I know, but I had things to get."

"You need to stay out of the mall." Shopping was her daughter's weakness. When Camille went off to college, Shante thought she might have to take another job to make sure her daughter wanted for nothing. However, God blessed her and her speaking engagements increased, providing the extra money she needed to help Camille. She suddenly realized she had been on the phone longer than she wanted. Frantically looking around the room for her key, she was paying no attention to Camille as she continued talking about her day.

"Mom . . . Mom . . . MOM," Camille shouted over the phone.

"I'm here, Camille," she said, still searching.

"But you aren't listening to me."

"I am, and I'm also looking for my room key. I have somewhere to go."

"With Max?"

"Stay in a child's place."

"That's okay. You don't have to tell me. You know I got the gift. Anyway, will you put the money in my account?"

"I'll do it first thing in the morning."

Shante said good-bye, found her key, and hurriedly left the room. As she headed for the elevator, she realized she had forgotten to ask Camille how pledging was going. She made a mental note to ask her the next time they talked. She was already late for her meeting with Max.

Shante burst through the door of the Japanese Gardens restaurant as if she were being chased. She looked around the large, open room for Max. She heard loud laughter coming from the back of the restaurant. She could see Max talking with two waitresses. They seemed to be having a good conversation. She knew he was talking to them in Japanese. He did it all the time. His late wife was Japanese. She had taught him the language, and he frequently went to Japanese restaurants so he wouldn't forget.

She leaned against the front counter and decided to give him a minute to have his fun. She was over thirty minutes late, so she was just glad he was still there. She stood at the door waiting to be seated. She tried to read a local real estate guide that was on the counter, but she could not keep her eyes off him. Even with age, she thought he was more gorgeous than ever.

She and Max had met in college. He was a Morehouse man and she was a Spelman woman. He was a member of Omega Psi Phi fraternity, and she was a

Delta. He was outgoing and involved in many campus activities and stood out in the crowd with his tall, dark-skinned, athletic body. He had always worn his hair short and with neatly lined edges. All the women wanted Max. His teeth were even and pearly white. His lips, perfectly formed and plump, were the stuff of dreams. He could have been a playboy, but he was quite the nerd. Although lots of women chased him, he was only interested in one thing: books.

Max was a voracious reader. Because of his vast knowledge, he could debate anyone on practically any topic. He could spit out dates, times, and events at the drop of a hat. Everyone knew he would be an excellent attorney, and he was. Many a girl dreamed of being Mrs. Maxwell Patrick. But his goal was to graduate with honors and go to Howard Law School, which he did, and that's where he met his wife, Meko. He actually met her on the DC Metro. She was lost and needed directions, and he helped her out. Tragically, she was killed in an automobile accident a few years ago. That had been a real bad time for him. Her heart had been heavy both for Max and for the loss of her friend.

Shante never expected to see Max or any of her friends again. Living with Kevin was hell, and he had isolated her from her family and friends. She had already lost her parents, both of whom died within a year of each other when she was a sophomore in college, and she relied on her extended family of aunts, uncles, and cousins for support. Kevin took them away from her and kept her a virtual prisoner.

When Shante finally got the courage to leave him, she ran to a place she knew he would not look for her: Charlotte, North Carolina. She knew he would search for her near her family in Jacksonville, and she did not know anyone in North Carolina. A few months after arriving, she ran into Max and Meko at the mall. Max had accepted a job at a law firm in Charlotte after his graduation, and they had moved there. It did not surprise Shante to learn Max had entered the ministry and was an associate pastor at his church. They renewed their friendship, and Meko and Shante quickly became friends and remained close even after Gwen, her childhood friend, moved to Charlotte with her husband. Thoughts of Meko's sudden death could cause waves of sadness to wash over her so she forced herself to think of something positive.

She focused on Max and smiled as she thought about how he had become the most eligible bachelor in town. He was a successful attorney, pastor of the Earle Street Baptist Church, and father of three very active little boys. The chase had started all over again. Women from the tri-state area flocked to his church in Charlotte because of him, bringing food and gifts for him and the boys. They lavished compliments on his children and over-worked themselves in the church to get his attention. None of it worked. His main focus was taking care of his boys—twelve-year-old Joshua, eight-year-old Jonathan, and four-year-old Jacob.

"Miss, your husband is waiting for you," a server informed Shante.

"Afraid I'm not married," Shante quickly corrected her. Pointing at Max and waving, she made her way through the black and red tables and chairs in the almost-empty restaurant over to where he was sitting.

"Did you tell that lady I was your wife?" she demanded when she reached the table.

"I was only kidding, Tay. Sit down," he said, looking at her sweatshirt. "You are always representing DST."

"You know I do what I do," she said, imitating Apostle Jenkins. They laughed.

"So how are the boys?" she asked, settling into her seat.

"They're great. Jonathan is thinking about trying out for the basketball team next year. He has been practicing in the backyard so much I have to make him come in and eat. I brought you their new school pictures," Max said, handing her three pictures.

"They're growing up so fast," she said, looking at the pictures of his sons—her godsons. These boys were one reason she was glad they had been able to keep their friendship secret from the church community. She did not want anyone to try to destroy her relationship with Max. They were only friends, but if people found out they would attach more to it than it was and then the rumors and lies would begin. They had been just friends while his wife was alive and had remained friends after her death, and Shante had been an important presence in the boys' lives.

"I know. It's hard to believe they are not babies any-more. Time goes by fast." He leaned over and took her hand. "Tay, I don't think I could've made it if it had not been for you."

She slowly removed her hand from his and picked up the menu. "Max, that's what friends are for. Have you ordered yet?"

She could feel him staring at her, and she became increasingly uncomfortable when he took her hand again. She knew he had feelings for her, but her feelings for him were not the same. She again eased her hand from his and tried to focus on the menu, not wanting to give him the faintest notion they were more than friends. She tried to keep her distance when it came to adding a different dimension to their relationship. She only wanted to be friends, nothing more. She would have loved to be in a relationship, but she was much too busy and had too much drama going on to be involved romantically with anyone.

"Take your order now?" the waitress asked.

"Tay, do you know what you want?"

"Go ahead and order me something. You understand the menu better than I do, and I trust your judgment."

"Boku wa sashimi teshoku," Max began his order of sashimi, rice, soup and salad. They continued their conversation in Japanese and they both began to laugh.

Shante wondered what they were talking about and fleetingly wished she spoke Japanese. She guessed they had said something about her because the server looked at her and grinned.

"What did you say about me?" Shante asked after she left.

"What?"

"Don't 'what' me, Max. I know you said something about me. You were probably talking about some Japanese aphrodisiac."

"I'm glad I got you away from that crowd. You're beginning to talk like some of them. Sex, sex, sex. Everything is not about sex."

"I know, but it seems to be an ongoing focus of the world."

"Am I like the world?" Max asked, suddenly serious.

"No."

"Good. I ordered you steamed shrimp. I know you like seafood."

"Thanks. How's your building program going?" Max's church was building. Construction had been going on for about a year and was almost complete. Max was proud he had completed the first phase of his ten-year building project, which would add a family life center and a school to the church campus.

Max began to talk about budgets and construction schedules, but Shante didn't hear anything he was saying. She had drifted off into her own fantasy, her mind going far afield. Maybe Bishop was right; her husband just might be at the conference. Maybe it would be nice to be married. Sometimes it gets lonesome traveling alone. It would be nice to look out into the crowd and see a husband supporting her when she preached. She thought about the places she had traveled. Instead of eating dinner with an old friend, she could be enjoying the romantic atmosphere of the island with her husband by her side. But then she remembered her busy schedule and reality brought fantasy to an abrupt halt. As she continued to block out Max's talk, she thought that she couldn't bring anyone into the chaos she called her life.

Returning to the real world, she shared a little of her sermon with him, highlighting points she intended to make about Solomon. He inched closer to her and placed his arm around her shoulder. She shrugged it off and reminded him that, although they were miles from the conference, someone could see them. He moved back to his side of the booth and continued listening to her discuss her sermon.

After dinner, they crossed the street outside the restaurant and began walking along the beach. Shante took off her shoes so she could feel the sand massaging her feet. She loved the beach in the evening. It was so peaceful. Following her lead, Max took off his shoes. They walked leisurely along, talking and laughing about their days in college, step shows, hangouts, and old friends. They shared funny church stories. They compared sermons and talked about music. Shante could feel the cool air send a chill through her body. Max took off his sport coat and placed it on her.

"What's in your pocket?" Shante asked.

"Oh, I forgot." Max reached into the inside pocket and pulled out a small jewelry box and handed it to Shante. "One of the vendors was selling these and I thought about you. Open it."

Shante opened the box and saw the silver cross inside. "Max, you shouldn't have."

"I know. I wanted to. Here, let me put it on." As she turned and lifted her short, flipped hair, he picked up the long silver chain and placed it around her neck. It draped slightly between her cleavage. She picked up the cross and looked at it. His hands slowly caressed her shoulders. A chill went through her. She turned.

"Thank you. It's beautiful." She hugged and kissed him on the cheek.

As he held her and felt her kiss, he whispered, "A little lower."

"Thank you, Max," she said in a much deeper voice, backing away from him. They both laughed. She knew what he was saying but she only wanted to be friends and nothing more. They continued their walk along the beach.

They had been walking for more than an hour when they heard music. It was coming from a luxury beach house; someone was having a party with a live band. The guests were dancing and laughing, apparently having a grand time.

"Looks like they're having fun," Max said looking at the partygoers.

"Yeah."

"Would you like to dance, madam?" He offered his hand, bowing and speaking in an overly exaggerated Southern accent much stronger than his natural Alabama one.

In her best Southern-girl tone, Shante replied, "Well, sur, rally I would."

She curtseyed and he bowed. He placed one arm around her waist and held her other hand as they swayed to the rhythm of the music. Max danced as if he was with the love of his life, holding her close and breathing in the very essence of the moment with her.

At that very moment, her life was good, dancing with an old friend on the beach, but it would be perfect if she had a special man in her life. She pushed the thought away; she couldn't focus on that now. Too much was going on in her life—the church, the community, Camille.

CHAPTER 2

Gail Jennings, Shante's assistant, was giving her boss a rundown of the day so far. "The Hunts are here for their session. Reverend Patrick called. You have several messages. I don't know what you preached at the conference last week, but you have gotten a lot of invitations this morning. I hope you brought me a tape. Reverend Johnson is on line one. And you are running late this morning, but you already knew that."

"Thank you, Gail. Please hold my calls and put the Hunts in the counseling room. I will be there in a minute." She went into her office and closed the door.

She loved her office. Pictures of members of her congregation, Camille, and other ministers she had met throughout the years adorned the walls. A framed copy of her ordination papers were on the wall behind her desk. A large cherry wood desk had neatly stacked trays on one end and a computer on the other. A large window faced the parking lot. On the far left side of her desk a sofa and chair with a large coffee table faced a television monitor she had installed so she could watch the service from her office. On the wall opposite her desk was a large bookcase filled with study guides, several versions of the Bible, and many other books and awards she had received lined along the shelves. The bookcase was also filled with small

African-American figurines and more pictures, and a large artificial flower in the center of the middle shelf.

Eating a bagel and drinking coffee, Shante pressed line one on the speakerphone. "Hey, girl."

"I just wanted to call you and tell you about yourself," Gwen crowed.

"What are you talking about, Gwen?"

"You showed your black behind at the conference. You preached those men silly. I bet you got several husbands out of that one."

"You need to stop."

"Girl, you broke down Solomon's building program. I know you made some of those old preachers go back and open up their Bibles again. You had them eating out of your hands."

"You know you really need to stop. I only preached the word God gave to me. Now change the subject."

"I'll change the subject. I'm glad you said that. Hmm, now what subject can I change to? I know—Maxwell Patrick. What's up with you two?"

"Nothing. You know he's our friend."

"Our friend? He's my friend, yes, but I don't dance with him on the beach."

Shante sat straight up. She had been so sure she and Max were too far from the conference site to be seen dancing. Her hand trembled slightly as she listened to Gwen. *I should have known someone would see us. I should not have danced with Max.* "What are you talking about?"

"Don't deny it, girl. We saw you. Ron and I did."

"We were miles from the conference site and you saw us? How?"

"It was such a beautiful night, Ron and I decided to walk along the beach. The waves were crashing against the rocky shoreline. We heard the music, and one thing lead to another, and I began to minister to my husband behind some large rocks. You know what I mean. We were just about to return to the hotel when we saw the two of you dancing on the beach. Ron began to minister to me because I wanted to say something. You know me."

"Yes, I do. Please don't say anything to anyone. It was completely innocent. Max thought nothing of it, and neither did I." Gwen was not always the soul of discretion, and Shante feared she would sooner or later tell someone about what she had seen. It was something that could easily be blown out of proportion. She just didn't want her name in the church community rumor mill.

"It didn't look all that innocent. Well, he at least looked as if he was totally into you. How long has this been going on, and why didn't you tell me?"

"Nothing's going on. It's no secret Max and I are friends. You knew that."

"Sure. But college friends, not dancing friends."

"You are too much. I've got to go. I have a couple waiting for counseling."

"Shante, is Camille still being initiated soon?"

"Yeah. You're still going, right? You know you can't miss it. The Delta legacy continues. I'll call you later in the week. I've got to go."

Shante hung up the phone and looked over the day's schedule. She usually did not have appointments on Monday, but she had made an exception in the Hunts' case, as their work schedule did not allow for another day. After this session ended, Shante would have the day to herself, and she was going to treat herself to a massage.

"Gail, I'm getting ready to go. Return my calls, please. And see if you can get additional information about the programs they want me for. You know what I'm looking for. If they will be charging to get into the program, send a letter of apology turning down their invitation. You can take off around lunch. I know you were extra busy while I was in Hilton Head last week." Shante was rapid-firing her instructions to her secretary at the opened door leading to the outer office.

"Thanks, Pastor. I know you said to hold your calls, but it's Reverend Patrick. This is his third call this morning. It may be important."

"I'll take it, Gail. What line?" She walked back into her office and began packing some papers and books into her briefcase. "This is Pastor Dogan."

"Hello, Pastor Dogan. This is Reverend Patrick. Sounds like you're on speakerphone."

"I am. I'm trying to get out of here and to the spa."

"Pick up the phone."

Shante stopped packing, closed the door, and ran to the phone. Max's serious tone made her think there was something wrong. Now that she knew Gwen had seen them on the beach, she was afraid the rumor mill had already cranked up. *Had he heard anything about them?*

"What's wrong?"

"Nothing. I didn't want anyone to hear our conversation. I tried calling you on your cell, but you had it turned off."

"The battery is dead. It's on the charger now."

"And your home phone?"

"I turned it off so I can get some rest and prepare for my sermon Sunday." *Why was he asking so many questions?*

"I had a great time at the conference. Woman, you preached. I was so proud of you. I wanted to tell everyone, that's my friend up there."

"I'm glad you didn't. We're already in danger of being on the front page of the church newspaper." She settled into her chair and turned to look out the window.

"What do you mean?"

"Ron and Gwen saw us on the beach."

"How?"

"They were there, she says ministering to each other, and they saw us dancing. I asked Gwen not to tell anyone, but you know how she is. Besides, I told her it meant nothing to you or me. We were just old friends dancing."

"Nothing?"

"Yeah, we're not seeing each other or anything. We know our relationship is strictly platonic, and that's what I like about it."

"Platonic?" Max asked, sounding disappointed.

Missing the change in Max's voice, she continued, "I hope Gwen doesn't tell anyone. That's all I need right now."

"I know you're busy, Shante. I'll let you go."

"All right, Max. I'll talk to you later."

She grabbed her purse and briefcase and started for the door when suddenly it opened. She jumped back, startled. "What are you doing here, Kevin?"

"I just came to see my baby," he said, walking closer to her. He tried to hug her, but she backed away. Hugging him was the last thing she wanted to do.

"We've been divorced a long time," she said. *Why was he here?* Usually, Gail would let her know when someone had come to see her. Perhaps Gail had already left for the day. She tried to think of a way of getting him out her office.

"No hugs or kisses for your husband?"

"Don't you have a wife at home? Where's Gail?" she asked, looking past him to see if anyone was in the office lobby.

"I don't know. She wasn't at her desk, so I just walked in. I saw your car outside and knew you wouldn't mind talking to me," Kevin said, closing and locking the door.

"You are not supposed to be here. I still have a restraining order against you. I'm going to ask you to leave now."

"Hey, baby, don't act like that. Come here and give me a hug." He held out his arms as he walked toward her.

"Kevin, if you put your hands on me, I'm going to call the police," she said, backing toward her desk.

He started laughing. "You won't do that. Not here in your precious church. You're too private for that. Now, can we talk? I promise you I won't put my hands on you."

Shante looked around the room to see what her escape options were. She knew how Kevin could be; his temper was short. He might go off at any moment. She opted to go along with whatever he wanted, just to get him out of the office. Besides, she smelled alcohol and, from past experience, she knew he was more dangerous when he had been drinking.

"What do you want?"

"I want you to do a revival at my church."

"Sorry, I can't do that." Shante hadn't realized she had spoken aloud until she heard Kevin's response.

"Why not?" he asked peevishly. "Are you too good to preach at my church, you boogie bitch? I remember when you weren't so holy. I remember a lot of things about you. I'm sure your members would love to hear some of them. *You are going to preach at my church!* I need the money." Kevin lunged at her, but lost his balance and almost fell against the desk. She dropped her briefcase and ran to the other side of the room.

"I'm calling the police," Shante said, but suddenly remembered her cellphone was on the charger sitting on her desk. Now panicked, she frantically looked around the room for something to protect herself if it came to that. And she prayed to God for help as she griped the cross that hung from a chain around her neck.

Kevin regained his balance and laughed when he saw how frightened she was. "Hey, I was just kidding. Come on now; I know you'll come to your senses. I'll have the church secretary contact you."

"Kevin, I'm not going to do it. I'm not going to stoop that low again. How much do you need?" she said, taking her checkbook out of her purse. She wanted to get rid of him as soon as possible. She was afraid of him, and he knew it. She feared he would follow up on the many threats to harm her if she did not give him what he wanted. He had power over her that even the law had not been able to break.

"You don't get it, do you? It's not about the money."

"Then what is it, Kevin?"

He turned and started for the door, but stopped short and swung around. She jumped back and gripped the edge of the sofa near her. Even though she had mentally prepared herself for a fight, she knew he would do nothing in the church except threaten her. Every muscle in her body ached; every nerve was on end.

"I want your little boyfriend, Max, to preach at my church, too, or something just might happen to those little zebras he has at home."

"Don't you touch those boys. This is between you and me. Leave them out of it," she shrieked. Shante found the strength to take one step toward him. "If you go near those boys, you will experience a greater hell than the one you put me through all these years."

Kevin laughed, a hint of derision in his voice, and walked out the door. Shante then rushed to check the parking lot below her office window. How did she miss his car when she looked out the window earlier? She finally relaxed when she saw him driving off, and she sat back in her chair and recalled their first meeting. There had been no clue then that he would turn out as he had.

She had met Kevin at a business conference in New York City. She was a junior executive at a marketing and advertising firm, and it was her job to work conferences looking for new clients and new products for her employer, A. L. Dixon and Sons. She had spotted Kevin the moment he entered the room. He looked different from the other junior executives and salesmen at the conference. He had a flair all his own. He had creamy pecan skin and was wearing a designer suit. He had strolled across the room as though he owned everyone and everything in it. Everything about him screamed confidence. She was so young—fresh out of college—and he was exciting to her. She had to find out who he was; it was lust at first sight. They began a hot and heavy whirlwind romance. Although they lived hundreds of miles apart; she in Atlanta and he in Virginia Beach, they always found ways to be together. About a year after they'd met, Kevin told her he had been saved and did not want to continue the life he was living—fornicating, drinking, frequenting clubs. He said he wanted to live a Christian life. He broke up with her that day.

She had lived to regret her decision to not just let him go, many times wishing she had walked away from the relationship. A month after he left, Kevin showed up at her office in Atlanta with two dozen roses. He said he could not live without her and had gotten down on one knee and proposed right in front of her co-workers. They had a big, elegant wedding at her home church in Jacksonville and a fabulous honeymoon in Maui. She thought it would last forever. And then he started drinking again, and life with him became hell.

It had begun as a way of relaxing after Camille's birth and his entering the ministry. He told her that the Bible says a little bit of wine is good for the body. She had not been all that conversant with the Bible and had taken his word for it. Then the violence began.

The last beating was so brutal she almost lost her eyesight. Her face still bore the scars under her right eye and along the left side of her mouth. She finally got up the courage to leave him. She took all the money she had and boarded a Greyhound in Atlanta to the farthest her money would take her: Charlotte, North Carolina. She gave up her good job, her home, and her car to get away from him. She was convinced she and two-year-old Camille would lose their lives if she had stayed. They lived in a homeless shelter for a while and she hadn't minded—she had peace. That is where she had met Bishop and Mother Thompson, who were doing outreach at the shelter. With their support, she finally got up the nerve to divorce him.

She had been shocked to hear he had been selected pastor of a small church in Matthews, a suburb of Charlotte, five years ago. She couldn't believe he was a pastor. She thought maybe he had changed; after all, she had. That was a long time ago, and she knew people did change. But, he hadn't. His drinking was worse. She'd even heard of him going into the pulpit drunk. He had a horrible reputation in the church community because of his drinking, gambling, and womanizing. Many people left his church because of his outrageous antics. Rank-and-file members wanted to fire him; however, the board elected to keep him.

Nowadays, when he wanted something he came and harassed her. He knew she was still frightened of him and he used this to his advantage, threatening her to get her to preach at his church. He knew she had a good reputation and crowds of people would come out to hear her preach. He was also aware of her good reputation in the community, and her word could get him into places he otherwise would not have access to. Shante knew exactly what he wanted: a good reputation. If she and Max preached at his church, it would help repair his tattered public image. She knew exactly what he wanted and she could not give it to him. She had made that mistake two years ago when she had preached at his church because of his threats. She had promised herself she would never preach out of fear again.

"Pastor, you're still here? I thought you would be long gone by now," Gail said, peeping into Shante's office.

"I was leaving, but I think I need to pray. You can go home now. Don't worry about returning those phone calls. You can start that tomorrow. Lock the doors when you leave. I'll set the alarm when I go."

"Is there anything wrong?" Gail asked, seeing a change in Shante's demeanor.

"No, I just need to pray. I'm fine. Remember to lock the doors when you leave."

"Okay, Pastor. Before I go, may I pray for you?"

"Yes, we all need prayer," Shante said, walking around her desk.

"Pastor, you don't have to act strong with me. Let's join hands." Gail began to pray.

"Oh, heavenly Father, we thank you for this day. We thank you for the outpouring of your spirit upon our lives. We thank you for your grace that is new each and every day. Now, Father, I come to you with a simple request. You said in your Word that I can ask you anything in prayer and you would hear my prayer and answer my call. Father, I ask you to touch my pastor. Whatever is going on in her life, give her the victory. Endow her with wisdom to stand and protect her. Father, I thank you that it is already done. In Jesus name I pray. Amen."

Moved by her prayer, Shante hugged Gail and then waited until she heard her lock on the door. She slowly made her way down the long hallway to the sanctuary and opened the door. The serenity in the room immediately embraced her. Going to the altar, she fell on her knees and began to weep.

CHAPTER 3

Max could not accept what he had just heard. *Platonic. Is that what she thinks of our relationship? Platonic?* Max thought as he hung up the phone. He had wanted to have lunch with Shante. He had waited all weekend to see her. He couldn't get his mind off of Hilton Head. He thought their relationship had finally gone beyond just friendship. He thought about that night on the beach, how they had walked and talked for hours. He relived how she felt in his arms when they were dancing. She could not have been more beautiful that night. He had longed to be with her. But she had taken no notice of how his heart raced as they danced, or had paid no attention to how his eyes brightened when he listened to her talk. He loved her laugh, her corny jokes, and the way she teased him about growing up in Alabama. He had been desperate to kiss her that night.

She would be a perfect mother for his sons; they loved her. They had drilled him for every detail about "Mama Tay" at the conference. She was the only mother Joshua had ever known. He was only a baby when his mother died. Without the merest hesitation, Shante had stepped in to help with the boys. She cooked meals for them. She even took Joshua to work with her until Max could find a nanny. She frequently took the boys to the park, movies, or shopping just to give him a break. He trusted her completely with his children. They loved her; he loved her.

Platonic. Max couldn't get that word out of his mind.

"Hey, Max, want to get some lunch?" Max's business partner, Gary asked, pausing at his door. "We're going to Smiley's."

"No, man, I've got to finish up something here," Max said. The truth was, he had lost his appetite. He loved a woman who didn't love him. *Lord, I don't know what to do. You said in your Word when a man finds a wife, he finds a good thing. But what does he do when she does not choose him? God, give me direction. I know in my spirit and my heart Shante is my wife. I love her. God, what should I do?* Max prayed.

When the phone rang he quickly picked it up, hoping it was Shante calling him back. But it was Bishop Thompson. Bishop was like a surrogate father to him. Friends since Max had arrived in Charlotte, he couldn't hide anything from him. Bishop always knew when something was wrong.

"Hello, Bishop."

"Hi, Max. How are you?"

"All's well, Bishop. How are you?"

"I'm blessed."

"How's Mother?"

"She's well. She starts chemo tomorrow. Pray for her. The treatment is worse than the disease. But, we know God is a healer. She will be all right."

"I'll keep her in my prayers. So what's up?"

"I was wondering if you weren't busy if we could have lunch today."

"Sure, Bishop. Where and at what time?"

"Let's meet at Kat's Place in thirty minutes. I feel like home cooking."

"That's fine. I'll see you there." Max hung up and sat wondering how he and his queasy stomach would get through any meal—much less a rich Southern one. Thinking about what Shante said was beginning to make him physically sick. But even though he didn't feel like eating he was glad to be seeing Bishop. Perhaps he could provide some insight into why, despite years of friendship, his relationship with Shante had not progressed to love—at least not on her part.

Max drove the short distance from his office to the restaurant. Only Bishop would come to the middle of the ghetto to eat lunch. Max belatedly wondered if his Mercedes would be safe in this neighborhood. Turning into the restaurant's parking lot, he saw people hanging out near the door. Some looked depressed and hopeless; others were probably up to something. Max got out of his car and looked around. What had been a neighborhood of well-kept houses owned by blacks had become one of run-down houses and high crime rates. Kat's Place had been there for more than fifty years. The granddaughter of the original Kat, or Katherine, was now running the restaurant. Even though her name was Janice, everyone still called her Kat. The restaurant was renowned for its good Southern cooking. However, eating was not on Max's mind; the word *platonic* was.

Bishop Thompson was not hard to find in the small restaurant. He was wearing a red-and-blue plaid suit, which reminded Max of an old zoot suit popular in the 1940s. Max walked toward the table wondering where he found his clothes.

Bishop Thompson was so wide he could not close his legs, which spread beyond the small table on both sides. He was so busy talking he didn't notice Max walking toward him. Bishop was a popular man in the community, as he and his wife had helped many people.

"Hello, Bishop," Max said.

"Max," Bishop smiled. "Sit down." He turned back to the man he had been talking to at the next table. "And when we got there, the Lord had already worked everything out," Bishop told the man. "You wait. He will work it out for you, too." And then he turned to Max. "Well, son, how are you today?"

"I'm fine, Bishop," he answered just as the waitress appeared.

"Can I get you something?" the woman asked.

"Trudy, you know what I want. Ask Irene to put some peppers in my greens and give me some buttermilk for my corn bread," Bishop said.

"I'll have the meatloaf. I'm not very hungry. Thank you," Max said. He still did not feel like eating and hoped he could get some of his food down without vomiting.

Bishop began talking about a meeting of the Mecklenburg County Ministers' Fellowship slated for the following week, outlining what he needed Max to do there. Max did not hear anything he said. He was in his own world, and Shante was the only one in it. He did not see when the food was placed on the table or hear Bishop's prayer. Nor did he notice Bishop devouring his food.

"You know she loves you," Bishop said without looking up from his food.

"What?" Max replied, his mentor's words having cut through the fog that had enveloped his mind.

"You heard what I said. Have you talked to her?" Bishop asked, placing his arms down on the small table and causing it to shake on its uneven legs.

"Who?"

"Don't act like you don't know who I'm talking about. You know who."

"I'm guessing you're talking about Shante," Max said, sighing.

"Guessing? Look, son, what's going on between you two? I saw how you looked at her at the conference. You can't hide it." Max didn't answer him. He was afraid all his emotions would spill forth and he would lose control. Bishop continued talking and eating at the same time. Then he took a break and looked at Max. "Did you talk to her?"

"No."

"Why not?"

"Well . . ." Max fell silent. He was reluctant to talk about such a personal matter in public. "Bishop, we shouldn't talk about this here."

"What's wrong with here? We're more at home here than anywhere else in the city. Now, tell me what's going on," Bishop said. "You love her, don't you? When the Lord spoke to me and told me Shante was getting married, I knew it was you. I know when the Lord speaks to me. Don't worry, son, it will be all right. You watch. God has it all worked out." Bishop began attacking his food again.

"Bishop, you need anything else?" the server asked.

"Yeah, bring me a piece of that sweet potato pie. What's wrong, son?" Bishop asked as the woman walked away. He seemed very concerned, and Max knew he only wanted to help him.

"She doesn't think of me that way."

"How do you know if you haven't talked to her?"

"She told me this morning. She said we have a platonic relationship and she liked it that way." Holding comment, Bishop just looked at Max and let him talk. "The first night of the conference, we went walking on the beach. We talked for hours. Someone was having a party at a beach house, and they had a band. It was the perfect night. We danced on the beach. We had so much fun. Dancing, walking, talking, laughing—"

"Anything else?" Bishop interrupted.

"If you mean sex, Bishop, no. It was more than that. It was a closeness I haven't felt in a long time. It was as if we had connected finally. She has been my rock since Meko died. If it hadn't been for her, I don't know if I could have made it. She's so good with the kids. I love everything about her—her walk, talk, style of dress, the way she laughs, preaches. I could go on. I even love it when she puts me in my place. None of the women I've met since Meko died compare to her. She's sincere and not fake. I loved her in college, but I was afraid to ask her out. She was so sophisticated. I got nervous every time I was around her. I thank God for her, but . . ." Max stopped.

"But what?"

"She doesn't feel the same way," Max said, looking down at the table.

"Where is your faith, boy?" Bishop asked firmly. Max looked up, surprised at Bishop calling him boy. Bishop had never addressed him like that. And his smile was gone. He seemed frustrated with him. "Do you believe this is your wife?"

"Yes, sir."

"Then put your faith on it and begin to call those things that be not as though they are. Hold your head up. It will be all right! I believe the Lord sent me to you today to tell you to keep the faith. Be encouraged. It's going to work out." Bishop's voice rose as he spoke as if he was gaining strength. He noticed Max had not eaten. "Now, son, eat your food. You'll need your strength. Now there's something I need you to do before the meeting," Bishop said, changing the subject.

Max began eating. His talk with Bishop was just what he'd needed. He made up his mind to talk to Shante as soon as possible and invite her out to dinner. No, he would do something special—maybe on their next First Friday outing.

CHAPTER 4

Shante and Gwen had gotten an early start on the long drive to Atlanta for Camille's sorority initiation. Shante looked forward to seeing her friend, Patrice Edwards, who served as dean of student affairs at Spelman College. It was a long time since the three of them were together. It was always loud and crazy when they got together. She longed to see her daughter Camille even more and could not wait to officially bring her into her sorority.

Shante and Gwen walked into Patrice's suite in the Rockefeller Hall Administrative Building and asked her secretary not to announce their visit. She expected them to arrive later in the day and they wanted to surprise her. They walked to her door and banged on it.

"What in the world . . ." Patrice blurted when she opened the door.

"*Ooh-oop!*" Shante and Gwen screamed, followed by an equally loud, "Hey, soror!" "I should have known it was the two of you. Stop making all that noise. I'm the dean now. You just can't come to my office acting all ghetto. Get in here," Patrice said, closing the door to her spacious, elegantly decorated office. Then they had a group hug.

Shante loved coming to Atlanta to visit Patrice. This was her girl. But that was not the case when she'd first met her in college. Shante had thought she was stuck on herself and arrogant. Patrice was petite and wore designer clothes, and her hair was always meticulously groomed. She took a lot of pride in her appearance, and there appeared to be a superior air about her. That perception changed after they'd taken the same class and worked on a project. Shante discovered Patrice was not at all like her public persona. She was from a small town in Georgia, was on scholarship, and was the first in her family to go to college. Her family and her church had joined forces to purchase clothes, books, and anything else she needed for college. Shante and Patrice had gotten to know each other and had been very close friends ever since.

"I've missed y'all so much. You're early," Patrice said.

"You know how Gwen drives," Shante said.

"You got here safe, didn't you?" Gwen replied, walking around the office.

"You ladies look good, but then we are some of Delta's finest," Patrice said, getting up and going into one of their old steps. Shante joined Patrice, and Gwen followed suit. About midway through the step, Gwen sat down in a nearby chair, breathing hard.

"Hey, y'all, I'm getting too old for this," Gwen said.

"You need to take your fat behind to the gym," Patrice said.

"I don't hear Ron complaining."

"That's because you're smothering him," Patrice said. The sound of laughter filled the office.

"You got me, girl. I know I can't keep up with you," Gwen said.

"Your new office looks good, Patrice. You have a great view of the campus," Shante said.

"I see you're representing," Gwen said, walking toward Patrice's sorority paddle on the wall. Gwen walked over to the corner of Patrice's office where she kept an assortment of elephants her sorority collects and noticed an unusual rustic-looking elephant amongst them. She picked it up. "Where did you get this?"

"Shawn gave it to me. He went to a medical conference in Austin, Texas, and he saw it there. He said it's hand made out of driftwood," Patrice replied.

"It's nice. I have never seen one like that."

"How are Shawn and the kids doing?" Shante asked.

"They're great. Tiffany is getting on my nerves about going to Europe for a year after she graduates this year. She is going straight to college. Travis only has two more years before he's out of the house. Y'all, I will be so glad. Then Shawn and I can really get our freak on," Patrice said, laughing.

"You are still nasty," Shante said.

"You should try getting yours, too. Maybe you wouldn't be so uptight," Patrice said, walking around the room very stiffly, teasing Shante. Patrice's good-natured imitation made her two friends laugh.

"You need Jesus," Shante pronounced. She loved her friend. She often prayed she and her husband's family would be saved and get to know Christ. However, she knew they enjoyed the life they were living, going to casinos, drinking and engaging in other activities that would be disapproved of by the church. They were good people. But they were not Christians. Patrice had no interest in the church. She thought most churchgoers were hypocrites. She often criticized televangelists and other religious personalities for what she saw as using the Bible to extort money from people instead of helping them. Still, Shante continued praying that she would come into the knowledge of, and find a relationship with, God.

"And you need a man," Patrice retorted.

"Oh, girl, you don't know about Max?" Gwen sat up, clearly glad for an opportune opening.

Shante knew then that nothing would keep her from relating what had happened at Hilton Head. She took a deep breath and waited.

"Max who?"

"Gwen, don't," Shante said trying to stop her. She didn't want to talk about Max and wished Gwen hadn't brought him up. She wanted to relax and not think about her problems. The memory of Kevin's unexpected appearance at her office and his sinister threats once again flooded her mind. It had been over a week and she still spent many sleepless nights praying for a solution. Her body ached with a tension that not even her regular exercise routine and massages could relieve. She had hoped this trip to Atlanta would help distract her and clear her mind so she could get the answers she needed. She didn't want to talk about Max, Kevin, or the church. She wished she could go back to her pre-Kevin days. Maybe she could have done things differently. And maybe she wouldn't have to listen to what Gwen was about to say.

"This is just Patrice. She won't tell anybody, and you know I've got to tell somebody," Gwen said, leaning toward them in the chair.

"What about Max?" Patrice asked.

"We're just friends."

"Dancing friends," Gwen said.

"How long has this been going on, and why didn't you tell me?" Patrice asked. Shante had wandered over to the window and was staring out, trying to separate herself from the conversation.

"Spill it, girl. I want every detail," Patrice said, looking at Gwen.

"We were at a conference, and Ron and I were on the beach ministering to each other—"

"Ministering? Is that what they are calling it now?" Patrice interrupted.

"Yeah, you know. A romantic stroll on the beach can do things to a woman and a man. It isn't often Ron and I do something spontaneous. The mood was right and the music was smooth . . ."

"Music? I know you weren't getting your freak on to gospel music."

"No. Just listen. Somebody was having a party at a house on the beach. They had a live band. They were playing some type of jazz, and the stars were out. We were relaxed . . ."

"Get to Shante and Max."

"I am. We were about to go back to the hotel, and we looked up toward some houses and saw Shante and Max dancing on the beach. Girl, he was all into her. She was smiling and laughing. You know that laugh she has. Then they walked back toward the hotel holding hands."

"What happened next?"

"I don't know what they did, but I know what Ron did after that. Lord help me, I love that man," Gwen said, leaning back in her chair and fanning as if the room was hot.

"Maybe I need to start going to church. You church folk seem to have more interesting lives than I do. Maybe I need to go to church more often so I can learn to minister to Shawn better," Patrice said as Shante continued staring out of the window.

"Patrice, where's the bathroom? That was a long drive, and I have to go," Gwen said.

"It's down the hall, to the left."

After Gwen left the room, Patrice walked over to Shante and leaned against the wall next to the window. "You want to talk about it?"

"Not really."

"What's up? Is it Max? Do you love him?" she asked, ignoring Shante's reluctance to talk.

"No, Max and I are just friends. It's Kevin. He's threatening me again. Not only is he threatening me, he's threatening Max's children."

"Oh, no, Shante. Did you call the police?" Patrice hugged her tightly.

"He was at the church. You know I can't cause a scene there."

"Can you die there?" Patrice asked sternly.

The thought never occurred to her. She didn't think Kevin would do anything like that in the church. The church was the only place she truly felt safe.

"You need to put that jerk in jail. What does he want now?"

"Something I can't give him . . . credibility."

"What?"

"He wants me to preach at his church again. He wants Max also. That's why he's threatening his children."

"Does Max know?"

"No, I haven't told him. I'm afraid."

"Of what, Shante? Dying?"

"No."

"Then what? Why did he come to you about Max? Does he think you're dating or something?"

"I don't know. He acted as though he had something on us. There's nothing going on. Yes, we were on the beach. Yes, we danced, but nothing else happened. You know I've been helping him with his children. Thanks for not telling Gwen you knew about Max."

"You know I got your back. I worry about you sometimes. If you need to, you can come and stay with me and Shawn."

"No, I'm not running from Kevin anymore. I'll figure something out."

"You need to let Max know about him. He's threatening his kids."

"I know, but I don't want to lose his friendship over a crazy ex-husband. Besides, you know how Max can be sometimes. People think he is a pushover, but he's not.

He may go straight to Kevin's church and jack him up. I don't want that to happen. I'm going to fast and pray about it. The Lord will give me the answer. He always does. Right now, my focus is on my daughter. How is she doing on line?"

"Don't change the subject on me. Are you going to be all right? I worry about you."

"Yeah. God will make a way."

"If not, I've got a baseball bat, and I can teach you how to use it."

They burst out laughing just as Gwen walked back into the room.

"What are y'all laughing at?"

"Old pledging stuff," Patrice said. Shante was glad Patrice didn't tell Gwen what was going on. If she did, Gwen would tell Max, and there was no telling what would happen. They decided, as if they had some unspoken communication, that for the moment it was best Gwen didn't know what was going on. "I'm glad you ladies are here. I can take off a little earlier now. Let me get my stuff. We have a lot to do before the ceremony."

Patrice gathered her things, and they walked down the hallway of the administration building reminiscing about the past.

∽∾

The sound of guys barking like dogs filled the air. Then there was a loud *Ooh-oop*! The chanting filled the night air and pierced the silence on the campus. The celebration had begun, and everyone was happy, especially Shante. She never thought her little girl would pledge her sorority, or any sorority; she was so independent and such a free spirit. But, tonight Camille had a big smile on her face.

Shouts of "D.S.T.," in honor of Delta Sigma Theta Sorority, filled the air. Shante, Patrice, and Gwen tried to keep up with their new sorors and the Omegas who joined them in the celebration.

"Camille," Shante yelled, trying to get her daughter's attention.

"Are you calling me, Mom—excuse me, *soror*?" Camille replied.

"Yes, soror, I am calling you. Come here. I want to take some pictures."

As her daughter ran toward her, Shante remembered the day Camille was born. She thought about how happy and scared she and Kevin had been when they brought her home. She remembered Camille's silliness when she began to talk. She seemed to have been born with a sense of humor, just like her father. She had become an outspoken activist in high school. There always seemed to be a cause to fight for. Now she looked at how sophisticated her daughter had become. Although she was still outspoken, she had a different air about her. Camille had graduated from peasant skirts and tennis shoes to form-fitting jeans and stilettos. She was so regal.

"How can you walk around campus with those shoes on? Your feet don't hurt?" Shante asked her.

"These shoes are comfortable, and I look good in them," Camille replied, hugging Shante.

"Let me get some of this," Gwen said, running to Camille and Shante and throwing her arms around them.

"Don't leave me out," Patrice said, joining the hugfest.

"Come on, sorors. Let's take some pictures," Shante said.

Someone started the music, and the Omegas began stepping. The Deltas began to dance. Shante found herself in the middle of the crowd trying to find a way out. Let the young people have their fun. All she could think about was getting back to the hotel and getting some sleep. She was weaving her way through the dancing group when a young man wearing an Omega shirt suddenly grabbed her and began dancing with her.

Shante had to laugh when Patrice hit Gwen and pointed to Shante and her dance partner and said, "It's about time she loosened up."

"I know," Gwen replied. "I hope she'll be all right. I think something is going on with her. Maybe tonight she can relax for a change."

❧

It was three in the morning when Camille and Shante got back to the hotel room. They were exhausted, but too hyped up to get to sleep right away. It had been a wonderful night. The step show was awesome. Afterward, Camille showed Shante how to do one of the steps they performed.

"Child, I am tired," Shante said, falling back onto the bed.

"As much as you partied, you should be. I have never seen you like this. What's up?" Camille asked as she plopped onto the other bed.

"Shouldn't you be with your line sisters instead of being here with your tired mother?"

"I can see them anytime. There's something going on with you. What is it?" Camille sat up on the side of the bed and looked at Shante lying across the bed with her eyes closed.

"Just a lot of church stuff. You don't want to be bored with that, do you?"

"Shoot, no! I don't see how you do it. If I were a preacher, I might cut some of those people."

"You're always talking about cutting somebody. I bet you don't even know how to use a knife."

"I can learn," Camille said, laughing. Then she grew quiet. "Mom, I got the internship I applied for at Sony Records in New York."

"What?" Shante said, sitting up on the bed. "That's wonderful. It will open a lot of doors for you. I'm so happy for you. It's what you wanted, right?"

"Yeah, and I have to be there two weeks after the semester ends."

"Two weeks! That's only six weeks away, Camille. We need to find you a place to live in New York. May will be here before you know it."

"Don't worry about that. The company has other interns, and they match us up with roommates. We're all going to be staying in the same place. We'll have classes in the morning and have to work at the studios in the evening. We may even help shoot a television show."

"Sounds exciting."

"It is, Mom. Opportunities don't come along like this often—doing what I like and getting paid for it. It's a wonderful life," Camille said, rolling over on the bed and talking on and on about her move to New York and all the fantastic things she was going to do while she was there.

Shante was listening to her daughter, but her mind still wandered back to Kevin's threat. He obviously wanted to make her think he had something on her, but she could not imagine what it was. It was impossible. She had nothing to hide other than the fact that he was harassing her. She was positive she had done nothing wrong. As a lady preacher, she knew she had to keep herself above reproach. To the people with whom she associated everything had to be straightforward, clean, unblemished. One little rumor could destroy everything she had worked for. There was no doubt about that, especially for a single, female preacher.

"Mom, are you asleep?" Camille asked.

"Just about. Let's finish this conversation in the morning," she said.

"It is morning."

"Then later this morning. I'm going to bed."

CHAPTER 5

This traffic is horrible, Shante thought. She was on her way to the church for a counseling session with a couple who were getting married in a few weeks. Realizing she was not going to make it to her appointment on time, she picked up the phone to call Gail, but it rang just as she was about to dial. She didn't recognize the caller ID, so she let it go to voice mail. However, before she could dial Gail, the phone rang again. Thinking the call could be important, she answered it. "Hello."

"Hey, Doobie." She didn't understand why Kevin continued calling her that name. On second thought, she did know. It was a name he had given her while they were married, because she used to wrap her hair and lounge around the house. She had tolerated it then, but now it irritated her and he knew it, which meant he did it to harass her.

"Kevin, how did you get my cell number?"

"Oh, baby, you know you can't keep anything from me."

"I'm going to hang up."

"You know I'll just call back. I need to talk to you."

"About what? Why are you harassing me?"

"Harassing you? Doobie, you know I wouldn't do anything like that. I just wanted to know if you have thought about when you and Max were going to preach at my church. We need to get it scheduled. That's all I want."

"I told you I'm not doing it," she screamed into the phone. Under no circumstances was she going to preach at his church. She had discussed it with Patrice, had prayed about it, and had decided it was her best course of action. Nothing he could do or say would convince her to preach at his church ever again.

"You'll do what I tell you. I'm telling you that you're going to preach at my church or else," Kevin yelled.

"Or else what? I'm not afraid of you anymore. If you call me again, I'm calling the police. I am not joking, Kevin. I'll send you to jail."

"And I'll send you to hell," he yelled into the phone as she hung up on him.

Shante pulled into the parking lot of a shopping center to calm down. She wondered how he had gotten her cell number. Long gone were the days when she enjoyed his phone calls. He was so funny, and his sense of humor had enchanted her over the phone or in person. Now she had to change her phone number whenever he managed to get it. But she couldn't just keep doing that; so many people depended on her.

She tried to pull herself together and began to pray. *God, help me. Show me the way. Remove any anxiety. Protect me from the attacks of the enemy. Father, you said you would make my enemy my footstool. I trust you. I believe in your Word. You are an awesome God. You are a faithful God. There is none like you. Now, Father, as I pre-*

pare to go to minister to Darryl and Terunda, give me the wisdom and knowledge to bless their union and counsel them in the steps they are about to take. In Jesus name. Amen.

∽∾

Shante sat in her office after her counseling session wondering what to prepare for dinner. With Camille in college, she no longer planned meals. She always tried to eat healthy, but today she felt like a hamburger.

"Excuse me, Pastor," Gail said, interrupting Shante's hamburger cravings. "Pastor Bryson's secretary called for a date you will preach at his church. You are booked up until the end of the summer. What do you want me to do?"

Shante couldn't believe he was calling her church trying to get them to put his revival on her schedule. How far was he willing to take his harassment? She debated whether to call the police and to tell them he was violating his restraining order, but did not want any negative attention brought to her church.

"Send him a letter telling him I will not be able to preach at his church." Why had she not seen this side of him before they got married? She was certain he was a good person inside. He loved the ministry. He loved his congregation. He was passionate about being a Christian and a minister. It was one of the reasons she married him. Ministry made him happy and gave him purpose. Now it seemed to be causing him so much sorrow. It was as if he had an evil twin living inside him, one who kept him from walking in the way he preached and in a constant state of despair and desperation. She lamented his fall from grace and prayed for God to change him.

CHAPTER 6

It was a perfect April day. The temperature was just right. The sky was a brilliant, cloudless blue. The gardens were in full bloom, and they had the place practically to themselves—hardly a tourist in sight. Shante and Max had left the intrusions of daily life behind and had escaped to the peace and quiet of the magnificent Biltmore Estate in Asheville, North Carolina. They walked in contented silence, basking in the beauty of the grounds. She bent to inhale the subtle fragrance of a perfectly formed yellow rose. He bent next to her. Their eyes met. She abruptly stood and continued strolling, leaving Max still bent at the yellow rose. Then he, too, jumped up and ran to catch up with her. They continued their silent stroll through the gardens until they came to a path leading to the Biltmore House, one of the grandest castles in the world and considered unmatched in America.

When they entered the House, Shante was immediately struck by how quiet it was. It seemed no one was making a sound, not even the few employees there. They were amazed by the sheer grandeur of the place—the architecture, the art collection, the Old World craftsmanship, the elegant furnishings—and its stupendous size (250 rooms).

They went up to the second-floor bedroom suites, each of which afforded a view of the vast estate. They went out on the balcony of one of the bedrooms and enjoyed a more sweeping view of the estate grounds and of the surrounding mountains. They were alone. Max came close to Shante and put his arms around her.

"Tay, I have something to tell you," Max said softly.

"What is it?" she asked, hearing the seriousness in his voice.

"When we were in college, I thought you were the most wonderful woman I had ever known."

"Thank you," Shante said.

"Please, Tay, let me finish. I would get so nervous when you were around, I didn't know what to do. Then we graduated and lost touch. Our lives went separate ways. We both got married. Meko died and you got divorced, and now we're back where we started, together. You are my everything—my peace, my joy, my comfort . . ." Max stopped, seemingly unsure what to say next.

"Max, what is it? What's wrong?" she asked, going to him and lightly, lovingly touching his back. "Whatever it is, Max, I can handle it. Are you seeing someone now?"

"No! That's not it, Shante. I guess what I'm trying to say is I love you. I've loved you for a long time. I wanted to tell you, but I didn't think you thought of our relationship that way. I mean, you don't have to say anything. I just wanted you to know," he said, both eager and afraid to hear her response.

"Is that all, Max? Is that why you're so serious?" she laughed. "I'm not laughing at you or what you said, Max. The truth is, I feel the same way about you. I'm relieved that it's out in the open now."

Max walked over and pulled Shante close. Their faces slowly came together; then their lips met . . .

The alarm jarred Max awake. "Dream interrupted," he muttered, rolling over and looking at the clock. It was six in the morning. Time to get the boys up and ready for school. *It was only a dream.* It was First Friday, the day he and Shante hung out together every month, and he had it all planned out. It would be just like his dream, but better. Wonder if Shante is up? On impulse, he decided to call her before waking the boys.

"Hello, this is Shante. I'm not available to answer your call. Please leave a brief message."

I'll just call her later. She may be in the shower and did not hear the phone ring. He leaped from the bed and read his scripture for the day, Proverbs 18:22: "Whoso findeth a wife findeth a good thing, and obtaineth favor of the Lord." Max said a prayer and started his day feeling light-hearted and expectant. Positive thinking is the key, he told himself.

∽∾

On the drive to Shante's house, Max's excitement about the day grew. Arrangements had been made with the Biltmore staff for a private tour of the main house, a carriage ride through the estate, lunch in a private dining room at the Biltmore Hotel, a tour of the winery, and a late afternoon snack beside the lake. Shante loved antique cars, and he was going to surprise her with a tour of an antique car museum in Asheville. He had even arranged for someone to pick up the kids. It was going to be a terrific day.

Max pulled into Shante's driveway and found her garage door closed; it was usually up when she was expecting him. He quickly parked and hurried to the door. She did not answer the doorbell. When she still didn't answer after a second ring, he became concerned. He got his cellphone from his car and dialed her house number. No answer. He then checked his messages to see if she had called him. There was one message from the night before.

"Hey, Max, this is Shante. I just wanted to talk to you before I boarded the plane. I'll call you later."

Max was perplexed. Shante usually told him when she went out of town. He reckoned something had happened and she had to leave on short notice. With all kinds of thoughts running through his mind, he quickly dialed her cellphone. *Where could she be?*

The ring of her cellphone awakened Shante. It was only 5:12. Who would be calling so early in the morning? "Hello."

"Shante, where are you?" Max asked.

"What?"

"Were you asleep? I got your message. Is anything wrong?"

"Max?" she said, finally recognizing his voice. She sat up and tried to shake herself fully awake.

"Yes, it's me. What's wrong? I'm at your house. I got your message. What's wrong?"

"You're at my house? Why?"

"It's First Friday. I had something planned for us."

"Max, did you forget I am preaching at a women's conference at Ray of Hope Worship Center? I'm in California. It's five in the morning here."

"I forgot," Max said, disappointed. Now he remembered; Shante had told him about the conference. He realized he hadn't even prayed with her before she left, something he usually did when she was traveling. "I forgot it was today. I'm sorry I woke you, Tay. It's just that I had something planned, and I didn't know where you were. I didn't even pray with you."

"Don't worry about that, Max. Can we do what you had planned next Friday?"

"No, I can't. I have a hearing, and I can't reschedule."

"Okay. I'm sorry, Max. I thought you knew. I would have called you earlier, but I had a lot going on at the church."

"That's okay, Shante. I'm sorry I woke you."

"Don't worry about it. I need to get up and exercise, anyway."

"Well, I'll let you go."

"Max, before you go, will you pray for me?"

Max began to pray for her. She closed her eyes and listened to his smooth, deep voice.

"Shante, you have a blessed time in California," Max said, trying to hide his disappointment.

"Thank you, Max. I'll be home tomorrow."

"Shante, I . . ."

"What, Max?"

"I-I, I'll miss you."

"Stop acting silly. I'll see you tomorrow."

"Do you have someone to pick you up at the airport?"

"I drove. My car is in the parking lot. Thanks for offering. Bye, Max." She leaned back onto the bed, and her mind wandered to Bishop Thompson's prophecy. At times she wished she were married. She hated traveling to preach alone. She fantasized that her husband would support her ministry and relieve some of the pressures she now faced alone.

Dressing for the fitness center Shante pushed the thoughts from her mind. She had to prepare herself for a long day of attending functions at Ray of Hope; and about the sermon she was to preach that evening.

❦

Max hung up and wondered how he could have forgotten about her trip. He called the Biltmore Estate and cancelled his plans. "God, will this ever work out?" Max prayed. Then he remembered what Bishop had told him. It brought him no relief. However, he promised himself he would not give up on his quest for a romantic relationship with Shante. He would plan something else special for her, and he wouldn't wait for the next First Friday to do it.

CHAPTER 7

"Good morning, Pastor. How was your trip?" Gail asked when Shante walked into the office on Monday morning. Once again, on her day off, she was in the office working. It had been a long few days. Her plane was late arriving from California on Saturday and she did not have time to rest as she had to prepare a sermon for Sunday. The two services on Sunday went into praise overdrive, and afterwards she had to meet briefly with the women's committee about the upcoming fellowship meeting. In addition, Max kept calling her throughout the day on Saturday and Sunday inviting her to dinner, and he wouldn't to take no for an answer. Her body had not overcome the jet lag, and she could feel it as she dragged herself into the office.

"It was blessed. The Lord really moved in that place. I thought we were never going to get out of there," she replied, handing Gail a CD of the sermon she had preached at the conference. She was tired, but she was still also excited about a meeting to stop a club from opening near her church.

"I'm glad to hear that. Oh, some people are already here for the meeting. I put them in the conference room."

"Thanks, Gail. Hold my calls, and please take some coffee into the conference room."

"I'm already on it. I also put some Krispy Kreme doughnuts in there."

"You know you're wrong for that," Shante said, laughing. She was glad she had Gail for a secretary. She was always on top of things. It wasn't easy finding a good secretary. Gail had been with her for three years. She'd had doubts about her in the beginning, because she was so young and she was right out of community college, but everything seemed to be working out fine. She had been a tremendous asset to the church. "I have to make a phone call. Tell them I'll be in directly."

It was going to be a long day. A group of ministers and other community leaders were meeting at her church to plan how to stop a gentlemen's club from moving into the neighborhood. Their initial strategy was to get the Mecklenburg County council to deny the rezoning application. If they could accomplish that, there was no way the club could move in.

They had been trying for weeks to get the names of the individual owners of the club. They knew the Annex Corporation was the corporate owner, but they needed the names of individuals they could approach directly. Shante felt if she could talk to the person in charge, she might be able to persuade him to donate the club as a tax write-off. It would be easier than going through all the drama of appearing before the county council. But Gail had researched the club's ownership for weeks and hadn't found out anything. She had a sense that the answer was right in front of her if only she could see it.

Four people were in the conference room when Shante walked in. She greeted everyone by name, except for a gentleman whom she did not recognize. She went over to him and introduced herself. "Hello, I'm Shante Dogan. I pastor this church."

"Hello, I'm Elder Richard Boyd. I pastor True Christian Believers Praise and Worship Center International. We're just moved into the old laundromat around the corner."

She sat down next to him. "So, Elder, are you new to Charlotte?"

"My wife and I moved here six months ago to start a ministry. We felt the Lord calling us here. You know my wife and I have been married over thirty years. I love her. There isn't another woman in the world for me. I don't know what I would do without her. She has definitely been my helpmeet. My wife is the most beautiful woman . . ."

Midway through the man's ode to his wife, Shante's mind started to wonder. She knew his kind—always praising his wife, wanting everyone to think he had a perfect marriage. Every time she encountered the wife of one of these types of men, she would see a woman looking depressed and worn out, or acting overly righteous to cover up the hurt inside. She could usually tell what kind of marriage the couple had just by looking at the wife. And whenever she encountered someone like Elder Boyd, she expected him to ask her to a private meeting or try to rub up against her. She decided to move before he tried to touch her leg, but before she could every seat had been taken. Every community leader seemed to be there. She stood and opened the meeting with a prayer.

The strategy session lasted more than two hours. Everyone was upset that someone would be bold enough to put a gentlemen's club near churches, schools, and homes—even a playground just two blocks away from the planned site. A plan of attack evolved and everyone agreed Shante would speak on behalf of the community at the council meeting on the following Tuesday.

As the attendees were leaving, Elder Boyd came to her. "Excuse me, Pastor, may I speak with you for a minute?"

"Sure," Shante said, shaking the hand of the last person leaving.

"I was really floored by your presentation today. You are a very intelligent woman."

"Thank you, Elder. However, my assistant, Gail, did all the legwork. It pays to have a good assistant behind you."

"I know. My wife is my assistant," Elder Boyd said, looking around the room before coming closer. "I have some questions about some of the points you made in your presentation. I was wondering if we could meet somewhere to discuss them."

"Elder, check my schedule with Gail. If there's a time you and your wife can meet me here at the church before the council meeting, she can set it up. However, I don't schedule meetings with male ministers outside the church setting. You know what the Bible says: Do not even give that appearance of wrongdoing. I try to live by that. So check with Gail. She can set something up for you. You know we have to be about the business of the Kingdom. Come on, I'll walk you out," she said, moving toward the door. It was just as she had thought. She knew she could not trust him. She had given him the benefit of the doubt, and he had failed. She couldn't believe he thought she was naïve enough to meet him to discuss issues. He probably thought she was new to the ministry. She thought he was a joke.

The council room was packed. People were standing against the walls. Max had hoped to get there early to support Shante, but his babysitter was a no-show, and he had to bring the boys with him. He hoped Joshua would be still and not act up. This was an important night for Shante, and he wanted to be there.

Max saw two chairs in the back and led the boys to those seats. Jonathan and Jacob shared one, and Max sat in the other with Joshua in his lap. Jonathan and Jacob began nudging each other. Max pulled out two video games from his grab bag and gave one to each of them. He gave Joshua a snack.

"Sir, there is no eating in council chambers," a guard told Max, pointing to Joshua eating his snack.

"I'm sorry. I'll put it away." But Joshua had already eaten it. He was relieved that he was spared having to listen to his son whining about his snack the rest of the night. Max looked around for Shante. He saw someone that looked like her, but when she turned around, he saw it wasn't her.

When Shante entered the room, it was as if a celebrity had arrived. People crowded around her, many walked up to talk with her. Some reviewed notes with her. A man got up and gave her his seat. Max took it all in as if he were watching a movie star on the red carpet. She looked so professional, so distinguished. Everything about her was perfect. Council members took their seats, and the meeting was called to order.

The council discussed a variety of issues involving budgets, highway infrastructure, and pay raises for county employees, and then the meeting was opened for discussion of zoning issues. Shante was called as spokesperson for the community leaders who had met at her church.

She addressed the council with elegance and style, self-assurance and passion. She spoke with authority on the increase in crime rates due to prostitution, gambling, and antisocial behavior a business like the club invariably brings to a community. She reviewed the negative experiences of other areas in the county that had allowed gentlemen's clubs to open in inappropriate locations. She described community concerns and presented a diagram of the proximity of the business to schools, churches, and playgrounds. When she finished, she received a standing ovation.

Max thought Shante exuded star quality as she delivered her address. She had mesmerized the audience. Max could barely contain himself as he proudly took in the whole scene.

When the crowd's applause died down, a small voice in the back called out, "You tell 'em, Mama Tay!" Heads turned. Joshua was clapping, yelling, "Yeah!" The crowd laughed. Max tried to cover Joshua's mouth with his hand, but it was too late; all eyes were on the boy. Shante saw Max and the boys and waved to them. She overheard a women in the crowd sitting directly behind her say, "Mama Tay, um-hum."

⌘

"I can't believe that bitch," Kevin said, driving down from the council meeting. He had gone to support his business partner, although he tried to make it appear he was on the side of those opposing the business.

He could not believe the council had voted against rezoning the gentlemen's club and had denied it a business license. It was going to be a classy joint, unlike the strip clubs in other areas. He was going to make sure of that. It was also going to be a private club, and only members of a certain caliber would be invited to join. He was not going to advocate prostitution—if the girls wanted to make extra money, they would have to do it on their own time. He wasn't going to interfere with that. But he was sure to make a lot of money, and it was all shot down because of Shante.

"How could she do this to me? She is messing with my money. I'm going to get that slut. She forgets, I know all about her. I knew her when she wasn't so high and mighty. Little Miss Holy. I ought to go to her house right now," he said, his voice loud and angry.

Driving down the street, Kevin's anger increased as he thought about seeing Shante with Max at the conference at Hilton Head. He recalled seeing them thru the window of a restaurant having dinner. It angered him thinking about seeing them dancing as he spied on them from a fishing pier. They had thought they could keep their little romance from everyone—including him. But he'd found out anyway. He never liked Max. He was too perfect in everyone's eyes. He was everything Kevin wanted to be—successful.

He continued thinking about Max and Shante when his phone rang. He saw from the caller ID that it was Pastor Foggy. Kevin knew he gossiped like a woman. This was perfect; he had a way of getting back at Shante. "Hey, Kev, how you doing, man? I saw you at the council meeting tonight. I wanted to holla at you after the meeting, but I lost you in the crowd. How you doing, man?"

"Hey, Foggy. I'm blessed."

"Did you see Pastor Dogan tonight? Man, she was on point. She showed those people on the council that some of us got some sense."

"Yeah, I saw her. It was funny seeing her, of all people, up there talking against a strip club."

"What do you mean?" Foggy asked.

"Man, she used to ride those poles like a professional. You didn't know?"

"Man, I've never heard that about her. I thought she was stuck-up. Everybody has tried to hit that. How do you know?"

"Foggy, we go back, way back. I knew her when I lived in Atlanta. She was something else. She wasn't preaching then. I tried to do everything I could to help her. She didn't listen to me. But I heard she was up to her old tricks."

"What?"

"Yeah, man, remember the conference at Hilton Head? I heard she was caught having sex on the beach."

"Nah, man, I don't believe it. The way she preached?" Foggy replied.

"You know those are the ones who like to get their freak on. Those are the hot ones."

"I know, man. Get with a Pentecostal ho, and it's a night worth paying for. Who was she with?"

"Maxwell Patrick."

"Reverend Patrick at Earle Street Baptist? You sure, man? He's pretty straight and narrow. From what I heard he hasn't messed with anyone since his wife died. He's taking all our single female members and a few married ones. They are all trying to get on him," Foggy said.

"Didn't you hear what happened after Dogan finished speaking tonight?"

"I did hear his son call her something. What was it? I know, Mama Tay. Man, all that was going on right in front of our eyes. You know it's always the quiet ones that are sneaking and creeping. Man, I didn't know that. Look, Kev, my other line is ringing. I'll talk to you later."

Kevin couldn't have asked for a better—or more willing—partner in misdeed. By morning this disinformation would be all over Charlotte and quite possibly the East Coast. He was going to show Shante not to mess with him.

⚉

Shante was finally able to get away from the reporters and the crowd of well-wishers after the council meeting. It seemed as if everyone wanted to speak with her about her comments. Other ministers wanted to talk to her about their next move, and the reporters wanted comments for their eleven o'clock news reports. Others wanted to celebrate their victory. She had made her getaway and had started her car when Max rang her cell.

"Shante, you should have gone to law school," Max said.

"I'll leave the law up to you. How did you get the boys to be so calm?"

"Believe me, it wasn't easy," Max answered. "Hey, we are going to get something to eat. Want to join us?"

"Max, now you know . . ."

"Come on. I know this little place not far from where you live. No one will see us. Besides, the boys want to talk to you. They are excited about the win and want to congratulate you. Come on, Tay. We won't stay long."

Shante agreed to have dinner with them on the condition they get carryout and eat at their house. She pulled into Max's driveway and waited.

"Yeah, Mama Tay. We won," Joshua shouted, running up to her. She smiled at Max as she hugged Joshua. Jonathan and Jacob were busy playing their video games, but they too came up and hugged her. Then went into the house and settled around the small table in the breakfast nook.

"You were just beautiful out there, Tay. I was so proud of you. The council had no other choice but to deny the rezoning after you finished with them. To get them to also deny a business license was a stroke of genius. Now they can't open a business anywhere in the county. Wonderful, just wonderful," Max said.

"You are good for a girl's ego. I think I'll keep you around for a while," Shante said grinning.

"And I believe I'll stay."

"Shante, did you ever find out who was behind the Annex Corporation?"

"No. Gail has been working on it for weeks. She told me she kept running into roadblocks. I tried calling the company myself. I kept getting an answering machine with a woman's voice saying they will contact us as soon as possible. Well, I guess it doesn't matter now. They won't be in our neighborhood or county. It would be nice to know who was behind it, in case they try to do this again."

"So what now?"

"We're going to contact the owner of the building tomorrow to see if he's interested in donating it for a new youth center. People in the community have a lot of ideas about things that benefit the neighborhood—an after-school program, for example."

"Any other use for a building that size? That's a pretty big place."

"Yes, there are a lot of ideas on the table. We're going to get together in a couple of weeks to really sort out our options."

"Speaking of a couple of weeks . . . I have a grant proposal you may want to take a look at. Come with me to the family room," Max said. He kept one eye on the boys as he spoke to Shante. "Don't forget about Josh's birthday party in two weeks," Max whispered.

"I haven't forgotten. Did you get the bike?" Shante asked.

"Yeah, It will be ready tomorrow. I'll bring it to your house. Is six o'clock all right?"

"That's fine, or you can bring it by the church earlier if you have to."

Max plowed ahead. "Tay. There's something I've been meaning to talk with you about."

"What's that?"

"Well, we've known each other for a long time. Since we were teenagers."

Shante smiled, recalling how they'd met. They were both freshmen in college and had been on campus only a few weeks and were trying to adapt to the heavy reading programs Morehouse and Spelman required. They met in the Shrine of the Black Madonna Bookstore in Atlanta. Ironically, they were looking for the same book, *The Falsification of Afrikan Consciousness* by Amos N. Wilson. There was only one copy left, and Max bought it and gave it to Shante with the understanding that when she finished reading it she would return it to him. She agreed and kept her word, even though she never actually read the book. Luckily Max had, and talked about it at length on their one and only date. In fact, he talked about it so much, she was able to pass the test just from listening to him. She decided to keep him around for a while. She didn't like to study, and they quickly became friends, although she felt no romantic chemistry between them.

"The boys love you," Max continued, walking as he talked.

"Is there anything wrong?"

"No, I'm just a little nervous."

"Really? Sit down and say what you have to say."

Max sat on the sofa. Shante was about to join him when Josh came in.

"Mama Tay, Mama Tay, come see my frog. His name is Ralph Junior. He's in my room."

"Ralph Junior? Where did you get that name?"

"We have a big frog in my class at school. His name is Ralph. My frog is little. That's why I call him Ralph Junior. Come on."

"Okay, but give me a minute. Let me speak to your father, and then I will come right up."

"No Tay, it's fine. He's been waiting to show you that frog since he got it. I'll wait until you get back."

As Shante and Josh headed up the stairs, she noticed Max sitting on the sofa with his head in his hands. "Max, are you okay?"

"Yeah, I'm fine. I think I'll go with you."

After Josh showed Shante how he fed his frog, he and his brothers headed for bed.

Walking to her car with Max, Shante sensed that something was weighing on his mind. "Max, are you sure you're okay? You had something to tell me. I'm listening."

"It can wait. But I could use a hug."

Shante embraced Max. He squeezed her tightly, which told her something was up with him. She always knew. She would talk with him about it later, when they were alone.

CHAPTER 8

It was Sunday, and Shante had been very busy all morning. She wished people would leave her alone before service; however, she had many visitors that morning. She was tired and hadn't even preached yet. She wished she could get through one Sunday morning without people unloading a lot of problems on her. She wanted more than a few minutes to focus on her sermon. Shante was closing the door to her office when she heard a knock. The elderly gray-haired man in the doorway was Trustee Tankersly, chairman of the trustee board of her church. "Hi, Tank, how are you doing this Sunday morning?"

"This is the day the Lord has made. Let us rejoice and be glad in it."

"Amen."

"Pastor, can I talk to you for a minute? It won't take long. You know the trustees and the brotherhood are going to get together to do some yard work around the church next weekend," Tank said, closing the door.

"I know. Is there anything you need? Sit down," Shante said, pointing to a chair.

"No, I won't be long. I thought you should know about something that's going around the churches," he said lowering his voice.

"Now you know I don't participate in gossip," Shante said, leaning on the edge of her desk. *What now?*

"Pastor, you've been here a long time. I've been here forty-two years myself. I think I'm a good judge of character. This time the gossip is about you."

"Tank, you say that as if no one has ever gossiped about me before."

"This is different. They say when you went to Hilton Head, you spent some time with a man." She could see he was deeply concerned.

"I spent a lot of time with a whole lot of men at the conference. It was mostly men there."

"No, Shante, you aren't listening to me. Rumor has it that you and Reverend Patrick spent the night with each other and people saw you having sex."

She stood up straight. This was nothing to shrug off. She knew he was serious because he called her by her first name. She was stunned to hear that someone had linked her with Max sexually. They had gone to such lengths to keep their friendship private. "What do you mean people saw us? How can they see what never took place?"

"Shante, I'm just telling you what someone told me. I'm not trying to judge you. Watch yourself. You know Chairman Deacon Curry has had it out for you since you denied his proposal for the staff retreat."

"His proposal was not properly completed. You know that. I just asked him to check his figures and rewrite his proposal and get back with me, which he never did. I did not deny his proposal." She walked around her desk and sat down.

"Church is about to start, Pastor. I only wanted you to know what's going on. Keep yourself clean. You know gossip has a way of blowing up all out of proportion. I'm on your side. I knew it wasn't you. I just wanted to hear it from you. I'll see you in the sanctuary."

Shante sat wondering what made people bring up drama right before service. But, she was determined not to allow the enemy to distract her. That was the problem, she thought, a distracting spirit that did not want the Word of God to go forth. She knew how to fight it with prayer. She went to the door and asked all four of the associate ministers waiting in the main office to come in for their morning prayer before service. They filed into her office and joined hands, and Shante prayed. After they left her office, she locked the door. She could hear service starting. She turned down the speaker in her office, knelt, and began to pray.

∽∾

Max was in his office at Earle Street Baptist Church preparing for his Sunday morning sermon. It was Communion Sunday. He always took time to be alone before service to clear his heart and mind. He decided to say his affirmations before service started.

"He who finds a wife findeth a good thing and receives favor from God. Father, I believe, I receive your Word, in Jesus name."

A knock at the door invaded his meditation. Where was his assistant? He did not like to be disturbed before service. He reluctantly walked to the door and opened it. There stood a very beautiful young lady who looked to be in her mid-thirties. She wore a big smile.

"Hello, Pastor. I'm Denitra Jamison. I was wondering if you had a minute. I would like to speak with you," she said.

"I'm sorry. You'll have to schedule an appointment to come in during the week to speak with me. Right now, I'm preparing for service," Max replied.

"Pastor, I won't be long. I need to discuss with you something the Lord revealed to me. It's kind of urgent," Denitra pleaded.

"Miss Jamison, please allow me to get my assistant." He tried to move past her. He knew what she wanted and he didn't have time for it. Too many women had come up to him with the same old line that the Lord had told them he was their husband. He was very tired of it and hoped it would stop once everyone found out about him and Shante.

"Your assistant? Why?" Denitra said.

"Ma'am, this is quite unusual. I'll have my assistant discuss the matter with you while I prepare for my sermon." Max tried to be polite and not cause a scene, but he had to get her out of his office. As she continued to talk, he slowly walked past her towards the hallway.

"Pastor, look at me. I'm your wife. The Lord told me this. We need to talk about it. I think you should take me seriously. I would not come to you if the Lord didn't send me here," Denitra yelled.

"Miss, you are highly out of order. Where is my assistant?" Max said, moving past Denitra into the outer lobby.

"I heard you were a great lover. I know all about Hilton Head—"

Max stopped her. "Miss, I don't know who you are or where you came from, but I'm trying to be nice. The Bible says the man finds the wife, not the other way around."

"Yeah, but—"

"Miss, service is about to start. Please leave. I have to prepare for service." Travis, Max's assistant pastor, entered the office. "This is Pastor Travis," he said, introducing the woman to him. "Ms. Jamison is visiting with us this morning. Could you please escort her to the sanctuary?"

"I know where it is." The lady left his office.

"What was all that about?" Travis asked.

"Nothing. Please see that I'm not disturbed before service."

Max returned to his desk wondering what she meant about Hilton Head. It sounded as if the rumor mill was churning again. He had grown tired of gossip and of the boldness of women like Ms. Jamison coming to him, especially in the church. God couldn't possibly tell hundreds of women they were his wife. It wasn't scriptural. It took all that he had to keep from telling them off. But, he couldn't focus on that now. He had to focus on his sermon without allowing his frustration to sidetrack him. He didn't have time to worry about idle gossip. There were more important things to take care of. Besides, whatever, it was, he was sure someone would call him and tell him.

CHAPTER 9

Two weeks had passed and Shante had busied herself fielding phone calls about her trip to Hilton Head and the minister's conference. It seemed to her that rumor spread with lightening speed. People finally had some dirt on her and Max, and they welcomed the opportunity to tell anyone who would listen. Shante attempted to assure everyone who had the nerve to ask her that it was only a false rumor. However, prominent members of her church began questioning her integrity and her relationship with Max. It had been overwhelming for her. With all she had done for the community and her church, she felt no one should question her integrity. Her only reprieve from the constant innuendos was Josh's birthday party. Only a few very close friends and members of his kindergarten class were invited to his party. Still, she felt people were staring at her as she tried to busy herself helping with the party.

"Happy birthday," everyone yelled as Josh blew out the candles on his cake. The high-pitched voices of children screaming filled the air at Max's home and he found it difficult to hear himself talk. Joshua was at the picnic table looking at the mountain of gifts he'd received, especially the one he most wanted.

"A big kid's bike," Joshua yelled excitedly, jumping on the small, electric blue dirt bike. "It's what I've always wanted. Thanks, Dad."

Max smiled broadly as he looked at Joshua. He was so proud of his son. At five years old, he had a near-perfect memory and was able to read simple books. Of all his children, Joshua looked most like him, dark skinned with a smile that could light up the room. Max wanted this birthday to be special. Joshua was entering another phase of his life. He would be going to school with Jacob—the big kids' school, he called it—and Max would no longer have to go to three different schools every day.

"Max, where's the helmet?" Shante asked. She had gone with him earlier in the week when Max had gone searching for the perfect bike.

"It's on the picnic table. I'll get it."

"While you're doing that, I'll go in the house and bring out the ice cream. This is a wonderful party, Max. Everyone seems to be having fun. Maybe later, I'll get the clown to teach me how to make balloon animals. Let me go get the ice cream," she said.

"Hey, girl, you need help?" Gwen asked, walking through the door of Max's custom kitchen, which he had designed himself.

"No, I think I can handle it. I'm just getting the ice cream. Thanks for coming to Josh's party. I think he loved the drum set you got him. Now you know Max is going to kill you," Shante said, laughing.

"He told me he wanted a drum set, so I got him one. I'm sure Max will appreciate it when he's making millions playing the drums, and when he wins his Grammys he'll get up and thank his Aunt Gwen for giving him his first set."

"Okay, Aunt Gwen, can you get those bowls out of the cabinet over there, the plastic ones on the second shelf?"

"Sure. So I see you know your way around the kitchen," Gwen said, walking over to the oak-stained cabinet.

"Don't start, Gwen. There are enough rumors going around about me now. I don't need another one started."

"I know, girl. When someone told me you used to be a stripper, I just laughed in her face."

What? Shante was stunned. Why would someone say something like that about her? How had such a rumor gotten started? She had tried so hard to keep her name out of the rumor mill.

"Didn't you hear that one? Yeah, someone said you used to be a stripper and that's why you fought so hard to stop the strip club from opening. I said to them we've been friends most of our lives, and I have never known you to be a stripper, but then you never know . . ." Gwen said jokingly.

"I didn't hear that one. I heard about me and Max having sex on the beach at Hilton Head."

"No, you didn't. Do you think someone saw me and Ron?"

"It's possible, but your name isn't attached to it; Max's name and my name are. I talked with Max about it when we went shopping for Josh. He said not to worry, that like all rumors, this one will go away as soon as someone else gets caught doing something, but . . ." She set down the ice cream container and sat at the small table next to the window. Gwen joined with her.

"But what, Shante?"

"Well, it's just that people are canceling my speaking engagements. I know it's because of the rumors. Can't people see how ridiculous all this sounds? I also had one speaker cancel with our women's ministry. She told Gail she couldn't be associated with our ministry at this time. It's embarrassing to walk into a room and know that everyone is talking about you and watching you, looking to see what you're going to do next. You know it's already hard for a lady preacher. Rumors only make it worse, and it eats at the heart of your integrity. Even today, it feels as if everyone is watching Max and me. I'm trying not to stand too close to him or sit next to him. As much as I love those boys, I'm afraid of what people are going to say. I thought for a moment of not coming at all."

"You know Josh would have been hurt. He loves his Mama Tay; you're his godmother. You had to come. You can't let all these rumors bother you. I know it's hard, but I also know how hard you work to keep yourself clean. You wouldn't do anything to hurt your ministry or the church image as a whole. Shante, I know all this will blow over soon. Just keep the faith."

"Gwen, you don't understand." The fear of losing her ministry was more than she could handle. She had learned of secret board meetings—the phone calls. Some were already plotting against her.

"Understand what?"

"Well, the board of the church called an emergency meeting today, and they're discussing me. They didn't ask me to come. Tank told me about the meeting. He said they would have another one with me soon. He thought I should know. I'm glad he told me."

"Oh, no, Shante. All this over rumors and gossip?" Gwen said, grabbing Shante's hand.

Shante began to cry. Gwen hugged her and prayed. "Father, we thank you for being the Most High God. We know that nothing is too hard for you. Right now, my sister Shante needs you. She needs your peace. You said in your Word that you would send us a comforter. Father, I ask that you send the Comforter to her right now and send peace into this situation. Father, we thank you that it is already done. We thank you that you have already given us the victory. In Jesus name. Amen."

"Thank you, Gwen," Shante said, wiping away her tears.

"I know that it's going to work out. Sometimes our faith is tested. Know that it's not God testing you, but the enemy. He wants you to give up, but I won't let you. I've got your back. Is there anything I can do?" Gwen asked stroking Shante's arm.

"Gwen, what if I lose my church? What am I going to do?"

"Shante, don't say that. Watch what you say. You aren't going to lose your church. I know it. I know things look bad now, but it will get better, you wait and see. Shante, you've got to keep the faith. Promise me something."

"What?"

"If you need anything—and I mean anything—please let me know. You know I'm here for you," Gwen said, drawing closer to Shante. They were hugging when Max walked in, startling Shante and Gwen.

"Hey, where's the ice cream?" Max asked. He stopped and looked from one to the other. Shante was crying. "Is anything wrong?" Max asked, looking at Shante trying to hide her tears.

"No, nothing's wrong. I've got to go to the bathroom," Shante said, running past Max.

"Gwen, what's wrong with Tay? Why is she crying?"

"You know women. We're hormonal. She's alright. I'm taking the ice cream out to the kids." When she got to the door, she stopped and turned to Max. "I don't know what's going on between you two—it's none of my business—but if you love Shante, you should support her now. She needs you. Do you love her?"

"Why are you asking me this?"

"Answer my question. Do you love her?"

"Maybe I should discuss this with Shante."

"That's all right. I think I know the answer. You should let her know. She needs to know she's not alone now. You know how private she is. She needs to know that her friends love her and will be there for her no matter what happens."

With that Gwen turned and walked out the door. Max wondered what was going on with Shante. He was aware of the gossip about them, but he thought she was handling it fine. He didn't see that she was having any problems; at least none that she'd revealed to him.

Shante returned to the kitchen and was surprised to see Max still standing there. "Are you okay?" Max asked, walking toward her.

"I'm fine," she said, moving around him and trying to avoid eye contact. She didn't want him to know what was going on, or even be involved, for fear his ministry would suffer, too. Besides, it was Joshua's special day, and she didn't want to ruin it for him.

"You're crying."

"It's my allergies. I'm fine."

"I haven't heard you use that excuse in a long time. What's wrong?"

"Nothing. I'd better go outside. It isn't a good idea for us to be seen alone in the house."

"I don't care what people think. I do care about what's happening with you. Talk to me."

"This isn't the time. I'm going outside."

Max grabbed her arm. He wanted to tell her he loved her. He wanted to hold her and comfort her. Something was definitely going on with her. Why wouldn't she talk to him?

"Let me go. Not now. We'll talk later."

Max released her arm, hoping she would talk with him later as she said. She walked into the backyard. Max followed.

Shante was looking around the backyard for Joshua, but there were so many children running around he was hard to spot. Then she saw him. He had on his bicycle helmet and was on his bike. Jonathan was helping him pedal. Something about the scene made Shante feel uneasy. She returned to the house and got her small bottle of anointing oil from her purse. She returned to the backyard and went over to Joshua.

"Let me help your brother. You guys go entertain the other guests," Shante said to Jonathan and Jacob.

"Mama Tay, I love my bike, and my helmet is cool, too. Can you teach me how to ride?"

"Yes, I'll teach you, but first there's something I need to do. Whenever you get a new vehicle—"

"Vehicle? Like a car?" Joshua asked.

"Yes, a car when you're older, but now your transportation is a bike, and whenever you get a new one, you should bless it so that God will always take care of you when you travel. Look, I have my oil. I'm going to bless you and your bike."

Shante put oil on the front and back fenders of the bike and anointed Joshua's forehead. She began to pray. "God, we thank you for your many blessings. We ask that you protect Josh as he travels on his new bike. Send your angels to surround him and keep him from all harm. We thank you that it's already done. In Jesus name. Amen."

"Thank you, Mama Tay. Now will you push me?" Joshua asked, hugging Shante.

From the other end of the yard, Max watched Shante with Joshua. He would have to tell her how he felt soon. He knew he wanted to marry her. To him, there was no separation between him, her, and his children. They were already a family.

CHAPTER 10

Shante was trying to decide whether or not to wear makeup. She only wanted to relax. It was First Friday, and Max was taking her to the Biltmore Estate. She was looking forward to it; she needed to get out of Charlotte, if just for the day. When he had first asked, she had declined, telling him she did not want to have First Friday until all the rumors had died down. But, he insisted they continue. He was trying to encourage her, but he didn't know about the meeting with the church board the following week.

She looked at the scars on her face and decided if it was only Max, she would go without makeup. However, since they were going to a public place where there would be lot of tourists, she needed to cover up her scars. She started applying her makeup and was interrupted by a phone call from Gwen.

"Good morning, Shante. How are you?"

"Hi, Gwen. I'm doing great. It's First Friday. Max and I are going to the Biltmore Estate. You know I love that place. It's so peaceful."

"You must mean your and Max's First Friday. It is not the first Friday of the month. It's only Thursday."

"I know, but I'm going through so much. I need a break. It will keep me from thinking about the meeting next

Saturday. We decided to do it today. Besides, I think Max needs a break from those drums you gave Josh last week." She laughed. "What's up? I'm trying to put my makeup on."

"Girl, I know that's going to take you about an hour. I'd better hurry. I just wanted to call and encourage you. You were in my spirit so much last night. I spent a lot of time praying for you, and Ron, and I prayed for you this morning. I know you'll be alright. I know God already has this thing worked out. I wanted you to know that we were praying for you."

"Thank you, Gwen. It's good to know someone has me covered with prayer. I appreciate your and Ron's friendship. I love you two."

"We love you back. I know you're trying to get ready. Tell Max I said hello. You have a good day."

"You, too, Gwen. I'll talk to you later."

"I know you will. I want all the details."

Shante hung up and went back to applying her makeup. Her doorbell rang. Max was there early; she was not even dressed. She ran to the door to let him in and found Kevin there looking as though he had not slept in days.

"What are you doing here? How did you find out where I live?" Shante demanded.

"I told you, I know everything about you," Kevin said, nudging Shante, trying to push past her.

"What do you want? You can't come in here," Shante said heatedly as she blocked the doorway.

"I can go wherever I please," Kevin said, pushing her back and forcing his way in. He pushed the door so hard the impact left a hole in the wall.

Shante screamed and ran to get the phone sitting on the table next to the sofa in her living room. Fear engulfed her when Kevin lurched toward her. She could smell the alcohol on his breath. His eyes were bloodshot and his speech was slurred. Stumbling slightly on the small rug on the floor, Kevin knocked the phone out of her hand. "You've been drinking," she said, backing away. Her heart raced, and she could hardly breathe.

"You think you're all that. I should have killed you when I had the chance."

"Kevin, I haven't done anything to you. What do you want?"

"You should have kept your mouth closed, standing there like you are all high and mighty. You think you know everything."

"Kevin, what are you talking about?"

"You know what I'm talking about—the Annex Club. You knew I was going to make a lot of money on that business."

"You were behind that club? How could you?" That was low, even for Kevin. She never imagined he would stoop so low as to put such a business in any neighborhood, much less one with schools and a park nearby. She could see the club from the church, and he knew her church was nearby. She was almost frozen by disbelief. She thought he had more respect for the church and God to ever do such a thing.

"You don't want me to be successful. You're always taking things from me. You took my daughter from me.

Now you're taking my money. Bitch, you're going to pay. How would you like it if I messed with your stuff?"

Kevin knocked a lamp off the table. Shante ran down and made it to the master bedroom in the back of the house before Kevin could close the distance between them. She closed and locked the door and leaned on it to catch her breath. She heard him coming down the hallway. Panic seized her. She ran to on the stand beside her bed and quickly dialed 911.

"Nine-one-one operator. What is your emergency?" a woman asked.

"My name is Shante Dogan. I live at 3307 Kingston Boulevard in the Greentree subdivision. My ex-husband, Kevin Bryson, is in my house. He's drunk. He's tearing up my house," Shante said in a panicked but clear voice. She could hear the terrifying sound of things being thrown about and of glass being shattered. She trembled with fear.

"He's in your house now?"

"Yes. I have a restraining order against him."

"Ma'am, I'm sending help now. Stay on the phone with me until help arrives. Did he assault you?"

Shante nervously held on to the phone as if hanging on for her life. "No, he didn't hit me. I ran. I'm in the bedroom at the end of the hall. It sounds like he's tearing up my house." A crashing sound made Shante jump. "Please hurry."

"Ma'am, they'll be there shortly. We have a unit on the way. Is he still there?"

"Yes. Oh, my God! He's trying to get into the bedroom," she screamed as the doorknob began to shake. She prayed as Kevin yelled and cursed at her through the door.

"Is that him yelling?"

She ran into the adjoining bathroom and locked the door. "Yes. I'm in my bathroom now. I can't get the window up." Shante said, trying desperately to push the bathroom window up. The window would not budge. Finally, she gave up and began looking around the bathroom for something to break the window.

"Ma'am, just stay where you are. The unit is almost there. Try to remain calm."

"He's not making a sound. It's too quiet," Shante told the operator. All of a sudden she heard him kicking the door. "Please hurry. He's trying to get in here." Her heart rate felt as though it had quadrupled. She was hyperventilating and made futile attempts to slow her breathing. It seemed like forever since she'd called 911. She shuddered, remembering what Kevin was capable of doing.

"Freeze! Put your hands up! Now! Move away from the door!"

Shante sagged with relief when she heard those words. The police had arrived. She listened intently to everything being said on the other side of the door. "They're here. I think they have him," she told the 911 operator.

"Ma'am, stay where you are until they tell you to come out. I'll stay on the phone with you."

"Thank you." Shante sat silently listening to the activity outside the bathroom door. A knock at the door made her jump.

"Ma'am, are you in there? It's the police. We have the suspect in the other room," a female voice said.

Shante walked to the door and cautiously opened it. The police officer was a welcome sight. She relaxed when she was sure Kevin was no longer in the room. She began crying. The officer took the phone and spoke with the operator and then hung up.

"Stay right here. Let me see if they have him in the car," the officer said.

She nodded, afraid to move without the police officer's consent.

"Ma'am, he's outside. You can come out now."

Shante walked through her house, surveying the damage Kevin had done. It looked like a tornado had hit her home. Holes were in her walls, furniture was overturned, picture frames had been smashed, and papers were strewn all over the floor. She bent down and picked up a picture of Camille and pulled pieces of glass from it.

"Ma'am, we need to ask you some questions. Are you hurt? Should we call an ambulance?"

"No, he didn't hit me. I ran," she said quietly.

"You did the best thing. It could have been much worse. Let's have a seat, and you tell me what happened."

Shante sat on her sofa and began describing the events of the morning to the officer. She also told her how Kevin had come to Charlotte and had begun harassing. She described his visits to the church and the threats he had made. She hoped what she said would be enough to keep him locked up this time.

The door opened and Max walked into the house and stopped short when he saw the destruction. Shante was sitting on the sofa talking with an officer.

"Max, thank God you're here," Shante said, running to him.

"What happened? Are you all right?" Max asked, hugging her. He looked around at the holes in the wall, the overturned furniture, and the shattered glass.

"Kevin. He found out where I live. He tore up my house."

"Are you okay, Shante? Did he hurt you?"

"No, he didn't hurt me. I'm fine. Too bad I can't say the same thing for my house."

"What was he doing here?"

"Tearing up my stuff," she said, looking around the room.

"Things can be replaced. Are you sure you're okay?" Max looked at her as if he was examining every part of her to see if she was hurt.

"Yes, I'm fine now."

"Ma'am, someone will be contacting you about this case next week. Sir, are you going to be here with her?" the police officer asked Max.

"Yes. I'm not leaving."

"Good. We're taking Mr. Bryson to jail. A judge will determine if bond will be set for him. Here is your copy of the report. If you have any questions, here is my card. You can contact me at this number," the officer said.

"Thank you for everything," Shante said.

Shante and Max stood in the doorway until the two police cars drove away. "Tay, are you sure you're all right?"

"I'm a little shaken up, but I'm all right."

"What happened?"

"I was getting ready. I heard the doorbell. I thought it was you. I didn't look through the peephole. I just opened the door. It was Kevin. He was drunk, as usual. He forced his way in."

"What was he doing here?"

"The question is how did he find out where I live."

"Did he say why he came over?"

"He was angry because . . . the strip club . . . it was his business."

"What?"

"Yeah, Max, the strip club was Kevin's business. He blamed me for closing it down. He thinks I was out to get him. I didn't even know he was behind the Annex Corporation. How could he keep that a secret? Gail tried to get the names of the owners. I guess now we know who was behind it. A preacher."

"I wouldn't call him that."

"There are a lot of things I can call him, but I won't. Look at my house. It's going to take a long time to repair this damage."

"I'll help you," Max said, pulling her toward him. As he held her, Shante began to cry.

"Why won't he leave me alone? I never asked him for child support. I try to stay away from him. Camille and I don't even talk about him. Yet he keeps showing up.

Not for the important things like when I told him about Camille's high school graduation, but for stuff like this. He just won't quit."

"That's how the enemy works. I'll help you through this."

"Thank you, Max," she said, pulling away from him and once again looking around the room.

"I guess we can start working on cleaning up this place. I'll have a contractor come out tomorrow to get an estimate on what it will take to fix the walls and windows," Max said, picking up chairs off the floor.

"We aren't going to Asheville?" Shante asked.

"I thought you wouldn't want to go now."

"I want to go now more than ever. I can't be in this place right now. I need to get away. I can start cleaning up when we get back."

"Are you ready to go?"

"Let me finish getting ready. I won't be long," she said, walking down the hallway, touching the holes in her walls along the way. She stopped at her bedroom door and put her hand in the hole Kevin had kicked in it. She wondered how she could have gotten involved with him and prayed that God would help her in this situation.

"Hey, baby, it's me." Kevin was talking on the phone after his bond hearing. "I need you to get ten thousand dollars and come and get me. I'm in jail. I know you can do it. You know I'm good for it. I'll give it back as soon as I get out. Baby, I need your help now. Come and get me."

Kevin hung up. An officer walked him back to his cell. He had been there all morning and was now sober enough to realize he was in jail. He didn't know why. He couldn't remember what happened.

⅋

The ride to Asheville was quiet. Max didn't know what to say, and Shante didn't want to talk. She only wanted to take in the view of the North Carolina mountains. As they drove around the curvy, narrow street leading to the Biltmore Estate, Max began to doubt whether this was the right time to tell her about his feelings. He knew she needed to be ministered to, but he didn't know how. Should he minister to her as a pastor, friend, or something more? Tension was in the air. He was desperate to diffuse it. After they had parked, he got out of the car, but Shante seemed frozen in deep thought. He opened her door, bent down, and placed his hand on hers.

"Do you want to talk?"

She shook her head. She couldn't look Max in the face. This trip meant more to him than he wanted her to know. She did not want to get into any heavy conversations; she only wanted to relax, to have fun. Shante got out of the car and walked past him.

"Tay."

"Max, I will not let Kevin destroy this day. Come on," she said, holding her hand out. He took it, and they started walking the Biltmore Estate.

They walked across the beautifully manicured front lawn with its lion-crested fountains, past the main house, and into the gardens. She looked at a rose like it was the very first time she had seen one. They walked through the greenhouses and out the back door into the gardens on the other side. She stopped at a small bush covered with brightly colored red and green leaves. She gently caressed them, hoping the softness of the leaves would take away the events of the day. Max came up behind her and placed his hands on her shoulders. She didn't turn around.

"You know I'm here for you. If you want me to, I'll punch him around a little," Max said, stepping back and assuming a boxing stance. She started laughing when she turned and saw his silly expression as he boxed the air.

"Maybe you can teach me a few things," Shante said, getting into the spirit of his antics.

"This is the first time I've seen you smile all day. You're beautiful."

"Thank you, Max."

"Come here," Max said, walking to her. "I don't want anything to happen to you. I'll protect you. You don't have to worry anymore, but I wish you would be more open with me."

"Open how?"

"You know what I mean. You keep things to yourself. You don't discuss your problems until after they've been solved. I'm your friend. I want to help you. Like today, I don't think that would have happened if you had a man in your life. He's only acting that way because you're alone and he thinks you're afraid of him."

"So now you want to be my protector? Kevin is a dangerous man," she said, backing away from Max.

"I can handle him. I'm your friend. I hate to see you hurting. Please let me be your protector—your friend."

"You are my friend, but I think I can take care of myself."

"Like you took care of yourself today?" She didn't answer. She walked away, leaving Max standing near the bush. "Hey, I'm sorry, I shouldn't have said that," Max said, catching up with her.

"I know you didn't mean any harm. Come on, let's go in the house. It's getting hot out here."

As they walked through the long covered walkway in the garden, Shante stopped to look at the flowers growing on a vine that covered the walls outside the house. "These flowers are beautiful. I wonder what they are. I would like to have this in my garden."

"You don't have to be strong all the time. Let me be strong for you."

"Max, please. I'm here to relax."

"It's okay. I'm here," he said.

"Max, don't."

"It's okay. I'm here."

The romance of the Biltmore Estate was always the forefront of their conversation on previous trips there. The endless flirting with each other was absent on this trip. Somehow, Kevin managed to distract her again. All she could think about was how to get him out of her life for good.

"I want to be here for you. Let me into your world. I want to keep you safe. I want to be here to comfort you when you need me. I want to be a part of your life, not just friends. Tay, I love you. I want to be with you all the time. I think about you all the time. I don't ever want you to have another day like you had today. I love you." He pulled her close and tried to kiss her lips. She quickly pulled away from him.

"No, don't do that," she said. "It's not the right time. I know you love me. I've known it for a long time. Max, I can't do that to you. You see I have a lot of drama in my life. People think I have a perfect life, but I don't. I'm not complaining. I'm doing what I like. I love the ministry. I love the people I work with, but all of a sudden, everything in my life has gone crazy. I've got problems in my church and in my home. I can't bring you into this. I value your friendship. I don't want anything to destroy that. If it means the end of our friendship, then I'll have to deal with that, too. I can't get you and the boys involved in my drama."

"You aren't doing anything to me. I want to be with you. Besides, I'm already involved. I know about the meeting next week. Ron and Gwen told me. I wish you had told me. I've been praying for you and asking God how to handle this whole situation. If it hadn't been for me, you wouldn't be in this position now."

"You didn't do anything wrong."

"I was at the beach with you. It's funny, but when the rumors started a few weeks ago, my ministry grew. I began getting calls from all over the place. People who have never spoken to me are now calling me up and inviting me places. The women . . . I don't want to even talk about the women. Yet, with you it's the exact opposite. Seems like your ministry has been hurt by all the rumors."

"You know why that is. It's because I'm female and single. There's a double standard for women in the ministry. One persistent rumor can potentially destroy a ministry. So far, I haven't lost many members because of this, maybe one or two. I am trying to be extra clean, extra careful. But it has been like walking on eggshells, like feeling as if I am being watched all the time. There is nothing I can do or say to make some people not believe the rumors. Some people simply cannot believe a rumor can be created out of thin air. Obviously, some board members believe them or they wouldn't be having this meeting."

"There is always an element in the church that wants to see you fail. You have to recognize that it is coming from the enemy. God says in his Word that you are victorious in all things. Look, I've known you for a long time. You're good people."

"Good people?"

"Yes, good people. I know everything will work out."

"Thanks, Max. I needed to hear that for the thousandth time. I don't want to talk about this anymore. Let's just try to enjoy this day. Come on."

Holding hands, they walked up the stairs leading to the first level of the house. Despite her upbeat words to Max, Shante thoughts kept returning to Kevin. She was trying to figure out ways of getting him to leave her alone. Preaching at his church flashed through her mind, but she quickly pushed it away. It had not worked that time she had preached there for exactly the same reason—to get him off her back. The harassment had continued. She felt a sense of absolute hopelessness.

Max was giving her a history lesson on the Biltmore and Asheville, but she was only half attentive, as her mind kept going back to how Kevin looked at her house. He had terrorized her, yes, but she still felt sorry for him. He was not always like that—so lifeless, so frustrated, so consumed by anger and resentment. What had happened to him to make him become so desperate in his life? The Kevin she knew before they were married would have never acted as he had today. He had been so loving and caring, so confident that he could do anything and be successful at it. Yet, today, he seemed so fearful and hopeless. Part of her wanted to get rid of him by any means necessary short of murder. Another part of her wanted to pray for him and help him get back on the right path. However, she felt her needs were more important, so she said a quick prayer for her situation. She knew if she prayed, God would give her an answer.

CHAPTER 11

Shante sat silently at the end of the long conference table, waiting for the board members to assemble. She greeted each one, but only a few returned her greeting; others talked quietly. This was a far cry from how they normally acted. Board meetings were usually friendly and upbeat. An air of fellowship would prevail. But not today. The air was thick with tension. No one seemed to be enjoying himself.

Shante looked at the assembly. She remembered how most of them were selected. After Pastor Anderson died, she had to reorganize the church structure. The board of her church was selected based on their relationship with God, their families, and the church. With the exception of three people, almost everyone on the board, which consisted of six deacons and six trustees, was selected by her. Their duties were divided; the trustees took care of the affairs of church administration and the deacons took care of the needs of the people. The two organizations came together once a month to discuss the total church program. Of all the people in the church, Shante felt they knew her best and could not understand why they would follow up on idle gossip. Finally, her thoughts were scattered when Tank entered the room.

"Hello, Pastor, how are you today?"

Trying to look confident, she replied, "I'm blessed."

"Well, we're about to get started. I'm going to get me some coffee. Do you want something to drink?" Tank asked.

"No, I'm fine. Thank you."

Tank crossed the room to the small table in the back and got his coffee. He then took his seat at the head of the table and informed the group that the meeting was now underway. He opened it with a prayer.

"As you know, we are here today to discuss some issues that have come up in our church. Pastor Dogan, we only want to hear your side. We have heard a lot of things lately. We know that it's mostly rumors, but some of us want to hear what you've got to say about all the gossip. We're going to try to make this meeting as short as possible. Pastor Dogan, we have the utmost confidence in you and your abilities. You have done some great things in our church, which has grown since you have been here. Membership has increased, and we have also acquired some choice real estate. Our church is well respected in the community, and we want to keep it that way. However, as I previously stated, there have been some rumors. Would you like to address them?"

"What rumors are you talking about?" she asked, trying to project a confident air.

"Let's start with your sleeping around with men," a less than friendly voice in the middle of the table called out.

"I don't feel my personal life is really anyone's business, but since this is a special meeting to discuss it, I will answer whatever questions you ask. I know my personal life can have an impact, good or bad, on this ministry. I wouldn't do anything to hurt this church. To address your concern, I am not sleeping around. I don't even have a boyfriend, unless you want to call the church my boyfriend. I'm here most of the time. I hardly have time for anything else," she replied.

"We are not trying to call you promiscuous, but there have been rumors," Deacon Curry said.

"What exactly are you talking about?"

"There was an incident at Hilton Head. Someone said you and a man were together."

"Who said that? I spoke with a lot of men there. There were mostly men at the conference. None of them came to my room. Neither did I go to anyone's room. It was a relaxing, successful conference—nothing out of the ordinary."

"We are not spending the church's money for you to go to these conferences and lay up with men," Deaconess Sarah Turner said.

"I am offended by what you said. You're calling me a whore to my face. I have tried to walk in the most right-eous way I know how. I've been celibate for years, not because I haven't had the opportunity, but because of my commitment to God.

"As for the church's money, as you know, each year I have an independent auditor come in and audit the books. They have found nothing wrong. I don't sign the checks alone. Everything goes through the finance secre-tary, treasurer, and chairman trustee. It takes two signa-tures to sign any check in this church. Each month, a copy of the church's credit card and receipts are turned over to the finance secretary. I put all these safeguards in place so there would not be any question of money and how it is spent. I don't use any church money for my personal expenses. All of you know that. I haven't had a raise in three years. As for conferences that I attend, I spend my own money, or if I am asked to speak, the group sponsoring the conference usually pays the expenses. I don't know how you can even say I'm spending the church's money at these events."

She could feel herself getting hot. She was outraged that these people actually believed the rumors. She couldn't believe what she was hearing. These people were not just board members; she considered them her friends. They had been through a lot together building up the church, and now they seemed to be turning on her. She tried to remain calm.

"Calm down, Pastor. Sarah, you were wrong in saying that. We're not here to point fingers. We really don't have any proof of, or direct knowledge of, anything except what Pastor just said. This meeting is a waste of our time. However, I know others of you have questions. Anyone else?" Tank asked.

"I have a question."

"Yes, what is it, Deacon Morris?"

"I want to address something Pastor just said." He turned and looked at Shante. "You haven't had a raise in three years? Why?"

"Maybe she saved some of the money she made as a stripper," another man in the back of the room said under his breath. However, Shante and everyone else heard it. She was livid. She rose to her feet, struggling to contain her fury.

"I have tried to be professional here. I can't believe you said that," she said to him. She paused and looked into the face of each person sitting around the table. To her, they all seemed to be waiting for her to act crazy. She decided she would not give them what they were expecting. Instead, she calmly said, "I don't know how that rumor started. I heard it, too. I can't believe any of you believe it. Most of you have known me several years. You know you can come to me and ask me anything."

She sat back down. "I don't sleep around, and I was never a stripper." She looked at Deacon Morris. "I don't know why I haven't received a raise."

"It never came up," Deacon Curry offered, not waiting for her to say anything else.

"Yeah, Pastor never asked for one," Tank said, after taking a long, deep breath.

"It appears to me that Pastor needs a raise. In the past three years, our membership has grown by at least five hundred members. I know with this number of people, there is a lot more work for her to do. Am I right about this?" Deacon Morris asked Shante.

"My workload has increased. I'm counseling more people now. We've started new ministries. I have taken on a more active role in the community because of the growth of the church. Let's not forget the changes in the IRS law that I have to keep up with and make sure the church complies with. It has been a lot of work. I hardly have time for myself. I haven't had a vacation in a while. It is rare that I get to see Camille," Shante said with a sigh, leaning back in her chair. It made her tired thinking about all the work she had to do.

"I think our pastor needs a raise," Deacon Morris said.

"Me, too. She deserves it. I can't believe we came here to listen to some mess. We have a good pastor. She's a hard worker. She's a woman of integrity. She has never given us reason to believe anything else. I want to make a motion that we give Pastor Dogan a raise," Trustee Kerns said.

"I second the motion," two voices in the back said before Tank could properly acknowledge the motion.

"Is there anyone opposing a raise for Pastor Dogan?" Tank asked. No one responded. Tank looked around the room. He looked at Shante. "I guess you have yourself a raise, Pastor. Congratulations."

Shante sat at the table looking surprised. She was speechless. She could not believe she had come in to defend her reputation and God had given her a raise. She wanted to jump up and start praising God at that very moment. She tried to remain cool. She couldn't wait to tell Gwen, Camille, and Max. She was ready to leave.

"We'll discuss the amount of the raise at a later date. Pastor, let us know what you think a fair amount would be," Tank said to Shante.

"I'll pray about it and get back with you," she said, about to jump out of her seat. She couldn't believe she could name her own raise. She began to silently praise God for blessing her.

"In addition to the raise, I think we should re-state very clearly what is expected of her," Deacon Curry added.

"Go ahead, state your piece," Tank said, motioning for Deacon Curry to continue.

"Well, she should know we expect her to act as lady-like as she can so she will be a proper representative of this church. We also want her lifestyle to be one that reflects a woman of high Christian morals and integrity. She has a lot of programs in place with clear checks and balances in respect to finances, and we expect that to continue. If there is evidence that she isn't living in a way that benefits this church, she could be relieved of her duties as pastor."

"Wait a minute, Deacon Curry. You're going too far. Are you threatening to fire her?" Tank asked.

"I can't fire anybody. I just want her to know that people are watching her and there may be consequences to her actions. She needs to know that everyone in here is not happy with the decision that has been made. No one is saying anything because there is no proof of anything other than Pastor Dogan being a good leader. I can agree with that. She has been a good pastor and good for this church. I only want her to be careful. That's all."

"Yes, I understand. But, who in here is not happy with this decision?" Shante asked. No one said a word.

"Does anyone have anything to add to this discussion?" Tank asked, looking around the room.

"I do," Trustee Makins said, standing up. "I just want to say I have confidence in Pastor. I believe she is a woman of integrity and good moral standards. I don't believe any of the rumors. They are just that: rumors. I hope none of you are participating in any of them. That wouldn't be Christian behavior. I want to commend Pastor for all the work she has done. I apologize to her on behalf of the board members for even putting her through this. I know it had to be hard for her. I believe she is an excellent pastor, and I hope she will stay on for years to come." He began clapping at the end of his comments. Others joined him, standing and clapping. Shante wanted to be happy, but she could feel the enemy working in the room.

"Well, if no one has anything else to say, I think we will adjourn," Tank said, wrapping up the meeting. "Pastor, don't forget to give me your thoughts on the raise soon," he reminded Shante.

"I will," she replied.

The meeting was adjourned and everyone except Shante left the building. After locking the doors, she went into the sanctuary and began to praise God for working things out for her. She also prayed for strength in the face of the opposition that had clearly not gone away. She knew she had the victory. It had been manifested that day.

◈◈◈

Shante was at her table looking through her mail as she spoke with Gwen on the phone. She was still basking in her victory at the board meeting. She had praised God all the way home. She knew the majority of her board was behind her and her position was secure—at least for the moment. She had to share the good news with someone. She thought about Max, but she was trying to separate herself from him. "They gave you a raise?" Gwen asked unbelievingly.

"Yes, and I get to name my own amount. Of course, it will be subject to negotiations, but I still will probably get a fat raise. I'm so happy, and I'm sure Camille will be, too."

"And she's in New York. She could have a ball there with your money. I am so happy for you, Shante. Have you told Max yet?"

"No, I've been trying to keep him at a distance since we returned from Asheville."

"Why? That man loves you. I don't know why you're tripping."

"Do you know how embarrassing it was to have Kevin come and my house all torn up? I felt so humiliated. I think I cried out of embarrassment."

"Max is not thinking about that. Do you know that Ron had to stop him from going over to Kevin's church and confronting him about you?"

"No, Gwen, he didn't," Shante shrieked. She placed her hands on her head. She couldn't believe Max wanted to fight Kevin. She had come to accept that she could not continue her relationship with him, but she didn't want to lose his friendship. She prayed silently to God for direction.

"If it weren't for Ron, he would have. Max was so angry. I think he could have really hurt Kevin that day."

"He didn't act like it."

"That's because he was trying to be strong and supportive of you, Shante. He was angrier than I've ever seen him. You should have seen him."

"See, that's why I can't get involved with him right now. I don't want anyone else to be caught up in all that is happening in my life right now. Max is such a nice guy, and he's still a nerd, even though he doesn't know it."

"True. But, Tay, you're going to have to learn to open your heart. Although you give out love, you've got to learn how to receive it. How can you love others unconditionally if you're afraid to allow yourself to be loved?"

"I'm not afraid."

"Then open your heart to love."

"I'm open."

"No, you're not. The Bible says that perfect love doesn't walk in fear. As long as you have fear, you'll never be able to receive love."

"I'm not afraid."

"Prove it. Give Max a chance. You said yourself, he's a nice guy."

"He is."

"Then prove it."

"Gwen, I have to go. I wanted to tell you about the meeting. I'll talk to you later," Shante said, hanging up.

How can she say that I'm afraid to be loved? I want to be loved. If I had to pick someone, Max would be the perfect guy. He's kind, compassionate, successful, and saved. He's my friend, and I don't want him to get hurt. Besides, Max is a preacher. Seventy-five percent of his members are women. He has them chasing him all over the place. I don't have time for that competition. I've got too much going on, and it doesn't seem it will end anytime soon. Besides, the board wants me to be 'ladylike' and exhibit high Christian morals. I've really got to watch myself now. I can't give even the appearance of wrongdoing.

Shante saw distancing herself from Max as the only option open to her—at least for now. It was too bad some people in the church can't see that a man and a woman can have a relationship without having sex. Even if nothing is going on, some people still speculate that there is and proceed to spread all sorts of rumors based on pure imagination.

∽

Max and his friend and business partner, Gary, walked the green around the ninth hole at Huntington Springs Golf Course. Max's game was off because his mind was on Shante and the meeting at the church. He had to fight the urge to call her to find out what happened. He said a special prayer for her and asked God to shine his divine favor on her. It was a perfect day for golf, but he just couldn't concentrate on it.

"Max, man, your game really stinks today," Gary said.

"I've got other things on my mind. I'm sorry I'm not much competition today. I'm worried about Shante and that stupid meeting at her church."

"Have you heard from her yet?" Gary asked.

"No. She promised she would call when the meeting was over. It's taking a long time."

"Yeah, that must be some kind of meeting. How is she holding up?"

"I'm sure she's fine," Max said, swinging his golf club. "I haven't spoken to her much this week."

"Are your plans working out?"

"Shante and I understand where we stand with this relationship."

"Really? So you told her how you feel, and she said the same?"

"Not exactly, Gary. I told her how I felt. She listened to me. She doesn't want to get involved right now."

"Get involved? With you?"

"In a close relationship."

"You two are already in a close relationship. I can look at the two of you and tell you guys are in love. Everyone can tell that. When you guys are together with the boys, you look like one big, happy family. What's the problem? Is there something you aren't telling me?"

"I think ghosts from her past are keeping her from getting involved."

"Ghosts? What do you mean?"

"I shouldn't tell you her secrets. It's personal. She confided in me, and I shouldn't run off telling everybody. She trusts me."

"That's it. She does trust you, and you trust her. Besides, I already know about Kevin. Shante told me about their marriage." Gary stepped up to the green, placed his tee in the ground, put the ball on it, and swung his club, sending the ball across the lawn.

"You know about him?" Max had begun walking towards the golf cart, but stopped when he heard Gary mention Kevin. He wondered how much Gary knew about the Kevin situation and how long he had known it.

"She called me about the incident at her house. She told me you were there. She said you wanted to represent her, but she thought you were too emotionally attached to the case. So I agreed to represent her when he goes to trial."

Max placed his club in the golf bag and put it on the back of the cart. "I'm glad you are representing her. She trusts you. With all the years we've been friends, she knows you are not going to run all over town telling her business. She's an extremely private person. She would not have gone to another attorney." Max paused. "Man, you don't know what it took for me not to go to his church and beat him down as if I were his father. You should have seen how Shante looked. Her house was destroyed."

"I saw pictures. It looked pretty bad. She doesn't want to do anything other than what the district attorney wants to do. I talked with her about a civil case, but you know her. She refused. Max, do you think you really want to get involved with a woman who has an ex like this? You know this can be a dangerous situation."

"I love her. I'm already involved. Because of me, she may be losing her church today. I don't know how to help her. I have asked her to let me help, and she refuses. I don't know what to do."

"You are acting like someone who doesn't know God. If you think Shante is your wife, then put your faith on it. Call those things that be not as though they were. Where is your faith?" Max sat silently looking at Gary. He had heard this before from Bishop. He knew the Holy Spirit was speaking through Gary.

"If you begin to pray and call that thing forth, God will give you direction and let you know which path to choose. He will let you know how to minister to her in a way that will draw her into a closer relationship with you and God. He will heal her heart and get rid of the ghosts of her past. You've heard this before. Why have you given up?"

"I haven't given up. I don't want to push her. If I push her too hard, she may leave. That would really hurt the boys."

"And you."

"Yes, and me. It's safer to keep her close rather than push her away. I have a much better chance with her near."

"Okay, man. Seems like you've thought about this. Don't give up. If you need someone to talk to, you know you can call me," Gary said, patting Max on the shoulder. "Come on, it's no fun beating you like this. Let's go get something to eat."

CHAPTER 12

Shante made her way through the hallway of the community center where the Mecklenberg Ministerial Alliance was meeting. It had been a month since the board meeting, and she was now feeling confident enough to participate in other ministerial activities. By now, she thought surely something or someone else had become the lead story on the gossip circuit.

As she walked past a few ministers, she greeted them cordially. She looked around and spotted Bishop Thompson at the snack table. He was wearing a bright red suit with red patent-leather shoes. He reminded her of a black Santa. She almost looked around the room for the Christmas tree. She tried hard to keep from laughing. Bishop was the only one she knew who had such a colorful wardrobe. She walked over and greeted him.

"Hello, Bishop," she said, hugging him, her arms barely reaching around him.

"Hi, Shante, how are you this evening?"

"I'm blessed. I thought I wasn't going to make it to the meeting tonight. There was so much going on at the church today. One of my sessions went way over time. I had to push it to get here, but I made it. How are you and Mother?"

"She's getting better every day. She was so happy to see you last week. You know she worries about you."

"Tell her I'm well, considering everything that's going on now."

"I know you're still not worried about all that talk. You know it's going to die down. Your church leaders showed you they have confidence in you. That is all you have to think about."

"I know, Bishop. I haven't been to one of these meeting since all this began. I didn't want to distract from the purpose of this organization."

"Distract? You're not a distraction. Other things are, other people are, but you aren't. Don't let talk take away your confidence. If you let that happen, you'll give the devil a foothold in your life. Remember, you are a winner. You already have the victory."

Bishop motioned for another minister to join them, but then Shante saw Gwen and Ron entering the room. She relaxed as soon as she saw them. She was grateful they were pastors, and glad they had decided to come to the meeting tonight. She took leave of Bishop and went to meet them.

"Hey Gwen, Ron," she said, hugging both of them.

"I'm surprised you made it to the meeting, Tay," Gwen said.

"Leave her alone. Hey, Tay, how are you tonight?" Ron asked.

"Why? I'm fine. Yeah, Gwen, leave me alone. You know I have been through it, and I have issues," she said, pretending she was crying and wiping an imaginary tear from her eye.

"Cut it out, Tay, before someone thinks you're really crying and tries to deliver you from some demons," Gwen said, laughing.

"There's Max. I'm leaving you two alone," Ron said, walking away.

"Tay, I'm glad you're here tonight. Are you feeling better now that it looks like everything is over?"

"You think it's over. It still feels like everyone is looking at me. You see that lady over there in the black ruffled skirt?" Shante motioned with a slight nod towards two women standing near a wall. "She's been staring at me since I came in. It's real uncomfortable."

"Her? That's Minister Hall. Girl, she can't see you. She's not wearing her glasses; without them, she can't see a thing. You don't have to worry about her, or anyone else. Get over it. You are yesterday's news. There are already rumors about someone else. Forget about all that. Look at all these people in here. No one is paying you any attention."

"I guess you're right."

"I know I'm right. Come on, girl, let's find a seat," Gwen said, taking Shante by the arm.

Ron went across the room filled with neatly lined chairs to greet Max, who was standing against the back wall waiting for the meeting to start leafing through his Bible, oblivious to people entering the room.

"Hey, Max. How are you doing?" Ron asked, extending his hand.

"Man, I'm blessed."

"Looks like a lot of people are going to be here tonight. Shante is here. Have you seen her?" Ron asked.

"Shante's here? Where?" Max looked around but didn't see her.

"She's somewhere in here with Gwen. I left those two alone to talk about whatever they talk about. I didn't want to be involved. So how is everything going at the church? I see your family life center is almost finished."

"It should be completed by the end of the summer. I'll be glad when it is. We're planning some great opening events. Did you get a call about speaking one night during the revival?"

"Yeah, I got it. You know I'll be there. How are you doing, Max? The last time we talked you wanted to hurt Kevin. I hope he doesn't show up here."

"I don't think he will. It's funny. All the stuff he has done, you never hear anything about him, but it seems like everyone has something to say about Shante. It's a shame. We ought to be focused on the Gospel and the healing and deliverance of others. Instead, we're focused on trash. Ron, don't get me started. I know all the pressure Shante is going through right now, and I don't know how to help her. Even if I did, I don't think she would let me. I'm glad she came here tonight. It shows progress. Where is she?" Max asked again.

"She's over there," Ron said, pointing at Gwen and Shante.

"I won't go over there. I don't want to give anyone any more ammunition. She's still not completely off the hook at her church, but things are getting better for her."

Ron left when Gwen motioned him to come over. Meanwhile, Max kept a steady eye on Shante, hoping she would sense his gaze and turn around.

"Hey, doc, how you doing, man?" a man asked, shaking Max's hand.

"I'm doing good, Marion. How are you?"

"Man, I'm blessed, but not as blessed as you. I saw that new family life center at your church. It looks awesome. You know, I've been hearing a lot of good things about you and your ministry. I want you to come and preach at my church sometime. I'll let you know."

Max paid scant attention to the man, so focused was he on Shante. Gwen saw him staring and poked Shante gesturing toward Max. Shante turned and tried to discreetly wave at him. Marion finally realized Max had tuned him out. He saw where he was looking and saw Shante wave. "That Dogan, she's a good one, isn't she? How is she? Everybody has been trying to get on that. I heard you've been hitting that hard. You think I can get in on it?" Marion asked in a whisper.

Max's reaction was swift and furious as his anger got the better of him. He turned and grabbed Marion by his lapels and slammed him against the wall. *"Don't you ever talk about her that way again. Man, I will hurt you,"* Max fumed.

"Son, no," Bishop called out, waddling across the room.

"Max, don't," Shante beseeched, in a loud, frantic voice.

Ron ran to the back of the room and touched Max's shoulder, trying to calm him down. All talking ceased, and everyone was looking at the men against the wall. "Max, let him go. Not here. He's not worth it," Ron said calmly.

Max released Marion and glared at him, the veins in his neck pulsating with anger. Marion straightened his jacket. "I'm sorry, I didn't know it was like that," he said, trying to get away as fast as he could.

Shante jumped up and ran out the door. Gwen followed her, while Ron continued trying to calm Max down. He saw people focused on him and instantly regretted what he had done: He had added fuel to the gossip and rumors that could hurt Shante even more. He rushed out and got to the parking lot just as she was pulling out of her space.

"Shante, wait. I'm sorry," Max called out, running toward her car.

"Leave her alone. I'll go talk to her," Gwen told Max.

"I didn't mean to. . . . What he said . . . it made me so angry. I didn't mean to hurt her. I just reacted. I shouldn't have done that. How am I ever going to make that up to her? I know she won't talk to me now," Max said, punching the air.

"You're going to defend the woman you love. It's what's expected of you. She'll realize that. Let Gwen talk to her," Ron said, trying to comfort him. "She'll get her to understand that. Come on, you've got to take me home. We'll talk along the way. It'll be all right, you'll see."

❦

"God, when will this mess end?" Shante asked, praying aloud as she drove. She took the ramp onto the Billy Graham Parkway. She wanted to get as far away from Charlotte as she could. Her phone rang and she reached over and turned it off. She didn't feel like talking to anyone but God. She knew He would give her the answers she needed. God would guide her through this process. *It's only a process. I'll get through this with your help, God. Let me learn the lessons I need to learn. Help me to grow in you. Teach me your ways, God. Show me your path. Lead me in the right direction.*

She had been driving about two hours before realizing she had just been circling the city. She expected Gwen and Max would try to contact her. She didn't want to go home. She didn't want to talk to anyone. She only wanted to pray. She drove onto Interstate 85 toward Gastonia, checked into a motel along the highway, and went into the room to pray. She could feel the presence of the Lord. She began to weep and question God about why she was going through all this tribulation. She reflected on her own actions, trying to determine if she had done anything to bring trouble into her life. She wanted God to show her what she was doing wrong so she could correct it. She wanted to know if she was walking in disobedience. So she decided to stay in the motel a couple of days to fast and pray for direction in her life. She called Gail and told her to cancel her appointments for the next two days. Then she went into the bathroom and took a shower.

Afterward, she knelt on the edge of the bed and began to pray. She had an overwhelming urge to call Max. She didn't want to talk with him. She tried to continue praying, but she couldn't focus.

"God, I don't want to talk with him. I only want to talk with you," Shante prayed, but the urge to call Max would not go away.

∽◈∾

Pacing the floor in his bedroom, Max was wracked with guilt for having lost control at the meeting. He had been looking for Shante all evening, going to her house several times. But he could not go again, because it was late and the boys were in bed. He asked God to have Shante call him. The door to his bedroom opened.

"Dad, I can't sleep," Joshua said, rubbing his eyes.

"Come over here." Max picked up his son and sat in a chair near the window and began rocking.

"What's wrong with Mama Tay?"

Surprised by the question, Max nonetheless answered, "Nothing's wrong with her."

"I heard you praying for her, and I thought something happened to her."

"Nothing has happened to her. I pray for her all the time. You've heard me. Sometimes we pray together."

"Yeah, but this time, you scared me. Dad, I'm scared. Can we call her?" Josh said, crying.

"Josh, it's late. We'll call her in the morning."

"No, Dad, let's call her now," Josh said.

Max hesitated; it was almost one-thirty in the morning. He prayed, *God, please let Shante call.* When the phone rang, Josh jumped up and ran to get it. "Mama Tay!" he squealed.

After talking for a few minutes, Josh handed the phone to Max.

"Shante, I need to talk to you. Will you hold on while I walk Josh to his bed?"

"I can do it myself," Josh said, heading out the door.

Max watched Josh walk down the hallway to his bedroom and then closed the door. "Shante, I'm so sorry. I didn't mean to cause a scene tonight. I just reacted. I didn't mean to embarrass you."

"Max, it's okay. I only called to let you know I'm fine. I left Charlotte. I'm in a hotel. I need to fast and pray. There must be something I'm doing wrong. I have to talk with God."

"It's not about you. You're not doing anything wrong. Where are you?"

"Something's happening. I don't know what it is. I've got to pray. I'll be gone for a couple of days. I already called Gail and told her to cancel my appointments. I wanted you to know that I'm all right. I understand why you did what you did tonight. I appreciate your being my friend. I wanted to let you know. I'll call you in a couple of days. I've got to go."

"Wait, Shante. Don't hang up. I didn't mean to hurt you. You've already gone through enough."

"I know, Max."

"I love you. Can I meet you tomorrow so we can pray about this thing together?"

"Josh said you were praying for me. That's all you need to do. Thank you, Max. I've got to go."

"Shante," Max cried out as she hung up. Max tried to call back but she had already turned her phone off. He knelt at his bed and began to pray. Sleep eluded him. He lay awake wondering if Shante would ever trust him, wondering if he would ever marry her.

CHAPTER 13

"Mother, it's me, Shante. I brought you and Bishop some food," Shante called out as she entered Bishop and Mother Thompson's roomy old house, using the key she still had from when she stayed with them. Shante had met them at the women's shelter where she was staying after fleeing to Charlotte. Her face was bruised and she was still recovering from Kevin's final beating. They had offered to help her get back on her feet, and she and two-year-old Camille moved in with them. The house had not changed since their stay there. She carried a large box of food through the dining room and into the kitchen and placed it on the table in the middle of the room.

"Hello, Shante, how are you today?" Mother Thompson asked, hugging her.

"Mother, I'm fine. How are you doing?"

"I'm doing so much better now. It's so good to see you. What are you doing here?" the small, frail-looking woman inquired.

"I thought I would cook dinner for you and Bishop today," Shante said. It had been almost a week since the ministerial meeting but she was still stressed out, so she had decided to cook. She figured Bishop and Mother could use some home cooking, since Mother was still recovering from breast-cancer surgery.

"Looks like you cooked for the whole neighborhood. Is that your peach cobbler I smell?"

"Yeah. I drove down to South Carolina to an orchard and picked the peaches myself. You know, they're in season now. Only the freshest ingredients for my . . ."

"Get-a-husband peach cobbler," Mother said, finishing for her and smiling.

"Yes, my get-a-husband peach cobbler," she replied.

"Child, Oscar don't need no mo' food that's gonna make him fatter. He's already rolling around the neighborhood now. I try to tell that man to watch what he eats, and he does; he watches it go into his mouth," Mother said, peering into the box.

"Mother, I made you smothered chicken. I know you like that."

"Thank you, baby. Come on in the living room. Let's sit a spell."

The living room was filled with pictures of family and friends. An oversized wooden fork and spoon were in the corner beside the fireplace. A picture of Martin Luther King, Jr., flanked by the Kennedy brothers, hung on the opposite wall. The pictures must have been there for forty years. Shante sat on the well-worn but still elegant European-styled sofa.

"Where are my manners? Shante, you brought the food; the least I can do is offer you something to drink," Mother said, going back to the kitchen.

"Mother, I brought sweet tea. It's in the box."

A large wooden table in front of the sofa was covered with pictures under a piece of glass. Shante had seen them a thousand times, but she still enjoyed looking at old school pictures of friends and family, as well as of church events. Looking at a picture of her and Camille taken shortly after they had arrived in Charlotte, she could see how far she had come. There was sadness in her eyes and brightness in Camille's, who had been too young to understand what was going on; life was still an adventure to her. As usual, Camille had a big smile, which made Shante happy. She was thankful to have met Bishop and Mother. It was the turning point in her life.

"I've got to get a new picture of the two of you to put in there," Mother said, handing Shante a glass of tea.

"Mother, you have other pictures of us, like that one over there," Shante said, pointing to a picture on the mantel. It was a picture taken at Camille's high school graduation. They looked so happy.

"I don't have much room on that table anymore. I need a larger one so I can put it right over there near the corner."

"I'll get you one soon, Mother. Where's Bishop?"

"He said he was going to the barber shop. I don't know why. He hasn't had hair in twenty years, yet he keeps going every other week. I think he likes talking with the men there. It's a social hall for him, a place where men can catch up on the gossip in the community and talk about women. So why don't you tell me what's going on."

"There's nothing going on. I'm at peace."

"Look at all that food you brought in here. When you start cooking and cleaning, it's a sign something is going on. I learned that when you lived with us. My house was never so clean, and Oscar gained fifty pounds." Mother knew her too well. She was one of the few people who did. She had spent lots of time talking with Mother when she lived with them. When she wasn't cooking and cleaning to relieve stress, she talked to Mother and, occasionally, Bishop. She wasn't saved when she met them twenty years ago. She got saved in this house. It held a lot of fond memories for her and Camille.

"I've got things on my mind. I'm working them out. I don't need to trouble you, Mother."

"I'm glad you came to see me. Oscar told me what happened at the meeting the other day. I tried to call you, but you weren't answering your phone. Child, you need to stop doing that. You may miss an important phone call."

"I'm sorry, Mother, I had to take some time to pray. I needed to be alone."

"You needed to hide."

"I wasn't hiding. I called people and let them know—"

"Let them know you were hiding. Child, you can't keep running away from your problems. You've got to learn to stand."

"Mother, I wasn't running. I really needed direction, so I decided to pray. What's wrong with that?"

"Nothing is wrong with praying, unless you're trying to avoid the issues."

"What issues are you talking about, Mother?"

"You tell me. You know Max did what he did because he loves you. Do you think he was going to sit back and let some lowlife like Marion bad-mouth you?"

"I know, Mother. I've got my board breathing down my back. I've got Kevin threatening me. I never have time for myself. Church growth is out of control, and it's taking more of my time. I'm not complaining. I enjoy what I do. I just can't get involved right now. I don't want to hurt Max."

"Or get hurt," Mother said. Shante walked to the fireplace and looked into the large mirror above the mantel. She was trying hard not to cry, so she stared into the mirror. "What are you afraid of, Shante?"

"Oh, you and Gwen. I'm not afraid of anything. I was afraid of Kevin. I'm not anymore. The last time I had him arrested, but he got out of jail the next day. We'll be going to court for that soon. Hopefully they'll lock him up for a while, and he can get sober and come out a better person."

"What are you afraid of, Shante?"

Shante turned around and looked at Mother Thompson on the sofa sipping her tea like an elegant Southern belle. "Mother, I've got to go. I hope you and Bishop enjoy the food," Shante said, looking around for her purse and keys.

"Running again. Child, come over here and sit down," Mother said, patting the sofa cushion next to her.

Shante walked around the large coffee table and sat down. She had the highest respect for her. Shante knew she was a woman of God and had great reserves of wisdom. Mother's prayers had helped her get through her separation and divorce. She looked to Mother for advice on raising Camille and about issues in her church. She knew Mother was an intercessor, and lived a good Christian life. She had come over hoping Mother could give her the answers she wanted and needed.

"I know you want me to give you the answers, but the answers are inside you. You're a praying woman. I know that. It's okay to pray, but you've got to stop running. What are you afraid of?"

"Gwen thinks I am afraid of love."

"Is she right?"

"No, I'm not afraid of love. I love people. People love me."

"Do you love Max?"

"Max is my friend."

"Do you love him?"

"Mother, nothing could ever happen between me and Max. He's a preacher, a coworker. I could never—"

"Never love him? What's wrong with being a preacher? Aren't you one?"

"Mother, do you know what I go through with male preachers? I can't go anywhere without some preacher hitting on me. Last year, I went to a church to preach. The pastor there told me they believed women couldn't have authority over men and that I had to preach from the floor, not the pulpit. I started to leave. I had to remember I had a mission that day. You know what he did after everyone left the office? Before we walked into the pulpit, he said he wanted to pray with me. We held hands and he prayed. And then he hugged me and grabbed my butt. I pushed him away and slapped him. It was difficult for me to preach that day while looking at his wife sitting in the front row. I felt sorry for her. Max is a nice guy, not like the others. His friendship means a lot to me. I don't want him to get hurt. I'm trying to wean him off me now."

"What about the boys? Aren't you their godmother?"

"Yes. I'll deal with that. I can support the boys without Max. I'll have to figure out a way."

"Are the two of you still having First Friday?" Mother asked.

Shante stood again and paced the floor. She didn't want to admit she looked forward to First Friday. It was her only opportunity to relax. She would hate to give up that day. She knew she would if she had to, but she didn't want to.

"Mother, you know First Friday is about helping Max," Shante said, trying to cover up her true feelings.

"I know it started out that way. What is it now?"

"Mother, you know when Meko died Max was having a real hard time. He wouldn't go into counseling. The only way I could get him to talk about his feelings was to create a day that he could be himself and express his emotions. It was a counseling session—nothing more."

"That was how many years ago—four, five?"

"It has been a long time, about five."

"What is it now, Shante? Is it still a counseling session?"

Shante didn't answer. She knew she needed First Friday just as much as Max did. She enjoyed his company. She liked the adventures they went on. She looked forward to planning a special day for the two of them and to seeing what Max had planned. Of all the days of the month, First Friday was the only one in which she could really be herself. She didn't have to get dressed up. She didn't have to wear makeup if she didn't want to. Sometimes she wouldn't even shave her legs. She enjoyed the compliments Max always gave her no matter how she looked. She remembered the First Friday last winter when she had the flu. Max came over with some chicken soup, her favorite movie, tissues, and cold medicine and nursed her back to health. He stayed even when she insisted he leave, saying he'd had a flu shot. He complimented her even with her eyes watering, nose running, and hair uncombed. She didn't want to give up First Friday. She walked to the corner knickknack stand and began to play with one of Mother's figurines.

"Shante, I'm going to ask you again. What are you afraid of?"

"Mother, I don't want to hurt him."

"Are you hurting him now?"

"Mother, I don't want to talk about this anymore."

"Shante, come here."

She walked to the sofa and sat down. Mother Thompson motioned for her to come closer. She slid over and put her head on Mother's chest and then jumped up. She had forgotten about Mother's mastectomy. She had felt the flatness of her chest. "Mother, I'm sorry. Did I hurt you?"

"Child, no. I'm fine. Come back here." She pulled Shante close to her.

"Mother, have you considered having implants?" Shante asked, sliding next to her on the sofa.

"Implants? You mean breast implants? Child, what do I need breasts for? I'm seventy-six years old. My children and grandchildren are grown. Oscar hasn't missed them, and I'm not going to have any children anytime soon or make any nudie movies."

"Mother, too much information," Shante said, smiling.

"Come here, child."

Shante put her head on Mother's chest. She could hear her strong, steady heartbeat. Mother caressed her head and she became more relaxed than she had been in several days.

"Shante, don't be afraid to love. You're going to have to learn to stop running and hiding. It's not going to help you or your ministry if you don't know how to stand. We all go through times in our lives like this when it seems like everything is falling apart. It's just a transitional period. Your blessing is on the way. It'll be over soon. Trust God. He'll bring you through fine."

Mother began to sing to her. There was a peace in the room. Shante felt like sleeping. She hadn't slept well since the incident at the meeting. She was glad she had talked to Mother, but she still needed answers.

～◈◈～

"Hey, Max, here's the Richardson brief," Gary said, coming into Max's office. "Angela and Treniece worked really hard on it. I've already reviewed it; it looks good. It's due tomorrow. Take a look at it for me, and we'll send it out by courier today. I know we got this one. They've already called to make a settlement offer."

Max sat looking out his office window, thinking about Shante. He had spoken with her briefly that morning. She was cooking for Bishop and Mother and couldn't talk long. If Shante was cooking, she probably was stressed about something.

"Max, the Richardson brief?" Gary said.

"I'm sorry, Gary, I was in another world," Max said, turning around to face his partner.

"I can see that. What's on your mind?" Gary asked, closing the door.

"Nothing. What were you saying about the Richardson brief?"

"It's complete. I looked over it. Angela and Treniece did an outstanding job. Here it is; take a look at it. It's due tomorrow, so we have to send it out today. What's up with you, man?"

"I've got things on my mind. Personal things."

"You want to talk?"

"No. I'll take a look at this and give it to Angela for the courier."

"Don't avoid the subject. You're still worried about Shante? Is she still upset about the fight?" Gary asked, sitting in the big leather chair facing Max's desk.

"Fight? There wasn't a fight."

"That's not what I heard. I heard you really messed Reverend Marion up. You know the church news. It was all over town by the next day."

"God, I really didn't mean to do that. He infuriated me. I only reacted. I wish I hadn't done that. What was I thinking?"

"You weren't thinking. Max, sometimes, you can have a little temper."

"What? I don't have a temper."

"Yes, man, you do. Maybe that's why Shante doesn't want to get into a relationship with you. She has already been in an abusive relationship. She may be afraid to get into another one because of it. You should check yourself. Think about it. The Spirit will let her know when to stay away and when to get into a serious relationship. Right now, she's staying away. If I were you, I would do an inventory on myself."

"Gary, that's so far from who I am. I don't beat or yell at my children. I didn't abuse Meko. I've never hit a woman. How can you say that, man?"

"You have never hit a woman, no, but look how quickly you hit Reverend Marion at the meeting. You reacted violently without thinking. That could have scared her. She loves you, but maybe she's fearful she would be hurt again, physically and emotionally. Take a look at that brief. It has to go out today," Gary said, taking his leave.

"I'll get it out," Max promised. He thought about what Gary had said and wondered if he was right. He would never hurt Shante or anyone. He never thought he had a problem with his temper. Was he now finding out something about his personality that he hadn't seen? He prayed that God would teach him how to help Shante. He did not want her to be afraid of him. He wanted her to love him. He didn't know what to do.

CHAPTER 14

Max's day at his law office was ending, and he was preparing to go by the church for meetings. Later, he was having dinner with Shante, Camille, and the boys. It had been a long summer. But Shante was feeling better now. It was August and Camille, after finishing her internship in New York, was at home for a couple of weeks before school began. His relationship with Shante had gotten better even though she still insisted on secrecy. He felt in time they would not have to hide and she could be open about their relationship. Things were beginning to look up for him. Max began singing to himself.

"Somebody's in a good mood today," Gary said, coming into his office.

"Ah, man, God is good."

"All the time. What are you so happy about? Where are you going? It's not five o'clock."

"I've got to meet with the contractor and decorator for the final walk-through of the family life center at two. I'm meeting with members of the program committee at five, then I'm having dinner with Shante and the kids."

"You guys are back in good standing now?"

"Yeah, man. The last few weeks have been great. Shante and I are talking to each other almost daily. We have been getting along great."

"If you're having dinner with Shante, why are you taking all this work home?"

"Shante is taking the boys shopping for new school clothes today. She volunteered, but at least she will have Camille to help her. At the end of the day—after all the shopping and dinner—I hope they will be so tired they will go to their rooms without my having to tell them to. I will then be able to work on the Richardson case. The hearing is next week, and we've got to be prepared. This is a big one for us, and I don't want to lose. I am going to memorize the evidence backwards and forward."

"I'm taking some files home, too. I agree, this is a big case for us. I'll call you about nine, and we can compare notes. Is that okay?"

"I should be at home, and Josh and Jacob should be in bed by then. We can go over our strategy. I think that secretary is going to crack on the stand. Her deposition seemed too rehearsed. We're meeting with the Stenopolis Law Firm tomorrow at ten to see what their investigators have found."

"Okay, I'll talk to you tonight, Max. I'm glad everything is working out with you and Shante."

After Gary left, Max began carrying boxes of files out to his car. He had just finished and was closing the trunk when Kevin suddenly appeared. Max smelled alcohol on his breath. "What are you doing here?"

"I wanted to ask you about a legal matter."

"You need to find yourself another lawyer."

"I want you. I know you're a Christian, and that's what I want in an attorney. I got this little charge."

"You can't play me, man. You know we're representing Shante. What do you want?" Max was trying to be cool. He felt himself getting angry.

"Did Shante tell you I wanted you to preach a revival at my church? I told her months ago. I didn't get a response, so I thought I would ask you myself."

"I'm not going to preach at your church. I have a lot of things going on right now."

"I heard. You're having a grand opening for your family life center. That looks like a nice place."

"Kevin, I'm a very busy man. I have something to do. If you want me to preach at your church, send me an invitation. That is what I ask everyone to do. I'll send you a response in writing. That's our procedure." Max began walking away from Kevin.

"You know I can get her back. I know all the buttons to push, and I've pushed them many times. I know what she likes," Kevin said. Max stopped walking. He wanted to turn around and punch Kevin. He prayed for strength as Kevin came closer to him. Max stared at him for a moment and walked away. "Walk away, you little punk. Buffed but sweet." Kevin was stepping in the parking lot and barking like a dog in a high-pitched voice, making fun of the steps Max's fraternity was known for.

Keep walking, Max. Keep walking. Max was relieved when he finally made it to the door of his office. If he had to listen to Kevin a minute longer, he probably would have hit him. He thanked God as he entered the office.

"Max, I thought you were gone," Gary said, coming down the hall.

Max pointed out the window at Kevin in the parking lot, stepping. "I'm calling the police," Gary said.

"No, don't do that. He's drunk. He'll get tired. Let's wait and see how long he's out there. Do you think God will allow me to knock him out one time and repent?"

"You know you can't do that. Are you okay?"

"Yeah. Just one time?"

"Max, if you think it, you'll do it, so don't think about it."

"Hey, do y'all see that guy in the parking lot?" Angela, Gary's paralegal, asked coming out of her office.

"Yeah, we see him. He's drunk. He'll leave soon. Look, he's leaving now," Gary said. "Come on, Max, I'll help you get your stuff and walk with you to your car. You passed the test. The heavens are smiling. Now what song were you singing?"

" 'Lovely Day'."

"Keep singing. Remember, you're having dinner with Shante tonight. Come on."

⋙⋘

"Camille, get Josh's hand. He's running through the mall again," Shante said. They had been shopping all day, and she was tired. It was tiring enough shopping with Camille. Now she had added three boys to the mix. She had worked hard to stay within Max's budget and still make everyone happy, but the only person happy was

Josh. Jonathan was mad because he didn't get a $175 pair of sneakers.

"Come on, Jon. You'll have to talk with your father about getting those shoes. He gave me a budget, and the shoes weren't in it. Stop sulking and come on. We're supposed to meet your dad in fifteen minutes. Let's get to the car. Jacob, where are your bags?"

"I've got them, Mom," Camille said. "He set them down in the shoe store. I knew he would forget them, so I picked them up."

"Thank you, Camille. You've been a big help today."

"You can show your appreciation when you take me shopping next week. You know I need some new clothes, too. Now that you've got your big raise, you can afford to buy me some designer stuff."

"You're going to make me pay for this, aren't you?"

"Only a little appreciation."

They made their way to the parking lot. Camille put the bags in the trunk while Shante buckled Joshua in. Jonathan and Jacob began pushing each other.

"Jonathan, Jacob, both of you get in the back and put your seat belt on," Shante ordered.

"Mama Tay, they're acting bad. I'm being good. Can I have some ice cream?"

"After dinner, Josh."

"I want it now," Josh said, kicking the seat.

"Josh, now you're acting bad. Wait until after you've had your dinner."

"How long is this going to go on? I'm never having kids," Camille said, getting into the front seat.

"Don't say that, Camille. You've known these boys since the day they were born. You know they're spoiled, just like you."

"I'm not spoiled."

"Yes, you are. Roll down the window, I can smell you over here," Shante said, sniffing and laughing.

She pulled into the parking lot of the restaurant and didn't see Max's car. They all got out and went inside. Twenty minutes passed, and Max still hadn't shown up. The boys and Camille started complaining about being hungry. Shante decided to go ahead and order. Just as the waitress was taking their orders, Max appeared. Her face brightened, and she put on a big smile.

"Mom, what is going on?" Camille whispered. "I've never seen you look at him like this. Look at you smiling and grinning. Close your mouth; you're drooling."

"Camille."

"I know, stay in a child's place, but you've got to remember, I'm an adult now."

"Fine, adult. Pay your own tuition and buy your own clothes."

"Checkmate."

"Hey, everyone," Max said when he got to the table. Joshua jumped up and gave Max a hug.

"Hey, Max," Shante said softly.

"I'm sorry I'm late. The decorator, contractor, and the design committee were having a difference of opinion, but we finally worked it out. I'm sorry I didn't call; I was trying to get here as fast as I could. Have y'all ordered yet?"

"Yes. I ordered you a steak."

"Thanks, Tay." He looked at his sons. "So, guys, how was shopping?"

They all started talking at once. Jonathan complained about not getting the shoes he wanted; Jacob was peeved he couldn't get a new video game with his clothes money; and Joshua still wanted his ice cream. But they all agreed Shante had helped them select some nice clothes.

After dinner, the bags were moved from Shante's car to Max's. The boys were tired and got into the car without complaining. Joshua was already beginning to nod off. Max walked Shante and Camille back to their car.

"Camille, when do you go back to school?"

"In two weeks. I can't wait to show my teachers the project I helped complete this summer in New York. It was awesome," Camille said.

"When can I see it?"

"You're welcome at our house anytime. Right, Mom?" Camille said, getting into the car.

Max took Shante by the hand and walked her around to the driver's side. "Why didn't you tell me Kevin wanted me to preach at his church?"

"What? You know about that? That was months ago, right after the minister's conference."

"Yes. Kevin paid me a little visit today."

"Please tell me he didn't come to your office."

"He was there. He met me at my car in the parking lot and pretended he wanted to hire me as his attorney."

"What happened? Was he drunk?" Shante asked. She had dreaded something like this happening. Her mind raced. She had to come up with something to prevent anything else from happening.

"Drunk is his middle name, isn't it?" Max asked, leaning against the fender.

"What did he say? What did he do?"

"It doesn't matter what he did. He acted like a total idiot. Why didn't you tell me?"

"I knew you wouldn't accept, so why even bother telling you? It wasn't worth mentioning." Shante nervously shifted from one foot to the other.

"You were right. I told him to go through the proper channels. I wouldn't preach at his church for anything. You're tired; I'm not going to waste your time talking about Kevin. Thank you for taking the children shopping. You've been a big help," he said, pulling Shante to him and hugging her. "I'm going to be up late working. May I call you later?"

"You don't have to ask my permission to call me." Shante tried hard not to hug him too tightly. She didn't want anyone in the parking lot to think it was more than a Christian hug. When she felt her body sinking into his, she quickly pulled away.

"I just wanted to be sure. Thanks again." He opened the car door for her and waited until she had driven off.

"Mom and Max sitting in a tree, k-i-s-s-i-n-g—"

"Camille, stop."

"Why didn't you kiss him? You know you wanted to. Heeeey, Maaax," Camille said, imitating her mother.

"You've got it bad, Mom. You should've seen your face when he came into the restaurant. You were glowing. I don't know why the two of you are tripping. You should go ahead and get married and get it over with. Everyone can tell you guys are in love. Admit it, Mom."

"Max and I are only friends," Shante said as they left the parking lot.

"Is that what he thinks? Max loves you, and you love him. You took his children school shopping. You know Max doesn't trust just anyone with his kids. He's so overprotective. But you . . . you can pick them up and take them out of the country and Max will just smile and say 'Go with Mama Tay.' You guys are so silly, but it's cute."

"Listen to you, sounding like an old lady."

"I've got wisdom. That's why you send me to college."

"Is that why I send you to college?"

"You know what I mean. He's probably going to ask you to marry him. Call me when it happens. It's all over him."

Shante turned up the volume on the radio. Although she had thought about it, especially when she traveled, she didn't want to get married at the moment, especially since Kevin was now harassing Max. She did not want Camille, Max, or the boys to be hurt by Kevin's violence. Too much was still going on in her life. Even though things had calmed down during the summer at the church, she still felt people were watching her. She tried to ignore the continuing talk, but there were times when it bothered her. She thought about what Camille said; she hoped she was wrong. She wished she hadn't let Max back into her life. She could not accept a marriage proposal. Then she realized that she was worrying about something that had not happened. She convinced herself that Camille was only playing with her mind.

CHAPTER 15

Gail was at her desk singing when Shante came into the office. Her sunny smile lit up the room. "Someone is awfully happy this morning," Shante said.

"God is good, Pastor," Gail said, smiling.

"Tell me about His goodness."

"I will, in time. Not this morning. Are you feeling better today?"

"What do you mean? I'm fine. There is nothing wrong with me."

"Well, you rearranged the pulpit furniture, redecorated the vestibule, and this morning, I noticed new slipcovers on the office sofa."

"You've been working for me too long."

"Are you doing better this morning?"

"Yes, I'm having a pretty good morning myself." Shante smiled as she thought about the thank-you flowers she had received from Max for taking the boys shopping. It was totally unexpected. She enjoyed getting them. It had been a long time since a man had sent her flowers. She began to sort through the stack of mail Gail handed her. "I think my first appointment is at ten. Is that right?"

"Yes, it's at ten. Mother Black wanted to talk with you about the senior missionaries."

"All right. I'll be in my office," she said, going inside and settling down at her desk.

Shante decided to call Max before she started her day.

"Hey, Max," Shante said in a low, even voice when he answered the phone.

"Good morning, Tay. I'm glad you called, but I can't talk right now. I'm getting ready to go into a meeting."

"I wanted to thank you for the flowers you sent me this morning. They're beautiful."

"I'm coming," she heard him say to someone. "I'm glad you liked them. Can I call you later? They're calling me."

"Sure."

"Good. I really want to talk to you. Have a blessed day. I'll be thinking about you."

"You, too," she said, hanging up. She began day-dreaming about Max, imagining what it would be like to be in a relationship with him and not have to hide her feelings, even though the thought of having feelings for him frightened her. But it scared her even more to think about what Kevin might do if he knew they were officially a couple. She also thought about how difficult it was for single ministers in the church community to date. She finally convinced herself to enjoy the moment and the flowers. If only she didn't have to listen to Camille, she would enjoy them more.

Shante was rummaging through her desk looking for the missionary report for her ten o'clock meeting when she came across an envelope from Max's law firm with her name on it. It contained temporary custody papers for the boys that Max had given her last summer when she had taken them on the church youth trip to Disney World. The papers gave her permission to seek medical treatment in his absence. She shoved the papers back into her desk and went to the door to ask Gail for the report.

"Yeah, I can't wait to see you again. I had fun yesterday," Gail was saying to someone on the phone. She turned and saw Shante. "Pastor, I didn't see you standing there. Hey, I've got to go. I'll talk to you later," she said and hung up.

"Looks like someone's in love."

"Not yet," Gail said, smiling. "He's a nice guy. Can I help you with something?"

"Do you have a copy of the missionary report?"

Gail gave the report to Shante and she had begun reviewing it when Mother Black came into the office.

"Good morning, ladies. How's everybody this morning?" Mother Black asked.

"We're blessed, Mother. You're early," Shante said, hugging her.

"I wanted to get the meeting over with. Can you see me now? I brought you ladies some of my pound cake."

"I'll go make some coffee," Gail said.

"Sure, Mother, come on in," Shante said, ushering her into the office.

Shante looked at Gail making coffee at the small table that sat on the other side of her office. She was dancing, not even noticing the background music had stopped. She was so happy. Shante wished she could be in a relationship that made her that happy and not be afraid to show it.

CHAPTER 16

People were on their feet praising God all over the sanctuary, including the balcony. Some worshippers were lying on the floor and ushers were fanning them to keep them calm. Others sat in their seats crying. The musicians were rhythmic, really praising with their music. The spirit of God was really moving in church. Shante had felt it the moment she walked through the door.

"Preach, Pastor," somebody shouted.

"Preach the Word," another urged.

"Glory," yet another cried out.

Shante looked around the sanctuary. This morning, she knew the Word coming out of her mouth was for her. She knew the congregation was only there to witness the Holy Spirit ministering to her. Tears flooded her face.

"God said he's doing a new thing in your life—now. There is a now spirit in the building. God said he's going to bless you and keep you. Don't worry about the trials and tribulations you're going through. It'll be over soon, because this battle is not yours; it is the Lord's. Some of you have been waiting a long time for the manifestation of the Lord. You've been walking in faith on the Word God gave you. You've fasted and prayed. You trusted even when it looked as though nothing was happening. Look at your neighbor and tell him God is going to move in your life—now." Shante gripped the microphone as she walked around the pulpit.

"God is going to move in your life—now," the crowd shouted, looking at one another.

"That's it. Look at someone else and tell him God is going to do it—now."

"God is going to do it—now," the crowd shouted again.

Someone began screaming. A man jumped up and ran up and down the aisle. The band played a fast, upbeat praise song. The church was in a frenzy. Shante began leaping.

"Now," Shante said.

"Now," the crowed echoed.

Ten minutes later Shante motioned the musicians to begin playing softly. The crowd calmed down. She began an altar call. Many people came for prayer. She tried to lay hands on as many people as she could, and she made sure the altar workers were available to minister to those who needed it. After altar call, she called for people to join the church. Several got up and came to the front. After accepting them, she gave the benediction.

She felt drained. Sweat had soaked through her clothing; however, she stayed in the sanctuary, trying to greet the people who were waiting to speak to her. When she shook the last person's hand, she headed back to her office.

"Mom, I got your clothes out of the car," Camille said, giving Shante her tote bag.

"Thank you, Camille. Try to keep everyone out of the office. I've got to change clothes and preach at another service at four. I'm not going to have time to eat."

"I got you something. It's on the table. When I saw how service was going, I slipped out and got you something to eat."

Shante rushed into the bathroom, took a quick shower, and changed clothes for the afternoon service. She wolfed down her food and headed for the door. Driving to the church, she tried to call Max but only got his voice mail. She wondered how he was doing and how his day was going. She had told him about the afternoon service. She hoped he would be at the church when she arrived. She wanted to see him. Sitting at a traffic light she privately imagined what it would be like to introduce him as her husband before she preached:

'This is my husband Max. Stand up, Max, and let everybody see you.' Listening to the parishioners respond with applause when he stood and waved, she continued. 'Ladies, him mine. Yes, fine, tall, dark chocolate, let me quit,' she would say jokingly, then continue, 'He is an anointed man of God and he has been a blessing to me . . .' The sound of a horn blowing snapped her out of her daydream and she continued her journey.

⚜

It had been a long day for Shante. Two morning services and an afternoon program that was overlong had drained all her energy. It was almost ten, and she was just getting into her home. She wanted to take a long bath in her Jacuzzi tub and go to sleep.

"Mom, Max called you," Camille yelled from the other room.

"Thanks, Camille. Did I get any other messages?"

"Yeah, Aunt Patrice called, too. She said it wasn't important. She wanted to see how you were doing. She said she'll call you back later in the week. I told her about you and Max and how the two of you are in love."

"Camille, you didn't." Shante tossed her purse onto the sofa and headed down the hallway toward Camille's bedroom.

"No, but I got your attention." She heard laughter coming from Camille's room.

"I'm not going to fool with you tonight. I'm tired. I'm going to take a bath." She walked down the hallway to her bedroom. There was hardly any sign that Kevin had trashed her home. She hadn't mentioned it to Camille. Camille probably hadn't noticed the walls had been repaired or that the color was slightly different. She went into her bedroom and closed the door. She lay across the bed and got the phone off the nightstand.

"Hey, Max, I know it's late. Camille said you called."

"Hey, Tay, I'm glad you called me back. I was up working on that case we have in Greensboro tomorrow. It's going to be a long week."

"I won't keep you long. How are you doing? How was service?"

"Service went well today. How about you?"

"Second service was unreal. We haven't praised like that in a long time. I felt such a release in my spirit. I know I was preaching to myself. Don't get me started—I may jump up and run around the room." She curled up on the bed, tightly clutching a pillow.

"I've been thinking about you, Tay—about us."

"What about us?"

"I wish you were here with me."

"Max, if I were there with you, you would be working and I would be getting ready to go to sleep. What time do you have to be in court tomorrow?" She rolled over on the bed. She loved hearing his smooth voice; it relaxed her.

"Nine."

"What are you doing talking to me? Greensboro is a long drive from here. You need to get some sleep. I'll let you go."

"No, Shante. Don't hang up. I want to talk with you."

"About what?"

"Nothing in particular. I haven't spoken with you all day. I want to hear your voice."

"My voice?" Shante said, making her tone low, calm, and slow.

"Yeah. Talk to me." Max's smooth voice relaxed her even more.

"What do you want me to say?"

"Tell me what you're thinking."

"I'm not thinking about anything."

"Then sing to me."

"Max, you know I don't know how to sing."

"You have a beautiful voice. Sing to me."

Shante knew she was crossing the line. She and Max were having a nothing phone call—one that was about nothing that could go on for hours. It came from two people who want to be together but are at a distance. It was a nothing phone call, but Shante didn't want to hang up.

"I'll talk."

"Sing."

"We can debate this all night, but you have a long day tomorrow. I shouldn't keep you on the phone."

"No, Tay, don't hang up. I'll sing to you."

"No, Max, please don't. I've heard you sing, and I think you should save your voice for a special occasion—like the Fourth of July during a fireworks show."

"You got jokes. I'm going to sing you something slow and sweet." Max began singing to Shante.

Something in his voice made her relax even more. She felt peaceful, loose, as if she had taken a long bath. She loved this man. She could never tell him, though. She was enjoying Max's singing, not noticing the bad notes he was hitting or the fact that he was singing out of tune. To her he sounded like Luther—even better. She wished she were there with him. She began to imagine his touch, the softness of his lips as they kissed. She wanted to feel his caress as they held each other.

No, I'm a Christian. I shouldn't have these thoughts. She shook her head to refocus her attention on Max. She felt as if she was lusting; something she taught others that the Bible looks down upon.

"What?"

Realizing she had spoken aloud, she tried to play it off. "Oh, nothing. I was talking to myself."

"How did you like the song?"

"It was interesting."

They laughed and talked a few minutes longer before hanging up. She was finally able to get into the bath she had been waiting for all day.

The following morning Shante went to the gym to work out. She was on the treadmill when Gwen showed up. "Gwen? You're in the gym? God does answer prayer," she said, laughing.

"Ha, ha. Funny," Gwen said, stepping onto the treadmill next to Shante.

"When did you decide to exercise? I thought you were allergic to it."

"Our anniversary is coming up. I tried on some new clothes to take with me on the cruise, and I couldn't get them in my regular size. I had to admit my clothes are tight. I thought I would try to lose a couple of pounds before we leave."

"Whatever it takes to get you here."

Gwen began walking. "Shante, help me. I'm dying over here."

Shante looked over at Gwen and saw her bent over and barely moving. Sweat was rolling down her face and soaking her t-shirt. "Gwen, you just started. You haven't been on the treadmill five minutes."

"It's only been five minutes? Is there anything else here I can do? This treadmill is a killer."

"Slow it down. You've got it set too fast. Start out slow. Try to walk a mile today. Increase it as you go along. Once you get into it, it'll come easy."

"That's easy for you to say, Jackie Joyner-Kersee." Gwen stepped off the treadmill, breathing hard. She leaned over and took in deep breaths.

"It's easy for me because I've been exercising a long time. Get back on the treadmill. Don't give up now. You're just beginning."

"Let me catch my breath. I'll get back on it. How's Max? Ron said he missed the fraternity meeting last week."

"He's been very busy. He's got a big hearing in Greensboro today. He said it might last all week."

"Now you know his schedule," Gwen said, smiling.

"You know I don't keep up with Max's schedule. We were talking last night and—"

"You were talking last night, were you?" Gwen walked over to Shante, who tried not to look at her, and began running.

"Cut it out, Gwen. You know I talk to Max all the time. Why are you acting so surprised?"

"What did you talk about?"

"I'm not going to tell you what we talked about." Shante ran faster, trying to ignore her.

"You already told me he's in Greensboro. What else?"

"Nothing."

"Nothing as in it's none of your business, or nothing?"

"Nothing in particular."

"I knew it," Gwen said, clapping. "You guys are having nothing phone calls. You're making progress. I'm glad to hear that."

"What are you talking about?"

"What did he say? 'What are you thinking about?' And you said, 'Nothing, what are you thinking about,' then he says, 'Nothing. Talk to me. Sing me a song.' A nothing phone call," Gwen said, laughing and clapping. "I knew it."

"You're talking silly," Shante said, too embarrassed to admit Gwen was right.

Gwen went back on her treadmill and began walking slowly. "Let me get my behind on this treadmill. Looks like I'm going to a wedding soon."

"Who's getting married?"

"You know."

"Don't hold your breath."

"Hold my breath? Right now, I'm trying to catch my breath. This exercise thing is murder and should be illegal."

"Stop complaining. Take it slow. You'll be okay. When we finish here, we'll go to the free weights, and I can take you through the routine. We're going to get you toned and firm for your anniversary."

"You mean there's more? God help me."

⚜

"Pastor, I wasn't expecting you this morning," Gail said when she saw Shante entering the office. She had not expected her to be in on Monday, since it was her day off.

"I won't be here long. I came by to pick up something I left in my office. I've got laundry to do at home, and I plan to study while I wait for it to dry. I've got to get a couple of books from my office." She went into her office and began looking through her bookshelf. Her cellphone rang and flashed Max's number. He was supposed to be in Greensboro.

"Mama Tay! Joshua! The car!" a young voice screamed over the phone.

"Jonathan? What's wrong?"

"Josh got hit. He won't wake up. Miss Mabel called an ambulance."

"Jon, put Miss Mabel on the phone." She tried to remain calm, but her heart had begun pounding as soon as she'd heard Jonathan's frantic voice.

"Hello."

"This is Shante, Miss Mabel. What's going on?"

"Joshua and his friend Brandon were riding their bikes on the sidewalk, and a car came out of nowhere and hit him. I called an ambulance. They're here now. He's unconscious. I tried calling Reverend Patrick. He's out of town working today. They're trying to get in touch with him."

"Oh, my God, Miss Mabel. He's in Greensboro. Which hospital are they taking him to?"

"They're taking him to Children's Hospital off 85."

"I'll be right there. Max is in a big hearing today. He can't take his phone into the courtroom. But I know there is some kind of way they can get in touch with him." After hanging up, Shante began a frantic search of her desk for the temporary custody papers Max had given her last summer and ran for the door. "God, take care of him."

"Pastor, what's wrong?"

"Gail, try to get in touch with Reverend Patrick. Tell him it's an emergency. Ask him to call me on my cell."

"Okay, Pastor. What's wrong?"

Shante ran out the office and to her car without answering Gail. She started her car and sped toward the highway.

The traffic on Interstate 85 seemed unusually heavy. There was a lot of construction on the highway. Shante took the opportunity to pray when she slowed down. "God, please help Josh. Touch his body, Lord. I know you are a healer. Guide the hands of the physicians. Wake him up. I know you are able. In Jesus name." *I better call Camille.* Her hands trembled as she dialed the number.

"Hello, Mom," Camille sang.

"Camille, I need you to meet me somewhere to help with the boys."

"Why? I don't feel like messing with those brats today."

"Camille, I'm on the way to the hospital. Josh got hit by a car."

"Oh, my God, Mom. Is he all right? Oh, my God."

"Camille, calm down. Meet me at Children's Hospital. Drive carefully. He's going to be fine. I'll be at the hospital soon."

She tried to call Max again, but the voice mail immediately picked up. She pulled off the interstate and drove the short distance to Children's Hospital. She pulled into a parking space near the front door. She tried Max again. Because she couldn't use her phone in the hospital, she sent Max a text message and then ran inside.

∽∾

"Your honor, I would like to call my first witness," Max said.

"Proceed, counselor."

Max began questioning the witness. He had been waiting for this moment; he was prepared. He had a team of attorneys and investigators working with him. He knew if they won this case, he could make millions. He only had to prove the accident was caused by mechanical failure, not human error. All the evidence was there, and he knew every piece of it.

As the attorney for the plaintiff in a worker's compensation case that involved a malfunctioning crane that injured a worker on a construction site, Max and Gary were excited that their small law firm had been selected to represent the worker. Not only were they handling the worker's compensation claim, they were handling the liability claim against the crane's manufacturer. Today they faced the team of skilled attorneys representing the manufacturer, and he felt as if he had trained like an Olympic athlete and he was ready for the challenge.

The witness had been on the stand more than two hours when Max saw a clerk go up to the judge and whisper something in his ear. Max thought nothing of it;

this happened a lot in court. Max finally finished questioning the witness, but before the defendant's attorney could begin his cross-examination, the judge intervened.

"Will both parties approach the bench?" the judge said. After Max and the defense attorney complied the judge said, "There is an emergency. Mr. Patrick, can you meet me in my chambers? We'll reconvene in fifteen minutes. Any objections?"

Max signaled Gary to go with him to the judge's chambers. The three of them went into the office; a North Carolina state trooper and the defense counsel followed them. The judge motioned for them to sit down. The officer stood behind the judge.

"Max, I know we're getting started on what looks like a long trial, but I have something to tell you." The judge's voice was somber. "Your office called. There has been an accident. A car hit your son Joshua this morning. They've taken him to the hospital. I don't know his condition. I'm sorry."

"What?" Max said, jumping up.

"Oh, no," Gary said.

"Is he okay?" Max demanded and began pacing.

"I don't know. You may use my phone to call your office," the judge answered.

Max ran to the phone and quickly dialed his office. "Treneice, what happened?" he asked the second his secretary answered.

"Miss Mabel called and said Joshua was hit by a car. He was unconscious. An ambulance took him to Children's Hospital. I don't have any other information.

Pastor Dogan called and said she was on her way to meet them there."

Max hung up and told the group what Angela had said. He was trying hard to hold back his tears.

"Max, Officer Henley will take you to the hospital," the judge said.

"No, I'll drive." He headed for the door, but Officer Henley and Gary stopped him.

"Max, I can't let you do that, not after all you've been through with your wife. Officer Henley will get you there quickly and safely. Gary can continue with the hearing," the judge said.

"Yeah, Max. You go and see about Josh. Let us know how he's doing," Gary said.

Max gave Gary the keys to his car and left the courthouse with Officer Henley in a police car with the lights and siren on.

⚉

Shante ran into the hospital and went straight to the admissions desk and spoke with the clerk. "My godson, Joshua Patrick, was brought here by ambulance. A car hit him. Where is he?"

"Ma'am, only relatives are allowed in the back."

"You don't understand. His father is out of town. His mother is dead. I have permission from his father to take care of his medical needs." She handed the clerk the temporary-custody papers. She looked at them and told Shante to follow her.

They walked through the automatic door and down a long hallway. Shante heard a child screaming; she knew it was Josh. Her heart was beating so fast that she thought it was going to jump out of her chest. They went to a room that was eerily dim, even though the overhead lights and a table lamp were on. Shante wondered why she had been taken there instead of to Josh. "Ma'am, the doctor will be with you soon. I'm going to make a copy of these custody papers for our records, and I'll bring them right back. Wait right here," the lady said.

She was convulsed by panic. Shante was familiar with these small rooms, or family rooms as they call them in hospitals. She had been in them many times with members of her church who had experienced an accident or death. She tried to stop her worst fears from taking hold as she paced the room waiting for someone to come in and tell her something. She noticed a phone on the wall by the door, and picked it up and called Max's office. Treneice told Shante she had spoken with Max and he was on the way. Shante called Max's cell phone and got his voice mail again. She left an encouraging message. She was dialing Gwen's number when the door opened.

"Hello, are you Mrs. Patrick?" a man dressed in a white lab coat asked. Shante repeated the details she had given the receptionist when she arrived at the hospital. "I'm Dr. Bouknight. I'm the emergency room doctor who is working with Joshua. He's a lucky boy," he said. "Here's his helmet." The doctor handed her Joshua's helmet. It was in two pieces.

"This protected his head. It was reported that he was unconscious at the scene, but by the time he got here, he was screaming. That's a good sign. We're going to let you see him when he gets back from X-ray. It's important that we don't move him too much until we know what's going on. After X-ray, we'll probably send him to get a CAT scan to be sure there is not a problem with bleeding in his head. He did take a nasty hit, but the helmet took most of the impact. I wish more parents were like you and insisted their children use a bike helmet. I need to talk with you a little about his medical history. Is he allergic to anything?"

"No," Shante said. She listened closely as he asked her a number of questions about Joshua's medical history. "Doctor, when will he be back from X-ray?"

"In a few minutes. There's one thing I have to tell you that may be a problem."

"What is it?" Shante tried to remain calm, trying hard not to show the doctor how frantic she was. She braced herself for the worst. "His arm is broken pretty bad. He'll need surgery to repair it. We have called in an orthopedic surgeon."

"Surgery! Is it that bad?" she asked, losing her battle to remain calm.

"One of the bones in his arm was sticking out when he came in. We think his bones are broken in a couple of places. We can't do anything to it until the surgeon gets here. We gave him something for pain. He'll be sleepy when you see him. It's only the medication. Do you have any more questions?"

"No."

"We'll let you know when you can see him."

After the doctor left, Shante began praying, but was interrupted by a knock on the door.

"Mrs. Patrick?" an officer said, coming into the room.

"I'm Shante Dogan, Joshua's godmother. I have permission from his dad to get medical assistance for him. His father is out of town."

"Maybe I should wait until his mother gets here," he said, turning to leave.

"His mother is dead. She died when he was a baby. You can talk to me."

"Witnesses said the driver of the car was acting as if he was drunk. He went up on the sidewalk, back out into the street, and then back on the sidewalk again before hitting Joshua. Some people had called the police when they noticed his erratic driving. Before we could get to the scene, he had already hit your son—godson. He left the scene of the accident. That's okay. We have the make and tag number of the car. We'll get him. Here's a copy of the report. We'll let you know when we arrest this guy."

Shante was stunned. Kevin was the first person she thought of who could do something as horrible as this. He had already threatened to hurt the boys. She never imagined he would actually do it. She thought he was only trying to scare her. "Officer, you have no idea who did this?"

"No, but we have a pretty good start. We need to find out who was driving the car. How is your godson?"

"He's going to need surgery to fix his broken arm. He'll be okay."

"That's good to hear. It could've been so much worse. Is that his helmet?" he asked, pointing.

"Yes. It's in bad shape, but it's not his head. I'm grateful."

"I hope everything works out for y'all, ma'am. I'll be getting in touch with you."

The officer left and Shante began to cry. She was relieved a broken arm was the only major injury Josh had. However, she couldn't stop thinking Kevin had caused the accident. She began to blame herself for it and for not telling Max about the threat Kevin had made regarding his children. She wiped her tears. She knew she would have to pull herself together so she could be strong for Max when he got to the hospital. She picked up the phone and called Gwen. She got her voice mail and left a message. The door to the room opened and Camille, Miss Mabel, Jonathan, and Jacob came in. The boys ran to Shante and hugged her tightly as they cried and told her how frightened they were.

"Mom, how's he doing?" Camille asked.

"He's conscious and screaming. He broke his arm. He's in X-ray now. Overall, he's doing well. The doctor said he should be fine."

"Miss Shante, I was right there. It happened so fast. The car came out of nowhere."

"Miss Mabel, it is not your fault. There was nothing you could have done. The officer said the driver was probably drunk. They have his tag number. Hopefully they'll get him soon, before he hurts anyone else." Shante sat down on the small sofa with Jonathan and Jacob beside her. "Josh is doing fine. He broke his arm. He's going to have surgery to fix it."

A nurse came into the room and told her she could see Joshua. Shante asked Camille and Miss Mabel to continue trying to contact Max, but to not tell him about the surgery. She then left with the nurse. They went down the hallway and into a small exam room separated from the others by a circular curtain.

∽∾

The siren on the police car was blasting as Max and Officer Henley sped down the highway. Cars were pulling over to let them go by. Traffic slowed down as they neared Charlotte. Officer Henley maneuvered the police car down the emergency lane. Max sat in the passenger seat without saying a word. His thoughts went back to the night Meko died.

He remembered it so clearly. They had been at the church for Bible study. They had driven separate cars that night because Max had come straight to the church from the office. Two ladies needed a ride home, and Meko volunteered to take them. Max left the church with the boys. He had gotten them into bed when he received the phone call to go to the hospital. When he got there, the doctors and police told him what had happened. Meko and the two ladies were driving down Beatties Ford Road. A man in a tractor-trailer truck had run a red light and had plowed into the side of the car. All three were killed instantly.

A tear ran down his cheek. Max tried to wipe it away before Officer Henley noticed, but it was too late. He noticed. He tried to reassure Max that everything was all right. Max called his home but no one answered the phone. He called the hospital, but no one would give him any information. Then his cell rang.

"Max, I'm so glad I got you. We've been trying to get in touch with you. We're at Children's Hospital. A car hit Josh. Mom's in the room with him. She said his arm was broken, but, he'll be okay. We haven't seen him yet. Where are you?"

"We're about thirty minutes from Charlotte. We'll be there soon. Are you sure that's all your mother said? Is there anything else?"

"She said he was screaming. He's going to be fine. That's what she said. I'll be here after Miss Mabel goes home."

Max could hear Jonathan and Jacob yelling for the phone. "Give the phone to them, Camille," he said. He tried to remain calm as he listened to his son. "Jonathan, you guys are going to have to be good and hold down the fort for me. Do what Camille says. Tell Jacob to listen to Camille. I will be there in a few minutes."

"Dad, we were so scared. We thought he was dead."

"Don't say that. Mama Tay said that he'd be fine. Y'all be good. I'll be there soon. Let me speak to Miss Mabel."

"Reverend Patrick, Miss Shante said Josh broke his arm. It all happened so fast. Josh and Brandon were riding their bikes, and a drunk driver came out of nowhere and came up on the sidewalk and hit him. I was right there with him. Brandon and I were knocked to the ground, but we didn't get hurt. It was so bad. It happened so fast." Max could hear her crying.

"Don't blame yourself. It wasn't your fault. Are you sure you didn't get hurt?"

"Yes, I'm sure."

"Camille is there with the boys. You can go home. I'll let you know how Josh is doing."

"Okay, Reverend Patrick. Call me when he gets out of surgery."

"Surgery! What's going on?"

"Oh, no. I shouldn't have said that. Miss Shante asked me not to. Joshua's arm is broken so badly he's going to have surgery to fix it. That's all I know. That's all she told me. She wanted to tell you herself because she didn't want you to worry. I'm sorry, Reverend Patrick."

"Thanks for telling me. I'm glad you did. You can go home now. I'll call you when he gets out of surgery." Max hung up the phone. What was really going on with Joshua?

"Your son's in surgery?" Officer Henley asked.

"He's having surgery for a broken arm. His god-mother is with him. How far do we have to go?"

"Not far. This traffic is heavy today, but I'll get you there shortly."

Officer Henley sped through the traffic. Max sat back and prayed.

"Mama Tay," Joshua said groggily.

"Hey, baby, how are you feeling?" Shante asked, rubbing Joshua's forehead. He had a cervical collar around his neck. He had scratches and a big bruise on one side of his face where he had hit the pavement. She looked at his arm and was shocked to see his bone sticking through his skin. She tried not to act surprised. She didn't want to scare him. She wanted so much to hold him and let him know everything would be all right. A nurse was busy adjusting the IV attached to his arm.

"Mama Tay, I hurt."

"I know, baby, but you're going to be fine. The doctor gave you some medicine." Joshua lay silently on the stretcher. "Excuse me, nurse. Can I hold him?"

"You'll have to wait for the doctor before you move him."

Shante sat next to Joshua's bed, feeling terrible that she couldn't hold him. She tried to comfort him as best she could by calmly talking to him and stroking his head. It didn't seem to relieve her anxiety or his pain.

The doctor came into the room. "Ms. Dogan, his X-rays look good. We don't see any broken bones other than the ones in his arm. His neck looks good. We're going to send him around to do a CAT scan now," the doctor said.

Two orderlies came in and took Joshua for the scan. Shante kissed him on the forehead before he left.

"You can wait here. He won't be in there long," the nurse advised Shante.

She sat down in the rocking chair in the corner of the brightly decorated room. She prayed for Max to get there soon.

⋙

Max and Officer Henley pulled into the parking lot of Children's Hospital. Officer Henley drove up to the front door, and Max jumped out before the car had come to a complete stop and thanked Officer Henley for getting him there so quickly. He ran to the front desk and asked for Joshua. He was immediately taken to the back.

"He's in this room here, sir," the lady said, pointing in the direction of the curtain around Josh's bed.

Max entered and saw Shante sitting in a rocking chair holding Joshua. They looked so peaceful. Joshua was asleep; Shante was humming. Max thought this was probably one of the most beautiful sights he had ever seen.

Shante sang "Jesus Loves Me" with her eyes closed. She hadn't noticed Max coming into the room. He walked quietly over to them and touched Joshua on his forehead. Shante opened her eyes and looked up at him. "Max, I'm glad you're here."

"How is he?"

"He's doing fine, but he's going to need surgery on his arm."

Max looked down at Josh's arm and saw the bone sticking out. "It looks pretty bad," he said.

"The surgeon is coming in to talk to you. Josh just got back from having a CAT scan. They're waiting for the results. The anesthesiologist spoke with Miss Mabel to find out what he had eaten today. Someone will be in here soon to take him to surgery," she said. They turned as the curtain to the room opened.

"Excuse me. I'm Dr. Phillips. I'll be performing the surgery on your son."

"I'm his father, Maxwell Patrick," Max said, shaking the doctor's hand.

"Well, as you can see, he has a pretty nasty break. Here are his X-rays." He and Max walked to the wall to view them. The doctor explained how the bone was broken and what he was going to do in surgery to repair it. "His CAT scan looked fine. He didn't have any bleeding in his head. He might have a mild concussion. After surgery, we're going to keep him a couple of days to watch him. Right now, everything looks good. When he wakes up after surgery, he'll be sore. We'll give him something for that. We're going to try to make him as comfortable as possible. Do you have any questions?"

"What happens after surgery?"

"Well, if everything goes well, he should be in a cast for six to eight weeks. It shouldn't affect his ability to use his arm. He should have normal growth in it. He's going to be fine. The bruising on the side he landed on should clear up soon. There's nothing to worry about."

"Good. Thank you, doctor," Max said, shaking his hand. After the doctor left, Max laid hands on Joshua's forehead and began to pray. Shante closed her eyes and listened while Max prayed for healing and for God to guide the surgeon's hand. After he finished, he left the room and went to find Camille, Jonathan, and Joshua. He located them and Miss Mabel, who did not leave, in the family room. He told them about Josh's injuries and his surgery. The hospital staff allowed them to visit him briefly before he left for the operating room. Jonathan and Jacob began to cry when they left the room. Max assured them he would be fine after the surgery. Camille offered to take them home and babysit as long as Max needed her. Before Miss Mabel left the hospital, Max made sure she had not been hurt in the accident and said he would contact her as soon as the operation was over.

Two patient transport assistants came into the room to take Joshua to surgery. Max and Shante walked alongside the stretcher as it rolled down the hallway. At the operating room entrance, they were told they could wait in the surgical waiting area. They kissed Joshua on the forehead and went to the waiting area.

"Do you want something to drink? There's a coffee maker and soda machine in here," Shante said. She noticed he was trying to hold back tears. She walked over and hugged him. Max squeezed her tightly.

"I was so scared. All I could think about was Meko."

"It's not like that. He's going to be fine, Max. Let's pray." She began to pray, and Max allowed himself to cry. "I don't know if I could have gone through this alone. Thanks for being here."

"There's nowhere else I would want to be right now."

Max continued holding her tightly. She looked so beautiful to him. He knew he wanted to be with her forever. She was his wife, the mother with which God had blessed his sons. He saw everything in her a wife was supposed to be. He touched her face and bent down and kissed her.

She didn't pull away; she relaxed in his arms. He felt the softness of her lips, and felt at peace in the arms of the woman he loved. They held each other tightly. For a brief moment, it felt as if it were only the two of them. They held each other closely as they sat on the sofa. She put her head on his chest, and he rested his chin on her head. They closed their eyes and prayed as they waited for the surgery to be over.

"Mr. and Mrs. Patrick? I'm Officer Jones. I wanted you to know that we caught the guy who hit your son."

"You did? Praise God," Max said, standing. "Who was it? Someone from the neighborhood?"

Shante stood and took Max's hand when he held it out to her.

"The guy's name is Lance Seawright. He lives in your neighborhood. It's a shame. He's only nineteen, and this is his third and most serious DUI. How's your son doing?"

"He's still in surgery. The doctor thinks he'll make it through without many problems. Thank you, Officer Jones, for coming by and telling us," Max said, shaking the officer's hand.

They returned to the sofa after the officer left. "Come here, 'Mrs. Patrick'," Max said, pulling Shante closer to him. Too tired and relieved to protest, she moved closer and rested her head on his chest.

CHAPTER 17

Three days later, Josh was discharged from the hospital. The trial in Greensboro had continued. Shante persuaded Max to return to work. She stayed at the hospital with Josh during the day, and Max took over each evening. Miss Mabel took care of Jonathan and Jacob during the day and they spent their nights at Shante's house.

"He's baaack," Camille said as Joshua rushed into the house past her. He couldn't wait to show Jonathan and Jacob his cast and the pictures a hospital volunteer had drawn on it.

"Hey, Mom. Max, I see he's back to normal," Camille said as they too came into the house.

"He is better than a few days ago," Shante said, "but he still has a long way to go. He'll need physical therapy after his cast is taken off."

"Tay, I'm leaving for Greensboro now. Are you sure it's okay for me to go? Josh just got out the hospital; maybe I should be here," Max said.

"Don't be silly. His arm is broken; he'll be fine. Look at him—he's all over the place. I'm sure I can handle it," Shante replied. "You go ahead. I got this."

"Well, if you say so. Do you need anything?"

"No, I don't need anything. You better get going if you are going to make it to the courthouse for the start of afternoon session. Come on, I'll walk you to the car."

Max put his arm around Shante's waist as though it was the most natural thing to do. "I'll see you this evening," he said, hugging her. I appreciate your doing this for me. The boys like having you around."

"And what about you?"

"I like having you around, too." He smiled and kissed her lips.

Watching Max drive away, Shante knew she had started something she shouldn't have. She didn't know how to stop it, or even if she wanted to.

Shante had finally gotten the boys settled. She helped Joshua put on his pajamas and read him a story before tucking him in.

"Mama Tay, are you staying at our house tonight?" Josh asked her as he lay in his bed.

"Not tonight. Your dad will be here in a few minutes. But I'll be here until you fall asleep," she replied.

"Are you going to live with us?"

"No. Where did you get such an idea?

"Cammy said you and Dad were in love, and when people love each other, they live together."

Note to self: Kill Camille when I get home. "That's true. I do love you and your brothers, but I can't move in here. I have my own house. What would Cammy do if I moved out?"

"She can live with us, too. She can have Jonathan's room—"

"And you need to say your prayers and get to sleep."

"Mama Tay?"

"Yes, Josh?"

"Do you love my daddy, too?"

Looking into his expectant eyes, she was silent. She knew what he wanted to hear. She wasn't sure she should tell him the truth. "Yes, Josh, I love your daddy, too. It's time for you to go to sleep now. Say your prayers."

"God, thank you for letting me come back home to my daddy and brothers and all my toys. Thank you for all the presents, and God, let Mama Tay and Cammy move in with us because we love each other. Amen."

"Get some rest, Josh."

She sat on the edge of the bed caressing the healing scars on his face until he fell asleep. She checked on the other boys and started down the stairs. Max was waiting at the bottom. He still had his suit on, but had loosened his tie and the top two buttons of his shirt. He was leaning on the railing looking up at her. She heard soft music playing.

"Max, how long have you been here?" she asked. "I didn't hear you come in."

"A few minutes."

She stopped one stair from the bottom, bringing her eye-to-eye with Max. "You look tired," she said gently rubbing the back of his head.

He put his head on her shoulder. She hugged him, and he squeezed her around the waist. He began rubbing his face against hers. She could feel his new beard as he slowly made his way to her lips. They kissed with a passion she hadn't felt in a long time. She felt every part of him touching her body. Their kiss grew deeper, and she didn't want to stop. His hands explored her back, touching every inch of it before moving to the small of her back.

Shante, wake up. You can't do this. You're a Christian. Do something quick. She didn't want to let go. She felt herself begin exploring him. She could feel his firm body as she pressed into him. *Shante, stop.* She reached behind her and grabbed his hands and moved them to her sides. She pulled away.

"Come on, Max. You're tired. Want something to eat?" She started walking toward the kitchen.

"No. Gary and I stopped and got something. How's Josh?"

"He's the neighborhood celebrity. That child is so outgoing—seems like nothing gets him down."

"Jon and Jake, have they been a problem?"

"No. They're upstairs watching TV."

They went into the family room and she sat on the sofa. He threw his jacket on the love seat and sat next to her. He leaned back and let out a sigh.

"A difficult day in court?"

"Not really, just long. Looks like this thing is going to last into next week. I was hoping it wouldn't take this long. Everything looks good for us now. But, you never know how the jury is going to react."

"Have you thought about staying in Greensboro until the hearing is over? The boys can stay with me."

"I can't do that. I still have to do things at the church. We still have a lot to do before the grand opening of the family life center."

"That's right. Do you need me to do anything?"

"Hold me."

"Come here." She knew she shouldn't go any further with him, but she convinced herself she was helping. Max curled up on the sofa with his head in her lap, and she massaged his temples. She caressed his head and body until she heard him snoring. *God, what am I doing? I have not only crossed the line, I have gone down the street. I have got to get out of here.* "Max, Max."

"Uh hum."

"I've got to go. You're tired and sleeping."

"I wasn't sleeping; I was meditating."

"It's late. I need to go."

"I don't want you to go," Max said, sitting up on the sofa and stretching.

"I have to go. Come on, walk me to my car." She went up and said good night to the boys, and she and Max then walked to her car.

"Call me when you get home."

"Okay."

They kissed goodnight and she made her way home.

"How could I have let it go this far? I kissed Max at the hospital because I knew he needed comfort. Now it has gotten out of hand. God, what should I do? I'm getting into dangerous territory," she said out loud.

She thought about the kiss and how she longed to be held like that again. It had been so long since she had felt such passion and energy. She had thought filling her day with work would keep her from thinking about sex and keep her lust under control. And it had worked for several years. But now, she had crossed the line. She had opened a door that shouldn't have been opened. She didn't know how to close it; she didn't want to close it.

"God, I'm trying to live a Christian life. Help me to resist temptation," Shante prayed. She thought about how her life had changed since she had become a Christian. She knew if she were the same person she was before she became a Christian, she would have been in Max's bed without thinking twice. She wanted to be in his bed. "God, help me."

She had been tempted many times, especially right after she had given her life to Christ. On a couple of occasions, she had given in to temptation. Each time she'd repented, she had turned around and had done it again. Then, one day a strong conviction came upon her. She couldn't do it anymore. She vowed to be celibate until she got married. She embraced her work and became very successful. She lost some things in the process—like time with Camille for instance. She distanced herself from any man who was interested in her. She knew her weaknesses and considered every invitation for dinner a date with temptation. Distancing herself was the only thing she knew how to do. No one in the church was teaching her how to resist. They only taught her to say no to sex, but temptation was all around her—like tonight. However, this was different; she really cared about Max. Maybe she cared too much. She would have to distance herself. But how? She would have to wait until Josh was all healed. At the moment, Max needed her.

CHAPTER 18

Shante sat in her office reviewing various speaking invitations she had received. There were fewer invitations than she had at the same time last year, and most of them were outside North Carolina. All of them looked promising, but she was interested in only one—Pastor Kay's family conference. There were no admission fees, and she was looking forward to preaching there. She put the invitations aside when Tank walked into her office.

"Hi, Tank. It's a blessing to see you this morning. How are you doing?" she asked, walking around her desk greeting Tank with a hug.

"You know I'm blessed, Pastor. Where's Gail?"

"She called in sick today, so I have phone duty. She rarely calls in. I told her to take a couple of days. She's been working really hard lately. She is helping the Women's Fellowship get their conference package together," she said, motioning to Tank to sit in the chair in front of her desk.

"Thanks. How's everything? I just wanted to drop in and talk with you to make sure you're doing all right."

"Tank, you don't have to worry about me. I'm doing fine. It looks like the rumors have died down some. I can really focus on my job now. I think I'm a little more relaxed."

"That's good to hear. Looks like you changed things around in here," he said, glancing around her office.

"I needed a change."

"Are you alone?"

"Yes, why?"

"Let's go for a walk," Tank said, getting up and walking toward the door.

She thought this was a strange request, but she joined him. As they began to walk around the parking lot of the church, she wondered if he was doing a Joshua walk. In the Bible, Joshua walked around the walls of Jericho seven times in order to defeat his enemy. She started counting the times they walked around the perimeter of the church. She sensed something serious was happening.

"I had to leave your office. You never know who is listening," Tank said.

"What do you mean by that? You make it sound as if my office is bugged—like some secret spy thing. Besides, who would bug my office? Nothing really interesting goes on in there. Now the counseling room . . ."

"Shante, this is serious. I wanted you to know Curry wants an independent auditor to come in and review the books to make sure nothing funny is going on. He is calling people and getting them all riled up for the next board meeting. I told you he had it out for you. Are you keeping yourself clean?"

"Of course. I'm walking a tightrope as it is. Why would he do a thing like that? I haven't done anything to him. I haven't done anything wrong. God, what's going on?" She stopped walking, trying to hold back the tears. *Never let them see you cry.*

"Come on, Shante, keep walking. You know this is nothing but the devil. I knew I couldn't trust that Curry. When Pastor Anderson lobbied to get him on the board, I knew it would be trouble. He's from the old school. I don't think he likes sitting under the authority of a woman. It's his chance to get a man in the pulpit."

"Where would he get an idea that something is wrong with the finances? You know all the trouble it takes to get money from the church. We have safeguards."

"He says he has a gut feeling. That is what he's telling everyone."

"I'm not doing anything wrong. Tell you what, Tank, call the board members and tell them to go ahead and approve an independent auditor. I have nothing to hide. I have all my receipts and copies of the ones I turned in. If there's a problem, it is not coming from me. I'll call an auditor today."

"That's just it, Shante. He thinks you and the auditor are friends and are conspiring to cover up discrepancies in the books."

"What? Where do people get these ideas, these lies?"

"Keep walking, Shante. He wants the board to select the auditor."

"That's fine. I have nothing to hide. Go ahead and approve it. If it's a fight Curry wants, he'll get one."

"If everything is fine, there won't be a fight. We can't afford to have any more negative attention brought to this church. People have finally stopped spreading all those silly rumors about you being a stripper."

"It's not my fault."

"I know it isn't. We could still do without the gossip. Seven," Tank said, stopping in front of his truck.

"A Joshua walk. Thanks, Tank. It's good to know that someone is on my side. Thank you for telling me. God always has a way of revealing the enemy's plot against you. I love, you Tank," she said, hugging him.

"Let me get out of here. Rose thinks I'm at the grocery store. I'll talk to you later. Remember, keep yourself clean," Tank said, getting into his truck.

She watched him drive out of the parking lot and then returned to the church and went to the sanctuary to pray. As she headed back to her office, she heard the phone ringing. She ran to pick it up, but it was too late; the caller had hung up. Then her cellphone rang. The ID showed it was Max. "Hey, Max. Is the hearing over?"

"No, we're on break. We're trying to get some lunch. We're waiting to be seated. I wanted to talk to you."

"About what?"

"I wanted to hear your voice. I miss you."

She went around her desk and sat down and stared out the window. All things considered, she should be stressed but the sound of his voice relaxed her. "The last week has been great. We have seen each other every day since Josh got out the hospital."

"I know, but today, I miss you. It's First Friday. We're supposed to be having fun."

"You're not having fun in court?"

"You know what I mean. I love you, Tay."

"I know."

"They're calling us. I'm riding with Gary. We may stop for dinner, so I might be late getting home."

"I'll be waiting. I'll go ahead and take the boys to dinner."

"I'll see you when I get back."

Shante sat for a moment staring out the window, playing with the cross Max gave her. She missed First Friday. Then a thought popped into her mind. Greensboro was a long way from Charlotte. They could have a quiet dinner there and have a chance to relax. She tried to shake off the thought. Tank had just warned her to keep herself clean. She wanted to be with Max alone for a change. A quiet dinner would not hurt anything. She reasoned that no one would see them so far away from Charlotte. She reached into her desk and pulled out her emergency makeup kit and ran to the bathroom to put makeup on. She wanted to surprise Max, so she decided not to call him. She locked the church, got into her car and headed to Greensboro. Along the way, she called Camille. "Camille, can you stay with the boys this evening? Max and I are having dinner."

"I thought Max was in Greensboro," Camille said.

"He is. We're having dinner there. Make sure you get to his house before four. I told Miss Mabel I would be there by then. Thanks, Camille. I owe you one."

"Tomorrow we shop. You can show your appreciation then."

She got on the interstate leading to Greensboro and began making her plans. She would have to stop and buy something to wear, as she had worn jeans to work. She wanted to get something sexy. Max made her feel special, and she wanted to look the part this evening. They would be in another city, so she could dress the way Max made her feel—like a woman, and not like the business casual style she always wore. It was the weekend, so they did not have to rush and could take their time hanging out. They both could use a nice quiet evening alone with each other.

When she arrived in Greensboro, she drove through downtown and began looking for apparel shops. She found a little dress boutique on Elm Street. She went in and tried on several dresses, finally deciding on a close-fitting black dress. It had been a long time since she was able to get dressed up. All her clothes were safe, conservative. On the few occasions when she could have dressed sexier—the singles ministry Valentine's dance, for example—she had chosen not to. As the pastor, she had felt it wouldn't be appropriate. However, tonight was different. She wanted to feel beautiful; she wanted to feel sexy. This little black dress made her feel feminine, like a woman. She wished she had gotten her hair done, but there was no time for that. She had to get to the courthouse before the hearing ended for the day.

"Your husband's really going to love that dress," the saleslady said.

"I'm not married, but I'm meeting a friend tonight."

"His eyes are going to fall out of his head. With that dress on, he'll be more than a friend."

Shante also selected shoes, a purse, and jewelry, but she realized she couldn't go into the courtroom in that dress; it would attract too much attention. "Excuse me, miss, do you have a shawl or city coat?"

The clerk showed her a lightweight city coat that matched the dress perfectly. "I'll wear these out. I'll put my jeans in a bag," she told the clerk. Seeing a small greeting card shop next to the boutique, she went in and purchased a card, asking for directions to the courthouse before leaving the shop.

Shante entered the large courtroom at four-twenty, and it was packed. Gary was questioning a witness. She saw Max seated next to a man and a woman at a table near the front of the room. She motioned for a bailiff to come to her. She gave him the card and pointed at Max. Max opened the card and looked around and saw Shante sitting in the back. He waved discreetly at her, and she waved back. She sat quietly in the back of the courtroom and began to wonder if she was doing the right thing. She debated whether to stay or leave, but Max had already seen her. She had driven all the way to Greensboro, and now had to fight the urge to run.

Then, she heard the judge say court was adjourned until Monday at nine. A sobering thought came to her: what was she thinking coming to see Max like this? But she convinced herself she was doing the right thing. She waited in the back for Gary and Max to come to her.

"Hey, Shante, I didn't expect to see you here," Gary said, kissing her on the cheek.

"Max and I are having dinner; Camille is watching the boys."

"Yes, we are." Max bent over and kissed her cheek.

"You guys were awesome. If it had been me on that stand, I would have cracked. I should drop by the court-house to see you in action more often," Shante gushed.

"That's because you're good people. I wish everyone were like you." Max couldn't wipe the smile off his face. His heart raced with anticipation, with the promise of the night's events.

"Max, help me take these files to my car. Remember we're meeting at the office tomorrow at ten. I don't want this trial to go on all next week."

"Shante, can you meet us in the parking lot out back?"

"Sure."

She drove around to the back of the courthouse where Gary and Max were loading boxes of files into the car trunk. She got out and went over to them. "You guys need any help?"

"No, we got it. We're just about finished," Gary said.

The late summer sun was causing sweat to pour down her face and back, so she took off her coat not thinking about the little black dress.

"Whoa, Shante!" Gary said, after he looked up and saw her leaning against her car. "You look hot, and I don't mean from the heat."

"Wow, Tay, you look . . . you look awesome," Max added.

She was slightly embarrassed, but thanked them for their compliments.

"I see the two of you have a special evening planned. Enjoy." Waving, Gary got into his car and drove away, leaving Shante and Max standing in the emptying parking lot.

"Turn around. Let me see you," Max asked appreciatively. She obliged, allowing him to take in every inch of the dress that was hugging every curve. He hugged her. "You look so beautiful. I haven't seen you dressed like that before."

"I wanted to look special."

"Well, you do, but you know what would make that dress look even more special?"

"What's that?"

"If you take the tags off," Max said, laughing as he helped her remove the tags. Though embarrassed, she couldn't help laughing, too. They got into her car, and Max kissed her passionately before driving to a local restaurant called the Piano Bar.

"A bar, Max? I'm not going in there."

"It's not a bar; it's a restaurant. You'll like it."

They walked hand in hand into the restaurant. They had arrived early and didn't have to wait for a table. Max requested one on the balcony.

"I see we're in the colored-folk section," she said, looking around.

"No, this is the best table. You can see the entire restaurant. Look at it. It's so romantic."

She looked around the dimly lit room. Couples were laughing and talking. The dance floor was empty except for one couple that was dancing as if they were the only ones there. They looked like they were so in love. This was definitely a date restaurant, she thought.

"Have you been here before?"

"A couple of times."

"Oh, yeah? With who?"

"Have you looked at the menu? They have the best steaks."

"Dodging the question?"

"I've eaten here with clients, and when I was with them I was thinking of bringing you here. Now we're here, and I only want to focus on you. You look so beautiful, Tay."

"Thanks." She began to feel hot. Was she having a hot flash or was she blushing? She hoped Max didn't notice.

"When I read your card, I wanted to run and pick you up. I'm so glad you're here. I wanted to be with you so badly today; I've been thinking about you all day. Wow, you look beautiful," he said taking her hand.

"You say that as if I usually look horrible."

"No, Tay, that is not what I meant. Today, you look special, as if you were expecting to have a special evening with someone special. I feel honored to be that someone." Max slid closer and lifted her chin and kissed her.

She moved away and pulled her dress over her breasts. "Max, we shouldn't do this here."

"We're not in Charlotte. No one will see us. Relax. Come here."

He kissed her again. He softly kissed her bottom lip and then the top one. She wanted to relax, but couldn't. She was afraid someone might see them. "I think we'd better order." She moved away from him and picked up her menu.

During the meal, Shante relaxed a little and began to enjoy the evening. "The meal was delicious. I'm glad you brought me here."

"Would you like to dance?"

He took her hand and led her down the circular stairway to the dance floor. The restaurant was crowded now, and a lot of people were waiting to get in. They found a space on the floor and began dancing. The scent of his cologne soothed the anxiety that had swept through her earlier. She was glad she decided to meet Max.

Shante could feel the cross that hung around her neck pressing into her body as Max held her. She felt as if she could stay there all night. She pressed her head into his chest as they danced. When the music stopped, they began maneuvering through the now crowded dance floor trying to get back to their table.

"Hello, Pastor." She spun around and saw Sarah Turner, a member of her church board, sitting at a table with her husband. She panicked. She did not need anyone to see her like this. She tried to play it off and act as if everything was normal.

"Hello, Sister Turner, Brother Turner. How are you doing?" She quickly released Max's hand and smoothed down her dress.

"I'm blessed, Pastor. Funny seeing you here."

"We're having dinner. You know Reverend Patrick, don't you?"

"Hello, Reverend Patrick. Well, Pastor, you look mighty beautiful today. I don't think I've ever seen you dressed like that before."

"Thank you."

"Shante, let's get to our table," Max said, taking her by the elbow.

"We've got to go. It was good seeing you." She could feel Sister Turner's eyes on her as they made their way back to their table. She wanted to run out of the building. She sat down and Max sat close to her. She moved away.

"Why are you doing that? Come here."

"No, Max. That woman is staring at us."

"So what? Come here."

"You don't understand. That's the board member that called me a whore. She said I was going around laying up with men on church money. Now she sees me in here with you in this dress. Not today. Please not today. We were having such a perfect evening."

"And it can still be perfect. Let's go."

The ride back to Charlotte was quiet. All Shante could think about was being seen in that dress with Max. She wished she had let Max ride home with Gary. She wondered how much Sister Turner had seen, how long she had been there. She hoped she hadn't seen them kissing or feeding each other. She knew she had seen them dancing. If she hadn't, she probably wouldn't have said anything. She considered calling Tank before a new round of rumors started. She didn't know what to do. She felt like crying.

"Let's take a drive along the lake," Max suggested.

"No, I'd better go home. It's getting late."

"Tay, you can't let that woman get you down. What can she say about you? She was in the same place."

"She was in the same place with her *husband*. Besides, I've got to take Camille shopping tomorrow, and didn't Gary say you guys were meeting in the morning?"

"It's not even eleven. We have another hour before your curfew," Max said, trying to make her laugh. His attempt fell flat. She didn't feel like laughing. All she could think about was the church meeting. First, it was Deacon Curry; now it's Sister Turner. She dreaded thinking about what could come next. The one day she'd decided she wanted to feel like a woman instead of a minister all the time was ruined by running into a board member. She asked God why she couldn't have any fun and be a woman just one day. She was tired, drained. She sat silently staring out the window as Max drove her car down the highway toward Charlotte.

Shante paced the floor of her bedroom, praying. "God, I repent of my sins. I knew it was against my better judgment to buy that dress, and the way I acted at the restaurant was not a good image of a woman of God. Forgive me."

She couldn't sleep. She had a deep feeling of dread. "God, I always try to walk righteous and holy in your sight. I got carried away today. I cracked under pressure. Please forgive me."

She sat on the edge of the bed and continued to pray. She tried to lie down. She was still restless. She tried turning on the television, hoping that a preacher on Christian television would provide some comfort. However, she didn't seem to understand anything the TV ministers were saying. She wondered what to do next. She picked up the phone and called Gwen.

"Hello," Gwen said sleepily.

"Gwen, this is Shante."

"Shante, is there anything wrong?" Shante imagined her sitting up in the bed.

"Who is it?" she heard Ron whisper.

"It's Shante."

"Shante? Is there anything wrong? It's two in the morning," Ron said.

"Tay, what's wrong?" Gwen asked.

She told Gwen all that had happened that day, about Tank and about the auditor. She especially told her about the dress. She began to cry so hard she could barely catch her breath.

"Was the dress really that hot?"

"A fire truck followed us to the restaurant. We were having such a good time. Why did that lady have to be there? It ruined everything."

"Tay, why are you so afraid of people seeing you and Max? You guys are good together."

"You know how people talk."

"I'd talk about you, too, if I saw you kissing in public."

"Bad judgment. It was plain ol' bad judgment. I thought I had my act together. I thought I could control lust. Here it is, back again."

"You love Max, don't you? Admit it."

"Max and I are friends."

"Tell me something, Tay. Have you ever thought about how Max feels about all this? You know he's crazy about you, and you're playing him."

"Playing him? I'm not playing him."

"Yes, you are, Shante. Have you ever thought about how he feels when he has to sneak around to see you?"

"Sneak around? We don't sneak around."

"Where did you go last First Friday?"

"We went out of town."

"And the time before that?" She didn't allow Shante to answer. "And the time before that? Do you see a pattern here?"

"Max and I love our adventures. It gives us a time to relax and be ourselves, you know, let go a little."

"Like today. Did you let go today, Shante? I'm sure Max sees it differently."

"What do you mean? Did he say something to Ron?"

"No, I'm just saying. That man loves you, and if you don't want him, you need to let him go. Why does everything have to be a big secret with you? Why are you always hiding?"

"I'm not hiding. You know how people talk. When I was dating Troy, everything was fine until church folk found out about it. Then we started having problems. He started listening to everything people were telling him about me simply because they were his members. There were all kinds of rumors and lies. Remember the lie that I was pregnant? Oh, yeah, don't forget Kevin, the devil in disguise. Why can't church folk mind their own business and stick to the work of the kingdom and worship?"

"Tay, I don't know about all that, but I do know God is trying to bring you out of something. You need to seek His face. It would be a shame for you to give up Max because of something somebody is saying about you, whether true or untrue. Look, Ron's up. I'd better go back to bed. He doesn't like me sitting up all night talking on the phone. I'm going to pray for you before I hang up."

Gwen began to pray. Shante closed her eyes and listened to Gwen's words. Initially, she thought it was a good idea to call her. She was beginning to think she shouldn't have talked to Gwen at all.

"God, forgive me. I won't do it again," Shante prayed.

She thought about what Gwen had said, but she didn't feel as if she was playing Max. Yet, she knew their relationship could not continue as it had been—nor could she let him go. She was in too deep. Her feelings were greater than just friendship for him. She couldn't talk to Gwen or Camille about how she felt; they would expect too much.

"God, help me. What should I do? Speak to me, God." She flipped through the television channels again. An old vampire movie caught her attention and she became deeply engrossed in it. When it ended, she could feel the chain and the cross around her neck. It felt like it was choking her. She took it off and wept bitterly because she knew how it felt to appear alive but feel really dead on the inside.

CHAPTER 19

The Earle Street Family Life Center's auditorium was packed for its grand opening. Extra chairs had been brought in, and some of the people had to watch the program on large digital television screens in an overflow area. Max and other program speakers sat on the stage. He rose to open the program.

"Truly God is blessing the Earle Street Baptist Church family," Max said.

"Amen," the congregation responded.

"This could have been a day of sadness, but God . . ."

"But God," the congregation answered.

"I know I have thanked you guys before, but I want to share my testimony with all the visitors we have here today.

A few weeks ago, I was in Greensboro at a hearing, and was called to the judge's chambers and was told a car hit my youngest son, Joshua. I was put in a police car and driven back to Charlotte," Max stated. He continued his testimony, holding up the two pieces of Joshua's helmet to the audience, who gasped when they saw it. He called Joshua to the stage to show the people he was healed.

Josh was sitting next to Shante on the front row alongside his brothers. He jumped up and ran to the stage to join his dad. "This is my son Josh. The enemy had it out for him. But God . . ."

"But God," the crowd repeated.

"They tell me that the man who hit him was only nineteen years old, and he was drunk when he came up on the sidewalk. I want you to know, not a day goes by that I don't pray for God to protect my sons. After their mother was killed in a car accident, I knew I had to cover them with a special prayer of protection each and every day. I pray for all my sons daily. I hug them and call good things into their lives. This is living proof that God answers prayer."

"Say it, Pastor. That's right," a few members of the crowd yelled.

As Max continued his testimony, walking back and forth on the stage, ministers surrounded him and shouted their support. He began telling the congregation about the goodness of God and then he leaped into the air. People were on their feet. Shante felt like leaping, too. Max began dancing in the spirit. As she watched Max dance, a thought entered her mind; there was nothing sexier than a man praising God. She shook off the thought and tried to become involved in the worship.

However, as the service progressed, she began to think about their relationship. She cared about Max and did not want to let him go. Frankly, she enjoyed sitting in the first lady seat with his sons. Today, she didn't care if anyone noticed she wasn't sitting with the other ministers. She was there to support her ministry friend, she would tell anyone who asked. Yet, she wondered why she could not break free from her self-imposed bondage and allow herself to openly be in a relationship with Max. She wanted it, but something was holding her back. She asked God to show her what it was.

⸎

Two weeks after the family life center opened, life appeared to be returning to normal. Max won the liability case in Greensboro and was now a very rich man. He was looking through a file when Gary walked into his office.

"Max, this is a new case that came in yesterday. Will you take a look at it for me? I think we need to send this somewhere else."

"I'll take a look at it. Are you busy?"

"No, man. What's up?"

"Close the door."

"Sounds serious. What is it?"

"Take a look at this." Max took a box from his desk drawer and handed it to his partner. When Gary opened it and saw a diamond ring, his eyes bulged. "It's for Shante."

"I'd better close this up; the glare is going to blind me."

"Nice, isn't it? Five carats."

"I can see how you spent the money we won on that case in Greensboro. Don't show that to my wife. She may get ideas."

"I think it's time. I'm going to ask her to marry me."

"Are you sure?"

"I'm sure. I've been praying about it. I even talked to Bishop about it. Our relationship is on a whole different level now. I would have thought nothing good could have come out of Josh getting hit by that car, but it seems like God used that to bring us closer together. We've been seeing each other almost every day. I really think it's time. I've got it all planned. Josh gets his cast off tomorrow, and we're going to celebrate with the boys."

"You're going to propose to her in front of the boys?"

"Sort of. I have it all planned out. She'll be surprised."

"I'm sure she will. Congratulations. I'm happy for you. She's a good woman," Gary said, shaking Max's hand.

"Yeah, she's a good woman, and I'm going to marry her."

"Good luck to you, man. Let me know how everything works out," Gary said.

"Everything will work out." Max returned the box to his desk and went back to his files.

❧

Shante's next appointment was late, so she decided to catch up on her reading. However, she was soon interrupted by Tank tapping on her partly opened door.

"Hello, Tank, it's good to see you. I didn't expect you to come in today."

"We need to talk, Pastor."

Shante sighed. Every time Tank showed up lately, it was to bring bad news. Today, he didn't look too happy; he looked troubled.

"Shante, I told you I was on your side. I have confidence in you. You've been a good pastor for this church, but something has come up."

"What is it, Tank?"

"The preliminary report came back from the auditor. Everything is not what it should be. The board wants to meet with you soon to discuss the findings. The auditor hasn't completed the entire report. He contacted us early because of some problems he found."

"What kind of problems?"

"The budget is not adding up correctly. I can't really go into details. Pastor, I thought I asked you to keep yourself clean. I thought I could trust you." Tank began walking around the room.

"Tank, what do you mean? I'm watching everything I do, say, wear, preach—*everything*. I did mess up that one time with Max in Greensboro when I ran into Sister Turner, but I told you about that. It was an innocent dinner. Nothing else happened. I know Sister Turner tried to make it look like more, but we only had dinner. I knew she would, that's why I told you. What else is wrong?"

"Shante, the board's going to meet with you soon. This is very serious. I trusted you. I've been defending you on everything. I hope you didn't let me down."

"What are you saying? Is there something wrong with the books? You know there are safeguards in place. I haven't even asked the church for money since the last meeting. I haven't used the credit card. If I need anything, I pay for it myself. I don't understand."

"I can't tell you everything, Shante. Let's just hope the final report will show that everything is clear. I wanted to give you the heads-up on what's going on. I wish I could tell you more. You're our pastor and you should know what's going on, because in the end, you'll be held responsible. I've been advised not to discuss this with you. I'm not supposed to be here saying this, but I've been praying, praying hard. This is serious. God, help us," Tank said, trying hard not to cry. She could hear him sniffle even though his back was turned, and he was pretending to be admiring a statue on her bookshelf.

"Thank you for coming to me, Tank. I value your friendship. You have always helped me and advised me. I want you to know I appreciate your support. I want you to believe me. I haven't done anything wrong. Whatever is going on, I'm sure I'll be cleared and it'll turn out to be just a mistake. Let's not get all upset. In the end, everything will work out, you'll see."

"For your sake, I hope it does." Tank moved toward the door, trying not to let her see the tears that had begun to flow.

"Tank, before you leave, come here." She walked around her desk and hugged him. They joined hands and prayed. "Everything will be all right, you'll see. This is another attack of the enemy, and we know how to fight it. This is God's battle, not ours. It'll be fine."

"For your sake—for all our sakes—I hope you're right, Pastor."

"I know I am. Now try not to worry about it. I'm sure whatever is going on is just a mistake. It'll all be cleared up soon. Let me know when the board wants to meet with me."

Tank nodded and walked out the door. She felt like crying. She questioned what was going on now. She had felt in her spirit not to use church money for any of her expenses. Knowing Deacon Curry and Sister Turner had it in for her, she had been careful not to give them any ammunition.

Shante sensed something was not right with the auditor. She tried to figure out what it could be, but could think of nothing. She decided to not allow it to ruin her day or take up too much time. She had work to do. Yet, she could not shake the feeling something was wrong. Shante tried hard to return to her work. The phone rang, and when Gail didn't pick up, Shante assumed she was in the ladies' room and answered the phone.

"Hey, Tay."

"Max, why are you calling on this phone? You should use my cell." His voice relaxed her; she looked forward to hearing it. She turned her chair so her back was to the door.

"I was thinking about you. I tried to call your cell but you have it turned off."

She checked her cellphone. "The battery is dead again. I need to plug it into the charger. Well, how's your day going?"

"Better since I'm talking to you. How's your day?"

She wanted to tell him what was going on. However, she didn't want to bother him with her troubles. She wanted him to be encouraged. The next day was a big one. If Joshua's arm was healed, his cast would be taken off, and they had planned a surprise for him. "Same old stuff. My appointment didn't show up this morning." She rocked back and forth in her chair.

"Are you busy this afternoon?"

"I don't have anything planned. We both have Bible study this evening."

"Do you have anything planned for lunch?"

"No."

"Would you like to take a long lunch?"

"Sure." She was ready to get out of the office. She wondered where they were going.

"I'll meet you at your house in thirty minutes. Is that fine?"

"I'll see you there." She got up and went to the outer office. Gail was not at her desk. She looked in the break room, counseling room, and the sanctuary. No Gail. She went into the ladies' room and could hear Gail's voice coming from one of the stalls. She knew the conversation. Gail was having a nothing phone call. Shante thought she would leave her alone. She left her a note and headed home. She was looking forward to seeing Max. She needed a hug.

Shante and Max sat on the chairs at the large kitchen island discussing the surprise he had planned for Joshua. They had finished eating a lunch of Chinese food and put away the containers when Max began massaging Shante's shoulders. "Are you trying to get something started?" she asked.

"Hopefully."

She closed her eyes and enjoyed every stroke of his hands, thinking how nice it was to be with him. Her breathing deepened as she felt his lips softly kissing her on the back of her neck. She reached back and stroked his head as he gingerly worked on her neck and shoulders. Spinning her around on the stool, he continued on the front with Shante giving in to every kiss. She felt his hands slowly go down her back and brace her buttocks. She wanted to pull back, but couldn't. He lifted her body up onto the granite countertop of the island and stood between her legs, passionately kissing her. She felt the hardness of her nipples as they pressed against his chest.

She wanted to stop herself but couldn't. Fornication was against everything she believed in, everything she represented, but this was different. It wasn't mere lust; it was love. She wanted to express it. How could she without crossing the line? She was never a tease. However, she wanted to feel his hard body against hers. She reasoned she could touch his body without allowing him to enter hers. So, she pulled his neatly tucked in shirt out of his pants, slipped her hands underneath and slowly moved her hand up and down his muscular back. Suddenly he stopped and backed away.

"We shouldn't . . ." Max said, breathing heavily.

"I know." She tried to catch her breath too.

"Well?"

"Well, what?"

"You want to go somewhere?" Max asked.

"Not really. I only want to be with you," Shante heard herself say as if she was having an out-of-body experience. His smile widened as he approached her.

"One day," Max said. "Not today, but one day."

CHAPTER 20

Shante, Jacob, and Jonathan sat in the lobby of the doctor's office waiting for Max and Joshua. She browsed through some old magazines until she heard the sound of small footsteps running down the hallway.

"Look, Jake, the doctor took my cast off, and he gave it to me to put in my room," Joshua said. "He gave me this cool pencil," he told Shante, showing her a pencil that looked like an arm in a cast.

"Does he need physical therapy?" she asked Max.

"No, there are no problems with his arm. He was able to do several things the doctor told him to do. There's no nerve damage, but he still has to wear a soft cast for a couple of weeks. At least he can take it off when he bathes. Looks like he's back to normal. Are you ready to go?"

"Yeah."

"Tay, we have a change of plans. It has been a long day. Do you mind if we go to my house and order a pizza? I picked up some movies from the video store yesterday. I haven't watched them. Maybe we can watch one tonight. I really feel like staying in."

"That works for me. How about the boys?"

"It'll be okay with them. You know they're pizza junkies. We'll have it delivered when we get to the house."

They got into the car and drove the short distance to Max's house. He had bought a house in the suburbs because it was convenient to everything, the schools were great, and it still allowed him privacy. As soon as they pulled into the driveway, the boys jumped out.

"Josh, buddy, we have something to show you. Come on, guys." They all walked to the garage and Max let the garage door up. As it began to rise, they could see the wheels of three new bicycles. When it was fully raised, they could see two new BMX bikes and a smaller version with training wheels. Each one had a bicycle helmet attached.

"Dad, you got us all new bikes?" Jacob asked.

The boys ran to claim to their bikes. At the side of the garage, Shante saw three adult bikes, one man's and two women's. "The purple one is yours, Tay."

"Mama Tay, you got a new bike too?" Joshua asked.

"You bought me a bike? Why?"

"Well, I thought you could go riding with us sometime. I got Camille one, too. She can ride with us when she gets back from school. Do you like it?"

"Yeah, it's nice. No one has ever given me a bicycle, not even for Christmas. Thank you, Max." She lightly kissed his lips and got on the bike and rode out of the garage and onto the driveway next to the boys.

"Oh, noooooo," Joshua piped up.

"What's wrong?" Max was concerned he was afraid to ride.

Joshua jumped off his bike and ran into the house. He came back with Max's bottle of anointing oil. "We have to pray for our bikes," he said, handing the oil to Shante.

"Give it to your father. Let him do it this time."

Joshua gave the oil to Max. He anointed each one on their foreheads with the sign of the cross. Shante took the oil and anointed Max's forehead. Then Max anointed each bike. They joined hands and prayed.

The boys sped off on their bikes down the sidewalk. Jonathan was already doing tricks on his.

"Don't go too far. The pizza will be here soon," Max yelled at them.

"I thought you were only getting Josh a bike. Looks like everybody got a surprise today except you. Can I get you something? What would you like?" Shante asked coyly, lightly rubbing Max's back.

"I'll get mine later," Max whispered in her ear.

"I'm going into the house. What movies did you get?"

"They're in the family room."

She went into the family room and looked through the videos on the end table. She picked up a copy of the television show *Martin* and went to the door with it. "Max, where did you get this *Martin* DVD? You know that is one of my favorite TV shows."

"It was on sale at the video store, so I got it. I planned to look at it when I needed a laugh."

"Can we watch it tonight after the boys are settled? Which shows are on this DVD?"

"I don't know. We'll watch it later."

The pizza arrived, and they all went to the family room and watched one of the videos. After they finished eating, Jacob asked if he could play his video game upstairs. Max said he could play, but for only thirty minutes. Taking Joshua with him, Jonathan said he was going upstairs to watch a show on public television.

Shante thought their behavior was strange; in fact, all of them were acting strangely. The boys were overly polite. They hadn't argued over seats or what to do after the movie. They even offered to load the dishes into the dishwasher. She assumed they were tired; it had been a long day.

"Tay, looks like the boys are all settled in now. Do you want to watch that *Martin* video?"

"No, Max, it's getting late. I'd better go home."

"Come on, Tay. It's only eight o'clock. One show is only thirty minutes long. Besides, we haven't had any time alone today. Stay just for thirty more minutes?"

"You convinced me. If it were something other than *Martin,* I would be out of here."

Max put the video on. She thought she heard the boys on the stairway, but when she turned around, she didn't see them. Max returned to the sofa and they cuddled. She kicked off her shoes and put her feet up on the sofa and snuggled up to Max more. "This looks like the episode where Martin proposes to Gina. I love this one." Shante laughed at the antics of the characters on the video. She knew the dialogue by heart. This was one of her favorite episodes.

"Mama Tay, I got you some flowers. I picked them out myself." Josh handed her a bouquet of roses.

"Thank you, Josh," she said kissing him on the cheek. "They're beautiful, but why didn't you give them to me earlier?"

Josh shrugged and walked away. She laughed. "I'd better go put these in water. Pause the video." She returned with the flowers in a vase and placed them on the end table. "Did you know about this?" she asked Max.

"I did. I thought he had forgotten about them. Let's watch the rest of the video."

She snuggled back into Max and continued watching the video, barely noticing Jacob come in.

"Mama Tay, I brought you and dad something to drink." Jacob was holding two wineglasses.

"Thank you, Jake. Put it on the table. You're so thoughtful." After he left she snuggled up to Max again.

"Dad, look what I found in my book bag," Jonathan said, handing Max a box.

Shante sat straight up. She looked at the video and at the box Max had in his hand. She looked at the table and saw the wineglasses. She looked at the flowers. She heard soft music. Someone had turned on the stereo, and it was playing her favorite song, Donnie McClurkin's, "Here With You". It always made her cry. "Oh, my God."

She watched Max get down on one knee with the box in his hand. He opened the box, and she saw the large oval-shaped diamond ring with smaller diamonds on each side. Her heart was beating fast. She could barely breathe.

"Miss Shante Elizabeth Dogan, I, Maxwell Theodore Patrick, am madly in love with you. Not a day goes by that I don't think about you. You are my life. I love everything about you— your smile, your charm, your wit, and your correction. I love the way you walk. Sometimes I ask

213

you to do things just to see you glide across the room. You have been my strength for the past several years. You are so good with my sons. They love you like a mother. When you're not with me, I feel like a piece of me is missing. I feel empty inside until thoughts of you fill me. I can talk to you about anything. I trust you. There is no one else for me. I want to spend the rest of my life with you. Will you marry me?" Max's hands were trembling as he looked into her eyes, nervously waiting for her answer.

She began crying. She looked toward the stairs and saw the boys sitting there—they, too, waiting for her answer. Max took the ring and put it on her finger. She was speechless. It was a perfect fit. How did he know what size ring she wore? She looked at the ring. She looked at Max. She turned and looked at the boys. It was all too much for her. She ran out of the house to her car. Max followed her.

"Shante, wait."

"Max, I-I . . ."

"Please say yes. I love you." He hugged her.

"Mama Tay, when are you coming to live with us? Jon said you're going to live in daddy's room. Dad can stay in my room. Are you moving in the morning?" Joshua asked, running toward them.

"Josh, go back in the house with your brothers," Max said.

Shante turned around so Joshua couldn't see her crying. Joshua turned and went into the house. Max turned her around to face him and wiped the tears from her eyes. "I know you're surprised, but I didn't expect this reaction. The ring fits perfectly. It looks good on you, Tay." He hugged her and whispered in her ear, "I love you, Shante Dogan. Say you will marry me."

This made her cry even more. She still couldn't talk. She looked at the house and could see the boys staring out the window. She opened the car door and got in and closed the door.

"Mama Tay, are you going to your house to get your stuff? Are you moving in with us tonight?" Joshua asked, running from the house again.

"Josh, I told you to stay in the house."

He stopped running and stared at Max for a moment, and then he looked at Shante crying. He walked to the car. "Mama Tay, what's wrong? Are you coming to live with us? Don't you love us? You said you loved my brothers and me. You said you loved my daddy, too, and when people love each other they live together. If you marry my daddy today we can live together."

This was more than she could take. She began to weep. The tears were flowing down her face. She couldn't look at Max or Josh. She couldn't look toward the house because she knew the other boys were watching them. She started her car and backed out the driveway and drove away, leaving Max and Joshua standing in the yard.

She looked at the ring as she drove down the street. She couldn't believe she didn't see this coming. She pulled over and took the ring off and put it in her purse. Her phone rang. It was Max. She sent the call to voicemail. Now she knew she had gone too far. She couldn't marry Max, not now. She began to weep loudly.

Shante ran past Gail as she entered the office. She had been up all night. No matter what she tried, she could not cover up the fact that she had been crying. She didn't want Gail to notice the swelling and puffiness around her eyes.

"Morning, Pastor. Whoa, you look bad this morning. Is everything okay?" She didn't want to face her. She did not want to talk to anyone.

"Pastor, before you go into your office, Reverend Patrick . . ."

She didn't want to hear about Max. She quickly opened the door to her office without acknowledging Gail. She stopped short. "Max!" She was surprised to see him sitting in the middle of her office. There were flowers all around. She closed the door and unplugged her phone and intercom system. She wanted to make sure no one in the office could hear their conversation. "What are you doing here, in my office, with all these flowers?"

"You didn't give me an answer last night. I thought you could give it to me today." There was a tremor in his voice.

"How could you bring this to my office? You know I don't like these people in my personal business. I can't believe you."

"I tried calling you last night."

"I didn't feel like talking to anyone."

"Well?"

"Well what?"

"I guess I know the answer. I want to hear you say it," Max said, trying not to cry.

"Max, I-I . . ."

"Say it, Shante."

"I can't marry you."

"You want to think about it? You want to talk about it?" He stood and walked to her. "I can give you some time. You don't have to make the decision today. How much time do you need?"

"Max, I can't marry you, or anyone, right now. I have too much going on. I told you I didn't want to bring you into it."

"Tay, we all have problems. That won't stop the love we have for each other. We can handle our problems together." He tried to hug her. She backed away and sat in the side chair. He sat on the sofa facing her. "Tay, look at me. Tell me you don't love me. Tell me you don't love the boys. Look at me, Shante."

She couldn't look at him. She began to cry. "How could you do this to them? How could you have them involved in something like this? I wish they hadn't been there. Oh, my God. Josh, my baby, he doesn't understand. How could you do this to them, Max?"

"They love you like a mother. They wanted to be there."

"No, you wanted to put pressure on me to say yes. That is what you were doing. You were trying to manipulate me. How could you?"

"I wasn't trying to do anything like that. We talked. They wanted to be there. They love you, and I do, too."

She got her purse. She reached in and took out the ring and handed it to him. "No. The answer is no. I can't believe you would use your own sons to get what you want. I thought I knew you."

"It's not like that. I don't want it back. Keep it. Think about it, Tay. Think about how good we'll be together." Max moved closer to her. She didn't move. She stood there with the ring in her hand, still holding it out to him. He pulled her to him and placed his head on her shoulder. "Don't do this to me, Tay. Don't do this to us. We're so good together. I love you," he whispered in her ear.

"You said that. Get off me. Take this ring. You have your answer. Please leave," she said, trying not to cry. She tried to act as if this were no longer having an effect on her, as if she were angry. She stood stiffly, her outstretched arm making it clear she was not going to keep the ring.

"Tay, don't."

"Here, Max. It's probably a good idea if we don't see each other again. Please leave."

"You're breaking up with me?"

"Breaking up? In order to break up, we have to be a couple. I told you we were just friends. I told you that, Max. I told you I didn't want a relationship with anyone right now."

He was stunned. "Tay, I thought . . . with the way our relationship was going . . . I thought . . . how can you throw our love away like that?"

"I never told you I loved you."

He stepped back. He knew she was right. She had never told him she was in love with him. When he'd told her he loved her, she had said she knew. He couldn't think of one time she had told him she loved him. "You're right. You never told me. I just assumed . . ."

"Max, don't make this harder on us. Please leave."

Her cellphone rang. She picked up the phone and looked at Max and asked him to leave again before answering the phone. Max walked out of the office with tears in his eyes. "Hello."

"Ms. Dogan?"

"Yes."

"This is the school nurse at Queen City Middle School. I have Jonathan Patrick here. He is upset. He didn't want us to call his father. He insisted we call you. I think something is going on. You're listed as an emergency contact in his records. I spoke with the principal, and she agreed that it was okay to call you. If you have a moment, he wants to talk with you."

"Please put him on the phone."

"Mama Tay, I know you love us. Why won't you marry my dad? Why won't you marry us?"

Tears began to run down her face. This was why she didn't want the boys involved in something like this. She knew she had taken the relationship too far, especially after Joshua's accident. She loved them. She wanted to be there to protect them from harm. She got caught up in the comfort she felt when she was with Max. She didn't want to hurt the boys. They were like her sons.

"Jon, I love you guys. Don't ever forget that. It's not the right time for your dad and me to get married."

"Are you going to think about it and get married later?"

She knew what he wanted to hear. How could she tell him she was no longer seeing his father? She couldn't tell him over the phone and while he was at school. "Jon, calm down. I tell you what. I'll pick up you and your brothers this weekend and we'll go somewhere and talk. We can go to the fun park and play laser tag. Would you like that?"

"Shante." She looked up to see Max staring at her. He had forgotten his keys and had returned to the office to get them off her desk. He had overheard her conversation with Jonathan. "Give me the phone."

"Jon, your dad wants to talk with you."

"Jon, I'll be at the school in a few minutes to pick you up. Tell them I'm coming to get you. I'm going to talk with Shante now." He handed the phone to Shante. "I'll let Jon know that you won't be coming to pick him up this weekend."

"What? Why not? I just told him I would. You're not going to make me look bad in this, Max."

"You're not going to bring the boys any deeper into this than they already are. It was my mistake to bring them into it in the first place. I'm sorry I did that, but I'm not going to let it go any further."

"Max, you can't take the boys away from me. They're my godchildren."

"They are my children, Shante. They are my sons. I'm not going to expose them to your little games. I won't let you do this to them," Max said, pointing his finger at her.

They stared at each other. Silence filled the office. Max shook his head and walked out.

Sadness rained down on Shante. She hadn't anticipated losing the boys. She couldn't imagine Max taking them away from her. She began to cry. She didn't want to lose her relationship with the boys.

"Pastor, I'm sorry to interrupt. Tank called and said the board will be meeting next week. Is everything all right? I heard loud talking. Do you want to talk?"

Shante tried to look strong. "Gail, help me put these flowers in your car. I want you to take them to the nursing home down the street and pass them out to the residents. I'm taking the rest of the day off. I don't feel so good right now."

"Okay, Pastor. If you want to talk . . ."

"I've had enough talking for today, Gail. Please take these flowers to the nursing home."

CHAPTER 21

Shante spent the next few days avoiding phone calls from Gwen and Bishop and Mother Thompson, knowing Max had probably talked with them. She pretended to be swamped by work, despite being unable to focus on the simplest task. All she could think about were the boys and Max. She wrestled with why Max had not waited to propose to her, especially with all the turmoil in her life—the board questioning her fitness and her integrity; Kevin harassing her and trashing her house; and unknown enemies spreading malicious gossip about her. Her heart hurt for the boys, and it pained her to think of the moment Max had proposed to her in their presence. She was at her desk trying to find something to take her mind off all her problems when Gail beeped her.

"Pastor, I'm sorry to interrupt you, but you have a visitor."

"Make an appointment. I'm not able to see anyone today."

"I think it's important. It's Jacob Patrick. He wants to see you."

"Jacob? What is he doing here? He is supposed to be in school." Then she realized it was late afternoon and school was already out. She hurried to the door and opened it. She grabbed Jacob and hugged him tightly;

she didn't want to let him go. He squeezed her and started crying. "Jake, come in here. Don't cry." Shante wiped his tears. "How did you get here?"

"I got a ride, Mama Tay."

"Does your dad know you're here?"

"No."

"I better call him and tell him where you are."

"Please, Mama Tay, don't call him. I wanted to see you."

"I've wanted to see you and your brothers, too. I miss you so much. After we talk, I'll take you home."

"You don't have to. I got a ride."

She thought it strange that a fourth grader would have a ride to her office, but figured he would get around to telling her how he got there.

"Mama Tay, Dad told us that we couldn't see you anymore. I'll probably get in trouble for being here. I don't care. I know you and my dad aren't getting married. I wanted you to—we all did. Jon is doing things to get in trouble. He got in a fight at school and was suspended for three days. Josh keeps asking to see you. Dad . . . well, Dad . . . sometimes when he thinks we're not looking, he starts to cry. He hasn't gone to work."

This news made her cry. These boys shouldn't have to be troubled by adult problems. It hurt her that they were hurting. She didn't want that; she didn't mean to do that to them.

"I know that God has a time for everything. That is what the Bible says."

"Yes, that is what it says."

"I know you may not marry my dad now, but there'll be a time for it. That is what God told me when I was praying last night. Don't worry about me. I'm going to help my dad until the time is right for you to get married."

She looked at him and knew God was using this child to send her comfort. This was Max's middle child. He was so quiet and reflective. Many times he was so quiet no one would know he was in the room. Sometimes she would sit and talk to him, and she found that he had wisdom unusual for a child. Max always said Jacob was his little preacher, and here he was ministering comfort to her. She hugged him again.

"I'm going to tell my brothers you're okay, and don't worry, you and dad will get married. It's not the right time. Can I come and see you? I have a ride."

"Yes, you can come and see me any time," Shante smiled. The thought of seeing him made her happy. There was a tap on the door, and to her surprise, it was Gary.

"Jake, we better go. I don't want your dad to get worried."

"Okay. I love you, Mama Tay." Jacob hugged her once again. Gary came a short way into the office.

"Jake, sit in the lobby. I want to talk to Tay a minute. Hi, Tay." He hugged her.

"Hi, Gary. Thanks for bringing Jake by. How did you do that?"

"He called me. I told Max I would pick him up from school and take him to his piano lesson. Shante, it's good to see you and Max look the same."

"What do you mean by that?"

"Both of you look bad, like train wrecks. I hope Max comes back to work on Monday. He's been out since . . . well, you know."

"Max is strong. I don't want to talk about it."

"But there is something I want to say. You guys love each other, and I hope you work everything out. Both of you are torn up about this. Look at you. You can't even look me in the eye. You're afraid I'll see your hurt. I saw it when I came into the room. The boys love you. If they want to see you, I'll bring them to you. Hopefully, Max won't find out."

"Thank you, Gary." She sat on the edge of her desk.

"I wish I didn't have to tell you this when you are going through a lot right now, but today I got news about Kevin from the district attorney."

"What did he say?"

"They're going to allow him to go through pretrial intervention since he has never been in trouble with the law. If he completes the program and pays the fine, they'll clear his record, and he won't serve any time—only some community service. He'll probably be required to go through some kind of counseling. He is not going to jail for destroying your house, but if he tries it again, he'll get some prison time."

"He's not going to serve any time for tearing up my house? It cost me almost four thousand dollars to repair what he did."

"He is required to pay restitution. You should get that money back. You can also sue him in civil court."

"I don't want to hear any more. I have too much on me right now. I can't take much more. With that board meeting coming up on Saturday, my nerves are being stretched to the limit."

"Board meeting? Anything I should know about?"

"I don't know yet. All I know is that our financial books are messed up, and they're looking at me."

"That sounds really serious, Tay. Let me know how everything turns out. Remember what happened at the last meeting and how God worked it out for you? He's faithful. I've got to go. I don't want Jake to be late for his piano lesson. I love you, Tay."

"I love you, too. Thank you so much for bringing Jake to see me."

"That's what godfathers are for." He hugged her and left.

Shante sat at her desk pondering how Kevin could have gotten pretrial intervention. She could not believe they would let him go. She had a restraining order on him and it had done nothing to prevent him from invading her house and threatening her, and it hadn't helped to convict him for his actions. She was beginning to think she had wasted her time going through the process to get the order. The legal system needed to do more to protect her and other battered women like her. Suddenly she remembered Jake, and she ran to the window to try to get a last look at him before he and Gary left the parking lot. It was too late; they had already gone. "God, I miss my boys. Thank you for bringing them back to me."

❦

Max shuffled to the door after the doorbell had rung for the third time. Bishop was at the door holding a big pot. Max was so drained he didn't notice the well-worn coveralls Bishop was wearing or the white socks sticking out from the too-short pant legs.

"Hello, son."

"Hi, Bishop. I didn't expect to see you here."

"Mother sent you some of her gumbo. She said you and the boys needed some home cooking, Creole style. May I come in?"

"Yeah." Max stepped aside and motioned to Bishop to come in. They went to the kitchen and Max took the pot from Bishop and asked him to sit at the small table against the wall.

"What's wrong with you, son? You look bad. Are you sick?"

"Jon got suspended for three days for fighting, so I'm hanging around the house with him. I'm making him clean the garage as punishment. He's not going to enjoy these three days."

"Why was he fighting? That's not like him. You have good sons. Is this something new?"

"Yeah, it's new. I don't know why he was fighting. He's not talking to me, but I have some idea."

"Well, what is it?"

"I think he's upset because of . . ." Max couldn't bring himself to say it. He had been trying hard not to get upset for the boys' sake. He didn't know how he could

227

talk to anyone about his pain without getting emotional. He had to be strong for his sons; they missed their Mama Tay. He missed her.

"Why is he upset?"

"Shante."

"What about Shante?"

"We . . . we're not getting married."

"I'm sorry to hear that, son. You were so sure she would marry you. What happened?"

"She said she didn't want to get married now." Max walked over and sat at the small table with Bishop, trying hard to hold back his tears.

"Maybe you sprang it on her too fast. Give her some time. She'll change her mind."

"No, Bishop. She said we shouldn't see each other again. She said she doesn't love me."

"She used those exact words?"

"She said we shouldn't see each other. I said we shouldn't throw our love for each other away, and she said she never told me she loved me. She was right. She never did."

"Son, I'm really sorry to hear that."

"How could she do this to me—to us—Bishop?" Max cleared his throat. "Our relationship had grown closer, more intimate. I thought we had the perfect relationship. She was only using me."

"Using you for what, money?"

"No. You know she would never take money from me or anyone. She wasn't using me like that. She was using me for comfort—emotional comfort. She was receiving, but she didn't want to give in return. I should have seen it coming. Why didn't God warn me?"

"Hold on a minute, son. You're angry, but don't get angry with God."

"I'm not angry with God; I'm angry with Shante. How could she do this to me and the boys?"

"The boys?"

"Yeah, they helped me propose to her. Josh kept asking her when she was moving in with us. It was so horrible." He dropped his face into his hands. The tears he'd tried to hold back escaped and seeped through his fingers.

"So that is why Jon is fighting. He's angry with Shante. Is he angry with you, too?"

"I told them they couldn't see her anymore."

"You didn't. How can you keep them from their godmother? You know those boys love her. Please tell me you didn't do that. I thought you had more sense than that."

"Everything happened so fast. I thought it was best at the time."

"How are the boys handling it? I know how Jon is. What about the other two?"

"You know Jake is quiet. He's not going to say much, anyway. Josh's silence scares me. It's been real quiet around here."

"I felt the sadness when I came through the door. I knew something was wrong. Agnes and I have been feeling it for a couple of days. We've been praying for you. That's why she sent you the gumbo. So what now?"

"I don't know." Max sat back in the chair and sighed. He really didn't know what to do.

"Have you been to work?"

"No."

"It's okay to take some time off when something like this happens, but you've got to get back to work. It's the best thing for you now. If you want, I'll talk to Shante."

"No, Bishop. Don't do that. She'll think I sent you."

"Well, okay. I won't go to her now. You know how close she is to Agnes. She may come over to the house to talk about it. Max, I want you to know that God is faithful." He looked around the room. "Where's Jon?"

"He is in the garage."

"Let me go talk to him."

Bishop pressed his hands down on the table and struggled up from his chair. He hadn't given Max the answers he desperately wanted. He suspected Bishop probably wanted him to find the answers himself. He was glad he was able to talk with someone about it, even if briefly. He wished Bishop had gone further and let him know what to do to get Shante back. He thought maybe he had acted too hastily taking the boys out of her life. His decision was having a negative effect on his boys and his home. *Bishop was right. There is a sad spirit in this house. It is time to change that.*

"Dad, can I go fishing with Bishop today?" Jon asked through the kitchen door.

"You're still on punishment." He saw disappointment in Jonathan's eyes. It was his fault Jon was being punished. He was the one who had told them they could not see Shante anymore. He had foolishly not considered its impact on his sons. So he decided to let Jonathan go with

Bishop. He knew Bishop could minister to him and help him understand what was happening. "Jon, come here."

Jonathan came into the house, and Max got up from the table and hugged him.

"Daaad," Jonathan said, trying to resist his father's hug.

"Jon, I want you to know I love you. I don't know how I'm going to do it, but I'm getting Tay back. I know she loves us; I know she loves you. She has a lot going on with her right now. It was the wrong time for me to ask her to marry me. I promise you, I'm going to bring her back to us. Wait, you'll see. Now I want you to go and have fun with Bishop today. Whatever you catch, we'll eat it for dinner tomorrow. I love you."

"I love you, too, Dad," Jonathan said, finally submitting to his father's hug.

"Now go on. Bishop is waiting for you. Take your jacket. It's a little chilly today."

Max watched as Bishop and Jonathan drove down the street. He put on a praise and worship CD and climbed the stairs to the bathroom to take a shower.

CHAPTER 22

"Hello, Pastor Dogan. I'll be right with you," LaDonna said as she continued styling a customer's hair. She had been Shante's hair stylist for many years, and Shante had a standing appointment for Friday mornings.

Shante waited for LaDonna in the lobby, idly looking through old hair magazines. She liked coming to this shop. It was clean, and LaDonna was a Christian. People there tried to encourage one another. There was no gossip or loud secular music, no conflicts with the stylists or profanity. Beautifully decorated, it looked like a salon one would see on a television makeover show. It was well lit and the atmosphere was happy and congenial. She had gone to many shops and had discovered this one by chance when she had stopped to ask for directions.

"Pastor, you can come in now."

As Shante walked over to LaDonna's chair, she received many hellos; everyone seemed happy to see her.

"I'm just getting it washed and wrapped today. I have a busy schedule, and I need to get to the church by one."

"Okay, Pastor, I'll hook you up. So how are you today?"

"All's well." Shante pretended to look at a magazine, conscious of her swollen eyes and the black circles under them due to lack of sleep and crying. She tried to cover up with makeup, but lately when she put makeup on, it didn't give her the coverage she needed. She hoped no one had noticed her face. After her hair appointment, she was going to buy some new makeup.

Shante flipped through a magazine while LaDonna parted her hair and scratched her scalp. "You're quiet today, Pastor. Is there anything wrong?"

"No, I've got a lot to do at the church."

"Well, if you need to talk, I'm here. Come on, let's go to the bowl."

Getting her hair washed was the part of the whole hairstyling experience Shante loved the most. LaDonna's fingers massaging her scalp and the warmth of the water relaxed her. Her mind was cleared of any thoughts about the proposal or the board meeting. She closed her eyes and worshipped silently to herself.

"Come on, let's go to the chair," LaDonna said after rinsing her hair.

Shante continued to pretend she was interested in the magazine she was holding, but her quietness was not lost on LaDonna. Usually, when she came to the salon, she would be encouraging someone or speaking an inspiring word. Today, she didn't feel like talking.

"Excuse me." Shante looked up. A tall woman with long, well-manicured fingernails was looking at her.

"Yes."

"I'm sorry to bother you, but I have something to tell you. You're a minister, right?"

"Yes, I'm a pastor."

"God is taking your ministry to a new level, a higher level. You've been in hiding. You're not going to be able to hide anymore. You won't be able to hide from your problems. You won't be able to hide from your responsibilities. You won't be able to hide from love. God is bringing you out."

"Miss, I'm sorry, but I'm not hiding from anything."

"Yes, you are. I don't know who you are, but God is pulling you out of your comfort zone. He has to do it. There is a greater work for you. God told me to tell you that you're getting married, too. Prepare yourself. There is work ahead for you."

The lady said this and walked out of the salon. Shante saw her get into a car and drive off. She was puzzled, but thought perhaps God had sent her to the salon that day. She wished she had told her the meeting was going to work out like the last one. The Word comes to bring comfort, but she had felt no comfort in anything the woman had said.

"You'd better listen to her. That's the prophet lady. She knows what she's talking about," LaDonna said as she continued wrapping Shante's hair.

Still pretending to read a magazine, she thought about the woman's words. She wondered if she should take her seriously. But she did not want to hear about getting married, and she felt annoyed when she thought about what the woman had said about hiding. To her, she wasn't hiding. What did that woman know about her? Could she have heard some of the gossip going around? Or was she really operating by the anointing of the Holy

Spirit? She decided to do what the Bible said—test the spirit by the spirit.

⤿⤾

Shante drove through the early morning traffic on her way to the board meeting. She had been praying all night. Once again, she had been unable to cover up the sadness on her face or the black circles under her eyes. She felt troubled in her spirit. As she prayed for peace, her phone rang.

"Good morning, Shante. This is Bishop."

"Hello, Bishop. What can I do for you this morning?"

"I know it's early. I wanted to call you and encourage you. I know you have that meeting this morning. Don't worry about it. It'll be all right."

"Thank you, Bishop."

"I've been in the ministry a long time. I've encountered all kinds of problems like this. Did you know I was put out of a church at one time?"

"No, Bishop, I didn't know."

"Yeah. They gave me all kinds of excuses. They accused me of all kinds of things, but you know what I learned?"

"What's that, Bishop?"

"I learned to be silent."

"What?"

"I learned to be silent. I learned not to argue with my accusers. Even when I wanted to defend myself, I learned to be silent. In the face of many lies and finger-pointing, I learned to be silent. I had to learn when to fight and when not to fight. I had to learn when to sit back and let God take care of my accusers."

"Is that what you think I should do?"

"When you go in there this morning, don't say anything. No matter what they accuse you of, don't say anything. I know you'll want to defend yourself, but don't. Even if they ask you a question directly, don't say anything. When you're silent, the only ones that have to give an account for their actions are your accusers. Leave it up to God to uncover and reveal truth. If you know you haven't done anything wrong, let God handle it. Everything covered will be uncovered."

"Thank you, Bishop, but I think I should defend myself. These are some serious accusations."

"Did you hear what I said? Don't say anything. No matter what they do to you, don't say anything. I'm an old man. I've been through this more than one time. I know what I'm talking about. Don't say anything. Please, Shante, listen to me."

"I'm listening to you. I respect your advice. I won't say anything. Pray for me."

"Good. I'll pray for you now."

Bishop began to pray as she pulled into the parking lot and into her reserved space behind the church. She sat in the car listening to him; she needed someone praying for her. After the prayer, she thanked him for his advice. She looked around the parking lot at all the cars already there. She sat in her car trying to psyche herself into going into the meeting early. She tried to figure out how she could get to her office without being seen by any of the board members. Her cellphone beeped. Someone had sent her a text message:

PRAYING FOR YOU. I LOVE YOU, AND SO DO THE BOYS. MAX.

Thinking of the boys made her smile, but then she was filled with sadness. She couldn't take dealing with Max and the board on the same day. It was too stressful. *I love the boys, too.* She got out of her car and hurried to her office. When she opened the door, Tank was sitting inside.

"Good morning, Pastor."

"Good morning, Tank. How are you?" she said, trying to sound confident.

"Are you ready? Everyone is here. We may as well get started."

"Go ahead. I'll be right in."

"No, I'm going to walk you in. You have to know there is someone who supports you."

She closed the door and hugged him. She was glad he was there supporting her. She had felt so alone in this whole process, but he made her feel there was at least one person in the church on her side. "Thank you. Let's go."

They walked into the crowded conference room. It appeared every deacon, deaconess, and trustee was in attendance. She saw a stack of papers entitled PRELIMINARY BUDGET REPORT sitting on the large table. Each chair had a packet in front of it. Shante sat down in her chair, and Tank called the meeting to order. The room was generally quiet, but a few people were whispering to one another.

"Deacon Curry, present the report," Tank said, motioning for him to stand.

Deacon Curry stood up and gave his reasoning for requesting a new audit of the budget. He went on and on about how he had a gut feeling something was wrong. He then directed the group to open their packets. Some members of the board gasped upon seeing the contents.

"As you can see, there is approximately $16,000 unaccounted for in our account." Shante looked at the figures and couldn't believe what she was seeing. She didn't understand how that much money could be missing from the church. She ran a tight ship when it came to the money. With so many safeguards in place, there was no way money could be missing from the account.

"Also, please note the questionable charges to the credit card," Deacon Curry urged the group.

"Look at the number of hotel rooms on here," Sarah Turner shrieked. "There's even one for Greensboro on the date of my anniversary. That's the day I saw Pastor in Greensboro. Don't deny it. Didn't I see you there?" Shante didn't say anything. She didn't even look up; she just kept on looking at the financial information in front of her. She didn't want to look into the eyes of Sister Turner. If she had she would have been compelled to answer her. She kept hearing Bishop say, *Don't say anything.* "Well, Pastor, are you going to deny that I saw you there that day bumping and grinding with Reverend Patrick on the dance floor? Are you going to deny I saw you there dressed like a tramp?"

She looked up. She wanted so badly to say something to her. She kept hearing, *Don't say anything.*

Everyone finally realized she was not going to respond, so they allowed Deacon Curry to continue. "This is a very serious report. We need to do a complete investigation. Once we have the final report from the auditor, I suggest we contact the police concerning this matter."

"Do you really think we need to call the police into this?" Tank asked.

"If there's a thief in this church, we need to find out about it as soon as possible. That person needs to be removed from our organization," Deacon Curry declared.

"Do you have any idea who this could be?" someone asked.

"There's only one person here who has access to the account, credit cards, and building—and that is Pastor," Deacon Curry replied.

"I'm sorry, Pastor. We have looked at everything. The credit card used was yours. We're trying to get evidence from the bank about the withdrawals. We can't accuse you of that. We can't accuse you of anything, but all the evidence points to you. I'm sorry," Tank said, stuttering as he spoke.

"We asked you to act ladylike. We asked you to watch your behavior. You couldn't even do that. First it was having sex with men on the beach, and then I saw you in Greensboro. You thought you could get away with it if you went to another city. But God allowed you to be uncovered," Sister Turner chimed in self-righteously. Shante stared at her without a word. "A tramp. I don't want a tramp as a pastor."

"Wait a minute, Sarah. You've definitely gone too far," Tank said, looking directly at her. "Give Pastor a chance to answer these charges. Pastor, you have the floor. Is there anything you would like to say?"

Shante shook her head. She had a lot to say, but was taking Bishop's advice to keep silent.

"Pastor, we're giving you a chance to defend yourself. If you have something to say, this is the time to do it," Deacon Curry said, trying to get her to speak.

"Please, Pastor, say something," Tank pleaded. Shante only shook her head.

"Well, you leave us no choice. I make a motion that we sit Pastor down until we have a complete report and a full investigation has taken place," Deacon Curry said.

"What are your grounds for sitting Pastor down?" Tank asked.

"We previously warned her about her character, yet we have a witness on the board who saw her behaving in a manner that was not godlike. Two, there are some questions about the finances of this church, and all the evidence at this time points back to her. Three, she hasn't denied any of the allegations. Those are my grounds."

Tank looked around the room. Several people nodded in agreement. "Pastor, I would like to give you one more chance to defend yourself," Tank said, looking pleadingly at her. She remained silent. "Then you give me no other choice. A motion has been placed to sit Pastor down until an investigation is complete. Is there a second to this motion?"

"I second," Sister Turner quickly jumped in.

"I'm not having any part of this," Trustee Faulkner said, getting up from the table and walking toward the door.

"Me either," a woman, said following him.

"I don't know what's going on, but something is not sitting right in my spirit about this whole thing. I wash my hands of it. I pray that the witch hunt you've been on doesn't backfire in your faces. I'm getting out of here." Another member got up and walked out the door.

"Is there anyone else who wants to leave?" Tank asked the group. "This is your opportunity. We need to have a quorum to vote on this issue." No one else left. Tank put the issue to vote. The majority voted to sit Shante down. They agreed she would continue receiving her salary until a full investigation was complete, but she wouldn't be allowed to preach, teach or counsel in the church. However, she would be allowed to represent the church in functions already scheduled outside the church, but she would have to be escorted by a member of the board. She wouldn't be allowed to schedule any new functions as a representative of the church until further notice. She wouldn't have access to any of the church's accounts. She was to immediately turn in her credit cards, and her security code for the church would be deleted from the system.

They agreed an associate minister Deacon Curry suggested would be acting pastor during the process. Deacon Curry said he had already contacted the minister, and he had agreed to take the position. At the end of the meeting, Tank escorted Shante back to her office. She unlocked her file cabinet and turned over her credit cards and her keys to the office.

"I don't know why you didn't say anything, but I believe you did the right thing. This is a witch hunt. There's something so wrong about this whole matter. I can feel it in my spirit. That's why I voted to keep you. There was no debate. It was so strange; I've never seen anything like it. Anyway, I can't talk about it now, not here. You have a lot in your office. You will have full access to your office, so you don't have to take anything out of here. Take this time to rest," Tank whispered.

Shante hugged him and thanked him for supporting her. She could see the enemy working in this whole thing. She took a few personal items from her desk and walked with Tank to her car.

"Pastor, this is a mess. I'm going to be praying. We all need to pray."

"Yes, we need to pray. I love you, Tank. Thank you again." She got into her car and drove away from the church. She pulled into the parking lot of a local store and picked up her cellphone. "Gary, this is Shante. I know it's your day off. We need to talk. Can we meet somewhere?"

"Sure, Tay. Sounds serious."

"It is. It's very serious. I don't want to meet at your office. I don't want to risk seeing Max. Is Ruby Tuesday's okay?"

"Yeah. In about an hour?"

"That's fine. I'll meet you there." She hung up the phone and dialed another number. "Hey, Patrice."

"Hey, Tay, how are you? I was just thinking about you. I was going to call, but you beat me to the phone. What's going on?"

"Can I stay with you for a few days?"

"What's wrong? You sound sad."

"I'll talk to you when I get there. I'll be there about six this afternoon."

"I'll tell Shawn. The kids will be happy to see you. You can stay as long as you need to. Does Camille know you're coming?"

"No, and don't tell her. I need a few days to get myself together."

"Okay. I'll be waiting for you."

"I'll see you at six."

CHAPTER 23

Shante arrived in the Buckhead section of Atlanta after eight. She was tired. The day's events and the long drive had worn her out. Even though Patrice wanted to know what was going on, she didn't push Shante to talk. Shante greeted Shawn and Travis. She was surprised at how much Travis had grown, and his voice was much deeper than the last time she had talked with him. Patrice took her to her room. She hugged her as Shante allowed the tears to flow.

"I know you probably don't want to talk about it now. You look tired." Shante shook her head. "I took Monday off. We can talk then when the house is quiet. Shawn will be at work and Travis will be at school. Unless you want to talk earlier."

"No, it can wait until Monday. I really don't feel like talking." She wiped the tears from her face. "Thank you for letting me stay here. I didn't know where to go. I won't wear out my welcome. I need a couple of days away from Charlotte."

"You can stay here as long as you want to. You're welcome here anytime. I'll leave you alone tonight. I put some extra towels in your bathroom. Help yourself to anything in the kitchen. If you need anything, let me know."

"Thank you, Patrice. I'm glad you're my friend. I love you."

Patrice left her in the spacious guest room, which was furnished with a large four-poster bed that was so high she had to climb a small step to get into it. She was glad the guest room had its own bath. She decided to take a shower and try to relax before going to bed. It had been a long day. She couldn't believe she didn't have to preach the next day. She was almost glad. The stress of wondering what the board members had planned was finally gone and the deed was done. She wondered what she would do next. Gary advised her not to talk to too many people about what had happened. He was doing his own investigation of the finances and planned to subpoena the church books and the auditor's report if needed. He told her not to worry; he would take care of everything. Yet she was worried. Shante lamented closing her consulting business to go into full-time ministry. How could they have sat her down? She fought to find understanding in the whole situation.

After taking a shower, she felt too drained to pray. Her prayer was simply that God give her wisdom and direction in this situation and that He protect her church and its members from the battle that was about to begin.

On Monday morning Shante woke up early and lay in the bed. She'd had a restless night and didn't feel like getting up. She felt as though every last piece of energy had left her. She had attended a local church on Sunday, but hadn't gotten all the answers she needed. She lay in bed and prayed quietly to herself. Afterwards, she forced herself up and put on her yoga wear and went downstairs to the home gym Patrice had given Shawn for his birthday. She hoped exercise would help clear her mind. She quietly walked down the dark hallway, down the basement stairs, and toward the gym. The lights were on and Shawn was lifting weights.

"Oh, Shawn, I'm sorry. I didn't know you were in here. I'll come back later."

"You're fine. I'm just finishing up. Help yourself to the equipment. I thought I was the only one who gets up early in the morning to exercise." Shawn continued lifting the weights. The muscles on his arms were bulging.

"I always try to get up between five and six to exercise, pray, and read my scripture. It helps me get my day started."

"I hear you. Exercising does help you get focused. The office keeps me pretty busy. God blesses me with new patients every day. I have to stay in shape just to keep up with the pace. Reading my Bible helps me stay positive with all the negative things I see. It helps me to focus on helping my patients."

"Read your Bible? I didn't know you and Patrice were reading the Bible."

"I read the Bible. I'm still praying for Patrice. When I got saved three months ago—"

"You got saved? Praise God. I've been praying for you and Patrice to get saved. I'm so happy." She walked over to Shawn and hugged him.

"I thought getting saved would make our marriage better, but it seems like the opposite is happening." Shawn sat down on the weight bench. She sat beside him.

"What do you mean?"

"I was in Chicago at a conference. There was a church conference in another area of the convention center. It was something about the music coming from that area that drew me into the meeting. When I heard the message, I knew it was time for a change in my life. I thought Patrice would be excited about it. She wasn't."

"I'm sorry to hear that. How has it affected her?"

"I'm not sure. She's so quiet. It's like she doesn't know what to say to me anymore. Before I got saved, we could talk about anything. Now it's hard to get her to talk to me. When we're together, she makes an excuse to leave the room. It's almost as if she is embarrassed to be seen with me. We don't go out to eat or to the movies anymore. I invited her to go to church with me. She went a couple of times. She didn't seem interested. Tay, I don't want to lose my wife. I love her. What can I do? I asked her to come to church with me yesterday. She said she had to stay here with you. Then you said at dinner that you enjoyed church. I knew she didn't want to go with me. She would rather stay at home all by herself before going to church. Travis went, though. I think he likes all the girls there." He smiled. "Whatever it takes to get him into church."

Shante jumped into pastor mode. She began counseling him about the changes that happened when becoming a new Christian and how it affected everyone around him. She advised him to take things slowly with Patrice, because she was probably watching him to see if he was true to his salvation. She also gave him scriptures that would give him hope. Afterward, they joined hands and prayed. She could feel the tremor in his hand. She knew the power of God was all over him. She prayed that their marriage would survive this transition and that Patrice and their children would get to know God the same way Shawn had. She also prayed for peace and blessing upon their house.

"Tay, I believe the Lord sent you to our home now. We need you here. Patrice needs you. She doesn't have many friends she confides in. She trusts you. You guys have been friends a long time. She'll listen to you. I know you're going through some problems of your own now, and I hate to ask you to help me, but Tay, we need help now. I feel the enemy really working on our marriage."

"I'll talk to her. Don't worry. Everything will work out."

"Thank you. I've got to get out of here and get ready to go to work. Patrice took today off. Hopefully, you'll have a chance to talk."

Shawn hugged her and left the room. She looked around. She was impressed with everything she saw. There was an elliptical, treadmill, stationary bike, free weights, and exercise mats. A television with DVD player was positioned on the wall facing the equipment. Two of the walls were mirrored, making the room feel larger than it was. She got on the elliptical machine and began to pray for Shawn and Patrice.

She ended her prayer and continued working out. She picked up the remote to the television and began going through the channels to find something to watch for the next thirty minutes. Her mind began to wander back to her own troubles. She still could not believe the church board had sat her down. She never expected that or the way they had spoken to her.

The more she thought about being called a tramp, the angrier she became until she realized she had been working out an hour without noticing. She went to her room and showered. She put on her sweat suit and went down to the kitchen. She could smell bacon; Patrice was up and cooking breakfast. Shawn and Travis were at the breakfast bar. Patrice was at the stove making an omelet.

"Good morning, everyone," Shante said, hugging first Shawn and then Travis.

"Morning, Aunt Shante. Come on, Pops, I'm going to be late for school."

"I'm coming. Morning, Shante," Shawn said as if this were his first time seeing her that morning. He walked over to Patrice, who was pretending she was concentrating on the omelet she was making. He kissed her on the cheek. She said good-bye without looking up. When the door closed, she looked at Shante and asked, "Would you like breakfast? I made cheese omelets with bacon. I have hazelnut coffee. Sit down. I'll pour you a cup."

"Thank you. Coffee will be fine. I don't feel like eating right now," Shante said, taking the cup from Patrice.

"You didn't eat much yesterday. You need to eat. It'll keep you from being depressed," Patrice said, going back to the stove.

"I don't have much of an appetite right now."

"Is it Kevin? Did he attack you again?"

"No, it's church stuff. My board met Saturday, and they sat me down."

"Sat you down? What does that mean? Did they fire you?" She stopped stirring the mixture in the bowl and faced Shante.

"No, it's more like I've been suspended with pay until they complete their investigation."

"Investigation? What investigation?" Patrice sat down at the table with her.

She told Patrice about being seen with Max and all the rumors that were out about her. She explained that she couldn't preach or teach at the church until they found out what was happening with the church finances. She told Patrice how Sister Turner had called her a tramp.

"Wait a minute. You mean you let someone call you a tramp to your face and you didn't say anything?"

"Bishop advised me not to say anything, and I respect him. He's a wise man. I wanted to say something to her real bad. She almost took me back to before I got saved. I wanted to cuss her out and jump across that table. It took everything in my power to sit there and take that from her."

"It's obvious she doesn't know you. As stiff and uptight as you are, anybody can look at you and tell you're not getting any. I don't see how you take that from those people. If it ain't one thing, it's another."

"I know. It's probably all over Charlotte now. The preachers are probably beginning to fight for my job. I wonder how my members are taking it. I should have gone to church yesterday and told them. It would've been easier on the church if I told them about the investigation. There's no telling what was said yesterday. I should've waited to come here."

"You did the right thing. You look bad. Did you tell Max?"

"Max? Max and I aren't seeing each other anymore," Shante said quietly, stirring her coffee.

"What? What happened? I thought everything was going great for you two."

"He asked me to marry him."

"Oh, Shante. What did you say?"

"I said no. He tried to use his sons to manipulate me into marrying him."

"How?"

"They helped him propose to me. They were there. It was so bad. Little Josh was so excited and kept asking me when I was moving in with them. I felt pressured to say yes. I kept quiet and left. The next day, I gave him back the ring, and we argued. I told him it was a good idea that we don't see each other."

"Tay, I thought you loved him. Didn't you tell me you thought you were in love with him the last time I talked to you?"

"That is what I thought at the time."

"So, you're sitting here telling me you don't love Max now?"

251

"I don't know what I feel. I know I didn't like him trying to manipulate me into marrying him. How could he use those boys like that? It turns out I didn't know him as well as I thought."

"You still love him. I can look at you and tell that. You told me Max was good to you. You said you enjoyed being with him. You called me many times and told me about how romantic he was. How could you change your mind all of a sudden? Love doesn't come or go instantly—not true love. You can't turn your love on and off. If you were in love with him, then you're still in love with him."

Shante didn't respond. She knew Patrice was telling the truth. She did love Max. She didn't want to admit it. She felt it wasn't the right time to be involved with anyone. She fought hard to hold back her tears.

"You should call him."

"I'm not calling him."

"Does he call you?"

"Yeah, and he started sending me text messages and e-mails when I wouldn't answer his phone calls. He sent me flowers Friday. He wanted me to know he was praying for me and for the outcome of this meeting. Anyway, he's probably heard about the meeting by now."

"He needs to hear it from you. You guys love each other, and you should talk this thing out instead of running and hiding out here in Atlanta. You need to give him a second chance. You told me yourself, he's good to you and his sons. You said he was everything you wanted in a husband. You said you could trust him. I'm only going by what you told me. How can you just throw it all away?"

"I've got too much going on now. My ministry is in trouble. All the work I put into the church is about to be destroyed. I don't even know what my next step will be."

"You need to stand up to those negroes at your church. That is the first thing you need to do. It's just like black folk to get jealous when you're successful. Someone probably saw how successful the church was becoming under your leadership and got jealous. Don't let them destroy what you and Max have. You need to call him and talk to him."

"I can't talk to him. I don't want him involved."

"He's already involved. Don't you think this has an effect on him? Didn't you say that woman saw you and Max together? See, he's already involved. You need to call him."

Patrice picked up the phone and handed it to Shante. "Here, take this. Call him. I'm going to take a shower and get dressed. Then we can go shopping. I'm not going to let you sit here all day thinking about your troubles. Call Max. He's probably worried about you. Call Gwen, too. She called here yesterday looking for you. She's worried. You're not answering your phone. Your friends love you, and you should stop shutting yourself off from them every time you have a problem."

Shante sat at the small table with the phone in her hand debating whether she should call Max and Gwen. She began dialing. "Hello, Mother."

"Praise God. Oscar, it's Shante," Mother Thompson said. "We've been praying for you. Where are you hiding now?"

"I'm not hiding, Mother. I'm at Patrice's in Atlanta. I'll be here a couple of days."

"Did you do what I told you?" Bishop asked after picking up the other receiver.

"I didn't say anything. Even when they were calling me names, I didn't say anything. I wanted to. I didn't say a word. They sat me down."

"We know, baby. Are you okay?"

"Yes, Mother. Patrice and I are going shopping. I think I'll buy something to cook them a special meal when we get back. You know, something to say thank you for letting me stay with them."

"Have you talked to Max?" Bishop asked.

"No, I haven't talked to Max in a couple of weeks. We aren't speaking to each other. I guess he told you he asked me to marry him and I said no."

"Did you think about it first?" Mother's soft voice echoed over the phone.

"I didn't have to. I know I don't want to get married now. I have so much going on. I can't bring Max into all this."

"He's worried about you. He asked if you called us. I'm going to tell him that you're fine and in Atlanta."

"No, Bishop, don't tell him where I am. You can tell him you heard from me, but don't tell him where I am. I don't want him to know. I'm embarrassed."

"Embarrassed? What do you have to be embarrassed about? Being sat down? I was sat down before. You get over it. Count it all joy. You're going to come out of this thing on top. I did and you will, too," Bishop encouraged her.

"People are praying for you. You don't need to be embarrassed. You have true friends here who know you and know you wouldn't do anything to bring shame to the body of Christ. You're a good woman. Come back to Charlotte soon. You're going to have to learn to look the devil in the eye and stand." Mother spoke with such authority it made Shante shiver.

"Amen, Agnes."

"I know you're hurting about this and about Max. You'll see that everything is working for your good. It was done for evil, but God will make it good. Believe this in your heart."

"I do, Mother. I've got to go. I'll call you later."

"Okay, baby. Let us know how you're doing."

Shante's cellphone rang just as she finished talking with Bishop and Mother. She looked at the caller ID. It was Max. She debated whether to answer and decided to take the call to prevent him from sending her a text message. "Hello."

"Shante?"

"Yes, Max," she said, trying to sound confident.

"How are you? I heard about everything. I was calling to see if you were okay."

"I'm fine. I'm getting ready to go shopping."

"You're in Charlotte?"

"No."

"I'm sorry, Tay."

"What are you sorry about? You didn't have anything to do with it."

"I'm sorry about everything—the proposal, the meeting, everything."

"You're sorry you proposed to me?" She was trying to start an argument so she would have an excuse to hang up.

"No, Tay, that's not what I meant. I'm sorry I proposed the way I did. I shouldn't have had the boys involved. I'm sorry the meeting went the way it did. I feel it's partly my fault. I was with you when that lady saw you in Greensboro."

"Max, I would love to talk now, but I have to go. Patrice and I—" She caught herself. She didn't want Max to know where she was.

"Patrice? You're in Atlanta? How long are you going to be there? Can I come and see you? We can talk."

"Max, I've got to go." She hung up. The phone rang; this time it was Gwen. "Hey, I was just getting ready to call you. This phone has been a hotline this morning. How is everything going?"

"Don't act like nothing is going on. How are you, girl? Ron and I have been praying so hard for you. You haven't been answering your phone. We were worried. Patrice told me yesterday you were with her. How are you holding up?"

"All's well."

"How can you say that? We heard they sat you down."

"That's true. They did what they felt was necessary. That is all I've got to say about that. I'm dealing with it.

Anyway, I needed the vacation. We're getting ready to go shopping."

"You mean you're not cooking and cleaning?"

"I'm cooking this evening and Patrice's housekeeper, Carmen, will be here to clean the house. I don't have to clean this big house. It's spic-and-span clean. It's good to be down here; it takes my mind off things."

"I'm sure Patrice will help you keep your mind off things. Don't stay too long. When you come back, Ron and I want you to come to our church. Oh, yeah, Pastor Kay called and asked if you're still going to do her conference Thanksgiving weekend. She said she tried to call you, but you haven't returned her call. She really wants you to preach at her church. Call her back. I have her number."

"I have it. I'll call her back. I really appreciate her letting me preach in spite of all the things being said. I'll definitely call her back. Thank you, Gwen. I hear Patrice coming. I'd better go. I'll talk to you later. Tell Ron I said hello."

"Shante, are you ready to go?" Patrice walked into the room wearing a light blue designer warm-up suit and blue-and-gray tennis shoes.

"Yeah. I don't think anyone else will call me. I've talked to everyone who has been trying to get in touch with me. I even talked to Max."

"Good. You'll see, everything will work out for you," Patrice reassured her.

Shante wanted to believe that. Her faith and everything in her told her to believe. However, doubt lingered. What would she do if she didn't preach? It was in her blood. It was her passion. How can it be taken away from her? She envisioned many scenarios as they drove through heavy traffic on their way to Lennox Mall. Finally, she thought of her invitation to preach at Pastor Kay's church and found a small glimmer of hope.

∞

Shante and Patrice sat at a table in a small coffee shop talking about their purchases. It was sunny, although the early October air was a little chilly. The coffee shop was packed with people looking for a bit of warmth.

"Thank you for taking me to that shoe store. These shoes are hot," Shante said, admiring the navy-blue stilettos she'd bought.

"It's one of Atlanta's best-kept secrets. Those shoes are nice. I'll bet Max would love to see you in them."

"Let's not get on that again."

"It doesn't matter how much makeup you put on, you can't cover up the sadness in your eyes. You love that man, and you need to tell him."

"Mom? Aunt Patrice? What are you doing here?"

"Camille? The question is, what are you doing here? Shouldn't you be in class?" Shante asked as Camille came up to them carrying shopping bags.

"My classes start late on Monday. My first class is at three. Mom, what are you doing in Atlanta? Why didn't you call me?"

"I was visiting Patrice. Sit down." She pulled out a chair for Camille.

"Mom, I'm so glad to see you."

"Why? Are you running out of money?" she asked, looking at Camille's bags.

"Funny. I've got money. I saw Dad last week, and he gave me two thousand dollars."

"What? Your dad came down here? I didn't know he knew where you were going to school. And he gave you money?"

"Miracles do happen," Patrice chimed in.

A waiter took Camille's order for a latte. "Yeah, I was surprised, too. I figured since he's never given me any money, this was a past-due child support payment and I took it. He owed me more than that. While he was down here, he could've paid some tuition, too. This is only a down payment on what he owes."

"Amen, sister," Patrice interjected.

"Don't be so hard on your dad. Now that's strange. Why all of a sudden would he come down here and give you money? That's not like him."

"I know, but two thousand dollars is two thousand dollars. Looks like I'm not the only one shopping. What did you get?" She began going through Shante's bags.

"Just some shoes."

"Mom, those are nice. Max is going to love those shoes on you."

Patrice laughed, openly enjoying Shante's discomfort.

"Didn't you say you had class at three? It's almost two. Don't you need to be going?"

"You're right. Are you staying tonight?"

"I'm staying with Patrice for a couple of days."

Camille looked from Patrice to Shante. "What time will you be home? May I spend the night? My first class in the morning is at ten."

"Is that all right, Patrice?"

"Sure, that's fine. You can come over when you get out of class."

The waiter returned with her latte. "Thanks. I'll see you guys tonight. Bye, Mom, Aunt Patrice." Camille gathered her bags and left, threading her way through the crowd.

"Now, that's strange. I wonder what Kevin is up to?" Shante mused.

"He's probably trying to look like the loving father now that he has those charges against him. He's probably trying to get Camille on his side."

"Patrice, he's not getting any time for those charges; he got community service and counseling. He owed me that two thousand dollars and more for tearing up my house. This is so strange. It's not like him."

"Maybe he's trying to change. Isn't that what you Christians do? Change?"

Shante suspected that was Patrice's way of introducing the subject of Shawn's conversion. However, she felt the crowded café wasn't a good place to have such a personal conversation. She decided to wait and talk to her later.

<hr />

Camille was trying to wrap Shante's hair. It had been a long day, and she was tired. She knew Camille wanted to talk, but she didn't feel like it.

"How are Max and the boys?"

"They're fine."

"Fine? That's all?"

"Yeah."

"You said no, didn't you?" Camille stopped combing Shante's hair and sat next to her on the bed.

"Said no? No to what?"

"You did say no. When Max asked me to help him pick out the ring, I didn't think you would say no. Why? Aren't you in love with him?"

"You knew about the proposal?"

"Yeah, Max called me and asked if he could marry you. I was happy for you. He came down here, and we went shopping for the ring. Why did you say no?"

"It wasn't time. There's too much going on right now."

"That's your excuse for everything. *There's too much going on now*," Camille said, imitating her mother.

"Camille, I have to tell you something."

"What, Mom? It sounds serious."

"It is."

"Are you sick?"

"No. There was a meeting at the church, and they sat me down. I'm not pastoring right now."

Camille jumped up from the bed and walked around the room. "Oh, no, Mom. How could they? When did this happen? Why didn't you call me?" Shante told her about Greensboro and the board meeting. Camille listened attentively but disbelievingly. "Mom, I know you didn't do any of those things. I don't see how you put up with it. Church folk make me sick."

"Don't say that, Camille. There are a lot of good people in the church."

"I know. But when something like this happens, where are those good people? Did anybody do or say anything to defend you? Who stood up for you?"

"Some people walked out of the meeting without voting. Tank tried to maintain an open mind, and after the meeting he tried to encourage me. I know Tank is on my side."

"But did he defend you, Mom? Did he stand up for you and call them to be the liars they are? No. He let you sit there and be accused of something you didn't do. Do they know how hard we've struggled over the years while you were taking care of them? Do you know how many times you missed my activities to take care of their families? Do they know, Mom? Did they appreciate what you did? No. That's how people are. They use you up, and when they don't need you anymore, they toss you aside."

"Where is all this anger coming from? I'm mad, but not that mad. You need to calm down and watch what you say."

"No, Mom. I'm tired of the way those people have treated you. They expect you to be everything for everybody and to be everyplace at the same time. You're not God. They're supposed to be so holy, yet they depend on you more than on God. And what do you do? You run yourself ragged until you collapse. And how do they show their appreciation? By trying to destroy you even more."

"That's not true. I enjoy what I do. I'm committed to what I do. I love the ministry. You know that sometimes we have to go through things. This is what I have to go through."

"Mom, you don't have to preach to me. I've heard you crying at night. I hear you pray. I know when you're hurting. Sometimes it seems as if I'm the only one who cares about you. It's a good thing I'm in Atlanta; I would tell those people some things."

"Please calm down. This isn't helping anything."

"You don't have to be strong for me. When I saw you today, you looked as if you hadn't slept in a while. You looked bad. Is this why you're not marrying Max? If it is, then you need to call him and tell him you've changed your mind. Don't let the people in your church keep you from being happy. Max makes you happy. I saw the two of you together. You had a glow about you. I can't remember ever seeing you like that before."

"I can't be with him now. It's not the right time."

"You can't? Is it because of the church or what Dad did to you?" Camille's question surprised Shante. She had tried to keep what happened with Kevin a secret from her. She had never told Camille about the incidents that had led her to leaving Kevin. Now, she wondered if Camille had known all along. "I know you don't want to admit it, Mom, but I'm an adult now. We can talk about things. I know how you got those scars on your face. I know Dad did that to you; I've known for a while."

"How did you find out?"

"Aunt Gwen. She thought I already knew, but I didn't until she told me. I wanted to ask you about them, but you never wanted to talk about him. Is it still hurting you? Does it still hurt to remember what happened? Are you afraid you'll get hurt like that again?"

"Max is not like your dad."

"That is my point exactly. He is not like Dad. They're completely different, but when you look at him, do you see all the hurt of a past relationship and fear getting into another? Is it that fear that is keeping you from loving Max? Are you still running and hiding like the day you left Dad?"

"So you're a psych major now?"

"I'm serious, Mom. Have you stopped running? That was a long time ago. You need to stop running. You can't be afraid anymore. Dad beat you into submission, and out of fear you ran and hid from him. You know people can sense fear. That's why you are being attacked at the church. The enemy sensed fear. And what did you do? What you always do; you ran and hid."

Shante sat on the bed quietly listening to Camille. She was right, and God was using Camille to minister to her.

"Is that why you're still running? Do you fear being hurt again?" Camille's voice rose.

"Maybe that is part of it. You don't know how it feels to look into a mirror every day of your life and see the scars of a bad decision. It was a bad decision to marry your dad. Now, I have to look at this reminder every day. Even when I try to cover it up, I'm still reminded of it. It hurts sometimes, but I keep moving. It keeps me from thinking about it."

"Mom, you've got to stop running. Come here." Camille took her hand and walked her over to the mirror. "Look at yourself. You don't have on any makeup. You're beautiful. This is who you are. You are a testament to the ability of the human spirit to triumph over adversity. You had a situation, but it doesn't have you. You overcame. When are you going to realize that? You are beautiful and intelligent, and I know you try to live right. When Max looks at you, he sees what I see; even more so because he's looking at you differently."

The tears began to fall down her face. Shante felt as if a weight had been lifted. Camille was right, and she wanted to change. But she didn't know how.

"Didn't you and Max go to college together? He was attracted to you then. Look at yourself. When Max sees you, he looks beyond the scars and the hurt, and he sees you—the real you, the beautiful you—just as God does. He looks beyond what you see as faults and sees the real you. The Bible says when God made us, he looked at us and said we were very good in his sight. Look at yourself, Mom. God made you, and you are very good. I'm going to tell you the most used phrase in the Bible: fear not. Fear not what people are going to do or say to you. You are redeemed from the hands of the enemy. Those people in that church can only do one thing for you, and that's move you to where God wants you to be. Look at Joseph. People did things to him to hurt him. They didn't know that God was using them to move him to where he needed to be, to fulfill something God had spoken in his life a long time ago. You should give Max another chance. He loves you unconditionally. But I can't tell you what to do. I'm just a child."

"No, you're not." Shante said, turning to face her daughter. "You're an adult—my daughter. You're full of more wisdom than I have given you credit for. You're right. Everything you said is right. Thank you for telling me. I love you."

"I love you, too, Mom." Camille hugged Shante and wiped the tears from her eyes.

"I'm glad I came to Atlanta. I needed this. Look at me. I look a mess. Let me freshen up, and then I think I'll go to bed."

"Okay, Mom, but you look great. Keep telling yourself that."

Shante studied her face in the bathroom mirror. She remembered how she got every scar. She tried to imagine herself without them. She could only see the scars, but she knew Camille was right. She was going to have to begin seeing herself as God saw her. Why had she allowed Kevin to continue to have control over her? And he knew he still had control over her mind and actions. She vowed to end his control over her. She made up her mind to do an inventory of herself when she got back to Charlotte and try to work on every area of her life. It was time she lived what she preached. She began to pray. Afterward, she went back to the bedroom; Camille was already asleep. She looked at her daughter. She was no longer her little girl, but a woman of great wisdom—and she was a gift from God.

⤞⤝

"Good morning, sleepy head. You really slept late this morning. It's after ten. You want some coffee?" Patrice said as Shante dragged herself into the kitchen.

"I'm sorry I slept so late. This was the first night in a long time I've slept through the night. I guess I was tired. Has Camille left yet?"

"Yeah, she left over an hour ago. She said she had to get to class. She didn't want to wake you. She said you looked so peaceful."

Shante sat down at the table. Patrice handed her a cup of coffee and sat down across from her. "Thank you for letting me stay with you. I think I'm going to go back to Charlotte this afternoon. Are you going to work today?"

"No." Patrice sighed. "I thought you would stay longer. I took a couple of sick days this week. I thought we could spend some time together. It's been so long since we hung out. Do you really have to leave today?"

"I want to leave. I want to get back to work. It's time I face up to my problems and stop running. Camille and I had a long talk last night. Did you know she knew about Kevin and me?"

"Yeah, we talked about it."

"How did everyone know but me? Anyway, I think my congregation should know what's going on from me. People can distort the truth so much, and I need to face my enemies and show them I'm not scared—that means Kevin, too." Shante took a sip of her coffee.

"If you have to go back, then I won't stop you. I wish you would stay."

"Patrice, is something wrong?"

"Well, we really haven't had time to talk since you've been here. Each time I wanted to come to your room and talk, I would hear you praying. I waited a couple of times, but, girl, you pray too long."

"I'm listening now."

"But you're ready to go home."

"I can wait. What's going on?"

Patrice didn't answer. She got up and went to the counter and poured another cup of coffee. "You want some more coffee? You haven't eaten. Can I get you something to eat?"

"Some more coffee would be fine." Something was going on with Patrice. She was not her usual loud, joking, trash-talking self, and she hadn't been since she arrived. She decided she would stay another day; Patrice needed her. "Is this about Shawn? Are the two of you having trouble?"

"How could he do this to us? How could he do something like that without discussing it with me?"

"What did he do?"

"He got saved. When he told me, I almost fainted. I couldn't believe he would do something like that. First it was Gwen, then you, and now my own husband. Why couldn't things stay as they were? We were so happy."

"Has it been that bad since he got saved?"

"No, it really hasn't been bad at all. I just don't know what to say to him. I loved him the way he was. He didn't have to change. Now everything is going to change. I'm afraid I'm going to lose him, lose my family."

"Why do you think Shawn getting saved will lead to your losing him?"

"We were so close. We could talk about anything. We had fun. We went out. We traveled. Our lovemaking was always so passionate and adventurous. You know, there were times when I went to his office in nothing but a coat and some shoes, and there were times when he would pay me a visit at work. We were happy. I could look at him and tell what he was thinking. He could look at me the same way. When the kids were young, we made sure there was at least one special day during the week we spent alone together. When he was trying to start his practice, we worked together to build it up. We were so good together. Now all that is over."

"Why is it over?"

"He's going to turn into one of those church folk you and Gwen are always telling me about—self-righteous and judgmental. They do horrible things to good people. Look at what they're doing to you. I don't want that to happen to Shawn, my children, or me. You know I would definitely hurt somebody. I won't let anyone destroy my family."

"What makes you think he's going to be like them? Has he done anything to make you think he's self-right-eous and judgmental?"

"No, but I'm afraid he's going to change the more he goes to church. I don't want to lose my husband. I love him. Sometimes I think he's looking at everything I do. I feel so uncomfortable having a glass of wine in the evening. After a long day, we used to snuggle, have a glass of wine, and talk. We haven't done that since he got saved. I don't know who he is anymore. We used to go out dancing. I'm afraid to ask him to go anywhere. Look at us. Look around you. We have a great life. We're successful and living in a prominent neighborhood. We have two beautiful, smart children who have their own successes. Travis has college recruiters running after him to play football for their school. Tiffany finally got that crazy idea of going to Europe out of her head, and she has settled into life at Hampton. We have money. We have everything." Patrice began to cry as Shante leaned over and stroked her shoulder.

"I know change can be hard. Let me ask you something. What has changed with our relationship? What has changed with your relationship with Gwen?"

"We don't go to strip clubs anymore." Patrice laughed nervously.

"Do you want to go to strip clubs?"

"No, I'm too old for that foolishness now."

"Has anything else changed?"

"Not really. We still have fun. We joke around as we used to. We don't get to see each other often. When we do, we pick up where we left off. The only thing that has really changed is that we're older and have adult children now."

"Then why does it have to change with Shawn?"

"I don't want him to turn into one of those church people."

"Patrice, I'm sorry I've given you the impression that church folk are bad people. If I had known it was having an effect on you, I wouldn't have talked to you about the trouble I've had in my church. I apologize. I didn't mean to give you a bad impression. The truth is, there are many good people—Christians—in the church. They're people of integrity. They're fun to be around. They make my work so much easier. They're faithful and honest. They know how to love unconditionally. They would give their lives for their friends and family. There are so many good people in the church. They are the ones who don't get attention. It's the loud ones, the troublemakers, who get all the attention. They are few in numbers. Is this why you haven't made a commitment to Christ? Because of what Gwen and I said?"

"I don't want to be like those people."

"You don't have to be. Being in a relationship with Christ is a personal thing. You have to know him for yourself. You have to believe that God loves you unconditionally. God accepts you for who you are. He wants to be a part of your life."

"How can God accept me? I love my life. I don't feel anything needs to change."

"But you feel something is missing, don't you?"

"I have felt it for a long time. I didn't know what was going on. When Shawn said he had gotten saved, something inside me wanted to be with him. It was as if he had the courage to do what I should have been doing. I don't know if God can forgive me for some of the things I have done—all of the guys I slept with before I met Shawn."

"How long have you known me?" Shante asked. "Haven't I been with a few guys myself and done some things, too? Remember that time at Freak-Nik when we entered that wet t-shirt contest?"

Patrice started to laugh. "Yeah, and Gwen won because her breasts were bigger than everybody else's."

"God forgave me for that. And what about that time I entered that amateur striptease contest at that club?"

Patrice laughed even harder. "You were so awful. Gwen and I were the only ones who screamed for you. We had some fun back then. We were so wild when the three of us got together."

"I can go on and on, but the point is God forgave me and he can forgive you, too."

"Yeah, but you were always different."

"Different how? I was a sinner, and one day I asked God to forgive me and he did. Yes, my life changed, but it changed for the better. Yours will, too. All you have to do is confess your sin, ask for forgiveness, and declare him Lord over your life."

"Is it that easy?"

"Yes, it is that easy. You don't need a preacher, a choir, and people praying over you. All you need to say is, 'God, I am a sinner.' "

"God, I am a sinner," Patrice repeated.

"Forgive me of my sins."

"Forgive me of my sins."

"I declare you Lord over my life."

Patrice repeated the words, tears spilling down her cheeks.

"Come into my life and cleanse me of unrighteousness."

"Come into my life and cleanse me of unrighteousness," she said softly.

"It's that easy. Now you're saved. Your life will change forever. Your marriage will be better."

Patrice continued crying. Shante went over to her and hugged her. She allowed Patrice to cry for several minutes. After Patrice calmed down, Shante returned to her seat.

"Now what?"

"Now you love your husband. Now you love your children."

"What should I do?"

"You go on living. Instead of going to clubs or casinos, you'll find a number of things to do together as a family and a couple. These things will only build you and your family up. Find a good church to go to together. I know someone here in Atlanta I can recommend, but you don't have to go where I send you. Your husband has a church now. Go with him. Spend some time with him studying your Bible. You'll find it will relax you and strengthen your marriage."

"You think so?"

"I know so. In my opinion, Christian men are so romantic, sexy, and passionate."

"Like Max?" Patrice asked.

"Yes, like Max," Shante said shyly. "Have you talked to Shawn since he got saved?"

"Not really. I didn't know what to say."

"Then it's time to talk to him. I'll tell you what. We can get ready and go to the spa. We both could use it.

We'll get the whole treatment—facial, nails, massage, sauna, the works—my treat. Then you can pay your husband a visit on the job. I'm sure he hasn't seen you in those shoes and a coat in a long time. He'll welcome the visit, and it'll open the door for you to talk. After the spa, I'll go home. You two don't need me around while you get reacquainted. Besides, it's time for me to go back to Charlotte and face my own issues."

"I'm so glad you came here, Shante. I love you."

"I love you, too. If you need anything, let me know, okay?"

"Okay."

"All right then, let's go. Before we get to the spa, can we stop and get something to eat? I'm starving."

"I see you're getting back to your old self. I'm glad. Come on, let's go."

CHAPTER 24

Shante drove into the parking lot of her church and prayed for strength to go inside. She didn't know what to expect; didn't know how people would respond to her when she walked into the building. Feeling stronger after her prayer, she squared her shoulders and went inside.

"Pastor, you're back!" Gail exclaimed, jumping from her desk and hugging Shante. "They told me you probably wouldn't be back this week. I didn't hear from you, and you didn't answer my calls. I heard what happened. I'm so sorry. I didn't know things were going to turn out this way. I'm so sorry." She began to cry.

"Why are you crying? No one saw this coming. Everything is going to work out, you'll see. Now dry your tears."

"But, Pastor, you don't understand. I really didn't want anything to happen to you, and I've been praying for you so much."

"Thank you, Gail. I appreciate your praying for me. I've got a lot of work to catch up on. Do I have any messages?"

Gail handed Shante the stack of pink message slips on her desk. "Here are the ones that came in this morning. Deacon Curry came by and picked up your other messages."

"Why did he do that?"

"He said he was in charge of the administration now. He asked for all the messages you had received. He said he needed them for his report."

"Did I have any personal calls?"

"I don't think so. But the copies of all messages are here in my book. You can take it with you into your office to check your calls."

"Thank you. How is the Thanksgiving food drive going? Do you have an updated report from Sister Moss?"

"Not yet, but it looks like it is going well. The storage room down the hall is filling up, and soon we're going to have to store donations in the conference room."

"I'll go in there after lunch and start sorting the items. Are we getting grocery cards?"

"Yeah, here they are. So far we have more than a thousand dollars in twenty-dollar gift cards. We'll be able to help a lot of families this year."

"Praise God. Looks like our drive will be successful this year. If you need me for anything, I'll be in my office."

Shante went into her office and closed the door. It felt good to be there, but it looked as if someone had moved things around. She buzzed Gail on the intercom. "Gail, has anyone been in my office?"

"Deacon Curry and Sister Turner. They had the door closed; I don't know what they did."

Shante became angry when she heard that. Now some of her personal items were missing. Her first impulse was to call them and tell them off. Instead, she prayed to God for direction. Looking around, she saw that a statue of a mother and child the Women's Auxiliary had given her was missing from the bookcase. Some of her books were also missing. She called Gail into the office and began doing an inventory of all the missing items, including personal ones. She asked Gail to draft a letter to the board listing everything missing. Gail went to her desk and began drafting the letter. It occurred to Shante that she should contact Gary before sending the letter out.

"Gary, this is Shante. Can you talk now?"

"Hey, Tay. Sure, what's up?"

"I'm back at work."

"You're back at work? Max said you were in Atlanta."

"I was. Now I'm back at work. I have a problem here."

"Another problem?"

"Yeah, someone has gone through my office and several items have been removed. Some of them are personal, including a statue that was given to me and some books signed by the authors."

"Did you make a list of the missing items?"

"Yes. Gail is typing it up now, and she is also drafting a letter to the board."

"No, don't do that. I'll take care of that. Are you planning to stay there all day?"

"Yes. I was going to return some phone calls and then sort through the donations for the Thanksgiving food drive."

"Have Gail help you with that. We have to make sure you're covered in case some of the stuff comes up missing. E-mail me the list of items missing from your office. I'll have Angela draft a letter to the board. Also, make sure you make a detailed list of the donations."

"I'll be sure to do that. Thanks, Gary."

"All right. I'll talk to you later."

Shante asked Gail for the list of missing items and told her to delete the draft letter to the board. She then began reviewing her phone messages. She returned a call from Pastor Kay and was invited to lunch at the pastor's office. Because she was casually dressed, she at first declined. But Pastor Kay persuaded her to come, anyway. Although she wasn't too keen on socializing for now, she did feel getting back into her regular routine would help keep her focused.

Shante returned a few other calls and then returned to thinking about the missing items. People were accusing *her* of stealing, and then she herself falls victim to theft. She remembered Tank telling her it would be okay to leave things in her office. Apparently, it wasn't, and whoever the thief was had a key to the building and access to the security codes. But she gave Deacon Curry and Sister Turner the benefit of the doubt. She would not stoop to their level and accuse them of anything. She would wait until Gary completed his investigation. She hoped that would be soon; she didn't know how much more she could take.

"Well, hello, Pastor Dogan," Pastor Kay greeted Shante with a smile. "Come on in and have a seat."

Shante looked around the spacious, beautifully decorated room. She thought Pastor Kay was a classy woman, as shown by her office decor. Everything in the office said *woman*. Flowers were everywhere. A large bay window had decorative pillows around its base. African-American paintings were neatly placed on the walls. A small formal dining area next to a sitting area had been set up for a meal.

Pastor Kay came from behind her desk and hugged Shante and then led her to a large sofa in the sitting area. "I hope you don't mind, but I took the liberty of ordering us lunch. You said you liked the Reuben sandwiches from Tasties Sandwich Shoppe, so I ordered you one with a salad and sweet tea. Is that fine?"

"Yes, that's fine."

"Can we talk while we wait for lunch to arrive?"

Although Shante knew Pastor Kay only casually, she felt they had a connection, being females in the ministry. Pastor Kay was relaxed and friendly, and spoke to her as though they were old friends.

"Of course. What do I need to know about the conference?"

"No, I don't want to talk about the conference. I want to talk about you."

"Me? What about me?"

"I heard they sat you down at your church. Is that true?"

"I guess everybody knows by now. News travels fast in the church world," Shante said quietly, embarrassed to have to acknowledge that she had been suspended. "You don't want me to preach at your conference, do you? Well, thank you for telling me in person. Most people just called and left a message."

"Don't jump to conclusions. I want you to preach now more that ever."

"You do?" Shante asked, smiling. She never imagined she would be allowed to preach at any church while on suspension.

"Yes, I do. I know God is doing something in your life and your ministry. I know the anointing is really on you now to bring forth the Word. I want you to preach two sessions—if that's okay with you."

"Really? Well, sure, I'll be happy to do that."

Shante couldn't help smiling, thrilled that Pastor Kay supported her ministry. She could hardly believe God was blessing her this way. She had begun to think everyone in Charlotte was against her. And here someone was asking her to preach at her church.

"How are you getting along? I know something like this can be hard on you. I know how I felt when I was sat down."

"You were sat down?"

"Yes, I went through what you're going through now, only I was an associate minister. Everything happened so fast. Some old preacher, a friend of my pastor, tried to hit on me. I rejected his passes, and the next thing I knew I was in a board meeting. People were sitting there calling me a lesbian and presenting all kinds of false evidence against me."

"That's awful." Pastor Kay's openness surprised Shante. She hadn't expected to hear her talking about this, having thought their lunch conversation would be about the conference. She was intrigued and wanted to know more about the pastor's situation and how she had handled it.

"It certainly is. We're supposed to lead holy lives, but when you try, it's used against you. I was sitting there wondering why I had to be a lesbian just because I was trying to live holy. It didn't make any sense. To make matters worse, they spread that word more than they did the gospel. To this day, there are people who still believe that lie. There is nothing I can do about it," Pastor Kay said resignedly.

"What a shame. How did you handle it?"

"It wasn't easy. I prayed a lot. I felt so alone. I didn't have anyone to talk to. I promised myself that I would not stand by and allow anyone else to go through something like that. Not on my watch. But you know the worst part about it all?"

"What's that?"

"It almost kept me from being in a true relationship. I started watching everything I did. I tried to make sure I was super feminine. I wouldn't wear those clergy collars, because I felt they made me look masculine. This got me in trouble with the church, as they required their ministers, male and female, to wear them. I would avoid any man who tried to begin a relationship with me. One guy who heard the rumor asked me to do a threesome with him and another woman. God, some of these men are shameless. Let's pray for them. Anyway, I avoided relationships at all costs. I tried to walk in the most holy way I could."

"Didn't you finally get married?"

"Yes, and I'm so blessed. When I met Don, there was something about him that I was drawn to. He had the most beautiful eyes, and he smelled so good. He had this wonderful laugh. The best part was that he was saved. He was so anointed, and when the spirit hit him, my God, he was so sexy."

"I know what you mean," Shante said, thinking about Max. Pastor Kay was talking about herself, but it was as though she was peering into Shante's life and seeing the essence of her soul.

"He knew I wouldn't go out with him, since I was being so cautious, so he would conveniently show up at various functions—like singles night at the church. I almost threw him away out of fear of what people thought. Then one night—skate night—we began talking, and the rest is history. I didn't care what people thought. It was the best decision I made during that time. Yes, people talked. Yes, they made up stories, but something inside me told me this man was part of my destiny."

"You could be talking about me and Max, but I really don't have the time to be in a relationship with anyone now."

"I heard about you and Reverend Patrick. So it's true? He's a good catch. I can see why the two of you are attracted to each other." She smiled. "*I don't have the time.*" She shook her head and laughed. "I've used that excuse numerous times. I even used it with Don. Luckily, he didn't listen to me—or I didn't listen to myself. You know, we make the time for what we want to make time for, even relationships."

"You're right."

"How are you and Reverend Patrick doing with all this going on?"

"I have no contact with him."

"That's too bad. Was it because of all the talk?"

"That was part of it."

"What was the other part? You were too busy?"

"Sort of."

"Shante I'm sorry, may I call you Shante?"

"Sure."

"Shante, you can't allow talk to keep you from love. I saw your reaction when I said Reverend Patrick's name. You love him. I can tell even though I haven't seen you two together. Just the mention of his name makes you light up. May I ask you what the problem is? Am I being too personal? If so, tell me and I'll end this conversation."

"It is personal, but my spirit is telling me to talk to you, to trust you." Shante felt she needed to trust Pastor Kay. She had to talk with someone about her problems and share everything she was feeling. Although she was trying to act confident, she was anything but. She couldn't continue holding things in and using nervous energy to cook and clean around her house, the church, and almost everywhere she went. She had to find another way of solving her problems.

"You can trust me. I've gone through what you are going through now. It's hard. I know it is. Don't shut everybody off. Find someone you can talk to. It doesn't have to be me. It can be someone you can trust. Don't hold it all in. Be honest with yourself and whomever you talk to. If you love him, don't deny it. Support that feeling."

"You don't understand. There's a lot involved."

"Like what?"

"Well, Max is a single parent with three boys."

"Aren't you a single parent?"

"My daughter is an adult and living in another city on her own. He has three little boys, ages five, eight, and twelve."

"What does that have to do with anything?"

"You don't know the release of having a grown child. It's like, now for the first time I can do what I really want, eat what I want, go where I want without having to account for my time, money, or love. I'm not responsible for anyone but myself. Yes, my daughter is in college and yes, she still depends on me, but it is not like when she was at home. It's so different now."

"You're afraid of giving up your independence?"

"I like being alone right now. It's been a long time since I've been alone—not lonely, just alone. I can sit at home in peace and quiet. I can watch TV, listen to music, or enjoy the quiet. I can pray so much better. I can study without interruption. It's wonderful."

"Do you think things will change if you and Reverend Patrick got together?"

"Sure they will. He has three young boys. There will be lots of activity around the house. It will be Camille times four. Each one, including Max, will be demanding my attention. There will be sports, and I don't like sports. There will be other school events like plays, recitals, parties. And I won't even mention all the youth activities in the church."

"Are you doing them now?"

"Not as much. I did spend a lot of time with them. Now I have to sneak and see them. Max doesn't know someone has been bringing them to see me. We still have activities together, but not as much. Maybe I should stop. Max doesn't want me involved in their lives now. I don't want to lose my boys. I love them so much."

"Your boys?"

"You know, Max's sons. I love them. I've known them all from the day they were born. I'm their godmother. I don't want to lose them; I don't think I could handle that."

"Are you using the boys?"

"Using them? How?" She adjusted her position on the sofa. An uneasy feeling came over her. She had never thought she was using the boys to stay close to Max. She loved the boys, and she wanted to be with them.

"To stay close to Reverend Patrick."

"I don't see Max and I rarely talk to him. I'm not using them; I wouldn't do that. He used them. I wouldn't do that."

"How did he use them?"

"He used them to try to get me to marry him. I felt so pressured when he asked with the boys nearby. They wanted me to move in right away. It was a terrible scene," Shante sighed.

"Can you tell me that you don't love him?"

"No, I think I do. I think about him all the time. Sometimes when I'm trying to fall asleep, I can smell him, and he's not even with me. The thought of his scent relaxes me, and I can fall asleep. Does that sound strange?"

"No, it doesn't. I've felt that way about Don myself. It was one way I knew I was in love with him."

A knock at the door was followed by her secretary coming in with food, which she placed on the table and left. Pastor Kay then continued her probing. "I hear everything you're saying. Are you happy? I've been where you are now. One day I had to decide if I wanted to be alone or if I wanted to be happy. You have to make the same decision. Do you want to be alone or to be happy?"

The last question was left hanging as they got up and went to the table. As Pastor Kay blessed the food, Shante mulled over her question. She wondered if she wanted the stress of a relationship. She couldn't start one now, not with an ongoing investigation into church finances. She might not even have a job or her freedom after the meeting to determine what the church should do about the missing money and her employment. What good would she do Max in prison? *What am I thinking? I haven't done anything wrong.*

"Excuse me?"

"I'm sorry. I was thinking out loud."

"That may be your problem. You could be thinking too much. Sometimes it's best to go with what you're feeling. I did with Don, and it has truly been a blessing. Listen to your heart. Pray about it. Stay in prayer. Ask God for guidance, and he'll direct you."

"I will, I have. I really can't focus on Max right now. I guess my biggest fear is that I'll lose my church and my ministry will fall apart. I don't want to lose my church. I love what I do. I love the people God has assigned me. My church is my life. What am I going to do?"

"Tell me, what would you do if you weren't preaching?"

"I guess I'd go back to being a consultant."

"Is that what you did before?"

"Yes."

"Did you like it?"

"It was financially rewarding. I liked being my own boss. That's about it. I didn't feel that I was helping anyone."

"Do you want to go back to that kind of work?"

"No, but I will if I have to. I don't want to."

"That takes me back to the question, what if you lose your church? What are you going to do? Will you continue preaching or will you run away?"

"I don't know. I don't want to lose my church."

"I'm going to tell you something—whenever it looks like you're losing, you're really winning. I've been there. Look around you. This is how God gave me victory. You know, my church never let me return to that pulpit, but God elevated me higher to a new pulpit. My ministry's growing. I have a wonderful marriage and family. I'm happy because I chose to be happy. I chose to live beyond what others thought of me. I chose to love in spite of what they were doing to me. You have a choice to make. You can allow them to make you crawl in a hole, or you can stand up, live, and be happy. You choose, Shante."

"Thank you for talking with me today. I needed this. I needed this real bad. Would it be okay if I called you to talk?"

"I'll give you my home and cell number. You can call me anytime."

"Thank you. You have been a blessing today."

"That's what I'm here for."

CHAPTER 25

On Thanksgiving, Bishop and Mother's house was full—children playing, men yelling as they watched a football game on TV, and women amiably chit-chatting. Mother was in the kitchen busy putting the finishing touches on the Thanksgiving meal.

"Hello, everybody," Shante said, practically having to yell to be heard over the noise. She was carrying several pies and cakes she had baked for the occasion. Camille, Gwen and Ron, and Patrice and Shawn, each carrying at least one box of food, followed her. This was Shante's year to host the annual after-Thanksgiving shopping spree they had started several years ago. Last year, they were in Atlanta. The year before that, Gwen had treated them to a shopping trip to New York. This year, she wanted to stay close to home; she needed the support of her friends. Besides, she had to preach at Pastor Kay's family conference, and she wanted her friends there to support her.

She worked her way through the crowded living room, hardly noticed by the men watching the game. She went through the arched doorways into the dining room. Several ladies jumped up and took an item from her, either taking it into the kitchen or placing it in the dining room.

"I think we have everything," Gwen said. "How many cakes did you make? Looks like you cooked all night."

"I knew a lot of people would be here today. I wanted to make sure I had enough for everyone." Shante looked around and was excited to see Bishop and Mother's granddaughter, Marie, who was in the Army reserves. She ran and hugged her. "Marie, it's so good to see you. I'm glad you were able to come. You look good. How are you? When are you returning to Iraq?"

"I've been over there twice. I hope I'm not called up again. I'm ready to retire from the reserves. This has gotten old."

"Hopefully, the war will end soon. Where are Bishop and Mother?"

"Pop is in the backyard with some of the guys looking at that old truck, and Nana is in the kitchen. She ran us out."

"Let me go in there and speak to her." She went into the kitchen and saw Mother busy at the stove. She couldn't believe it was only a few months ago Mother was dealing with breast cancer and chemotherapy. She seemed to have recuperated well from the disease and its treatment. There had been no sign of the disease spreading or returning, and Mother had been trying to live a normal life. She had gone on with life, acting as if nothing had happened to her. Shante thought how very few things bothered Mother. She wished she were that strong.

Although Shante had tried to carry on every day as normally as possible, not a day passed without her thinking about the investigation and the effect it was having on her church and members. When people talked to her, they only wanted to talk about the church's problems—everyone, that is, except her friends and Pastor Kay. For the past few weeks, she had been in counseling with Pastor Kay. It was good to finally talk to someone about the abuse and continuing harassment at the hands of Kevin. She was beginning to gain insight into why she acted the way she had. She now realized she needed to heal from the pains of her past.

She stood in the doorway of the kitchen watching Mother work, the smell of food producing in her a sense of well-being. She loved coming to Bishop and Mother's for the holidays. With both of her parents gone and without siblings, this was the closest thing she had to being with family. She looked forward to the holidays—the people, the camaraderie, the food. "Hello, Mother."

"Hey, baby," Mother said, looking up from the stove. "How did everything go at the church this morning?"

"We fed more than three hundred people at the church and delivered more than a hundred meals to shut-ins today. That's in addition to the four hundred families we were able to assist with food boxes and gift cards this year. We finished faster than last year. It was such a blessing. At one point, I thought we were going to have to do a loaves and fishes prayer. People kept calling the church for help. We kept on fixing plates, and everything worked out."

"That's good. I know you're tired. Sit down."

Shante sat down at the table. It was covered with bowls and pots filled with food. "Everybody said you ran them out of the kitchen."

"That's because none of them can cook. While you're sitting there, put the rolls on the pan for me and we can get that in the oven."

Shante lifted the foil from a large pan in the middle of the table. It contained a perfectly roasted turkey, and she couldn't resist the urge to taste it. She was about to pinch off a piece when Mother said, without looking up, "I wouldn't do that if I were you. Finish the rolls. That's all I need you to do."

"Agnes, when are we going to eat?" Bishop asked, walking through the door, several men on his heels.

"You'll eat when I get finished."

"Mother, you need help with anything else?" Shante asked, greeting Bishop with a hug.

"Shante, how are you? How did everything go at church this morning?"

"Everything went well. We were able to help over four hundred people this year."

"That's good. I'm going to watch the game." Bishop left them alone. Shante finished arranging the rolls on the pan and put them in the oven. She sat back down at the table and offered to help, but Mother told her to go ask the other women to set the table because dinner was almost ready. She was walking towards the dining room when she thought she heard Joshua.

"Mama Tay!" It was Joshua coming through the kitchen door. She bent down and hugged him.

"Josh, what are you doing here?"

"I'm having Thanksgiving. I made you this at school." Josh handed her a paper turkey made from a tracing of his hand. She suddenly realized she had been set up. She was sure Mother and Bishop had planned this, and had invited Max to dinner. They hadn't mentioned it to her. If they had, she would have cooked dinner at her house, and they knew it. She had successfully avoided Max for the last several weeks. There was no way she could avoid him today.

"It's beautiful. Thank you. Where are your brothers?"

"Mama Tay."

"Jacob, Jonathan. Come here. It's so good to see you," Shante said, pulling both of them into a big hug. She was so happy to see them that she couldn't wipe the smile off her face.

"Hello, Shante." She turned and saw Max dressed in jeans and a sweater. She was happy to see him and fought the urge to embrace him.

"Max, I didn't know you were going to be here today."

"Bishop and Mother invited us. Hello, Mother. It smells good in here." Max walked over and kissed her on the cheek.

"Mother, the rolls are in the oven. I'll check on them in a few minutes," Shante said, leaving the kitchen. The boys raced outside to play with the other children. She went into the dining room and joined the other women at the table.

"Did you see Max? He looks good," Gwen whispered to Shante.

"Did you know he was going to be here?"

"Mother asked me not to tell you. Doesn't he look good in those jeans?"

"I'm going outside with the children," Shante said.

"Don't do that. Sit down; talk to us," Patrice said, motioning Shante to come sit beside her. "Max does look good. He always has. You should find some time to talk to him today. It'll get rid of some of that tension you just brought in here."

"I'm not tense. I'm fine with him being here. It doesn't bother me. I'm glad he's here; I can see the boys." Shante tried her best to act as if it wasn't bothering her, but it was. She tried not to look into the kitchen at Max, who was talking with Mother. But the sight of him was distracting. She heard Gwen and Patrice laughing. She glared at them. "What's so funny?"

"You," Patrice said. "You know you want to talk to him."

Shante looked at Gwen and then Patrice. "You knew he was going to be here, too."

"I had to tell somebody," Gwen said.

"Lighten up, Shante. She only told me and Ron, and I told Shawn and he told the mailman." Gwen and Patrice laughed louder.

"Y'all are real funny."

"Ladies, come and help me get this food on the table," Mother said, entering the room with a dish filled with green beans.

Everyone went into the kitchen and picked up a serving dish and placed it on the dining room table. Shante went to get the rolls out of the oven. Max was still there, leaning against a cabinet. Shante acted as if she didn't see him looking at her. She quickly took the rolls out of the oven and set the pan on the butcher's block lying on the table. She picked up a bowl of candied sweet potatoes and headed for the table.

"No, put that back. Go cut those cakes over there on the counter," Mother said, pointing in Max's direction.

"Mother, I can help with this. I'll cut the cakes later."

"No, you can cut them now. Marie can take those sweet potatoes."

"Where's your cake knife?"

"You know where it is."

Shante looked around the room as if she didn't know where the knife was kept. But she knew it was in the drawer directly behind Max, and she would have to talk to him to get the knife. She sighed and moved across the room. "Excuse me, Max, I have to get the cake knife and cut the cakes."

"Oh, I'm sorry. Let me get out of your way." Max moved to the other side of the cabinet. "How have you been?"

"Uh, busy."

"I heard you guys helped a lot of people this year."

"Yeah, we helped a few." Trying not to look at Max, she pulled open the drawer to get the knife.

"I called you yesterday to see if you would like to go to a movie after dinner today."

"I got your message. I was at the church," she said, trying to concentrate on cutting a pound cake.

"Well?"

"Well what?"

"Would you like to go?"

"Max, I don't think that would be a good idea."

"I'll go if she doesn't," Marie interjected. Mother yelled for Marie to come to the dining room. Shante listened closely, but heard no talking coming from the dining room. She knew they were listening to their conversation.

"Max, let's talk about this after dinner."

"After dinner . . . we'll talk?"

"I promise," she said. Their eyes met and Max smiled and left the kitchen, joining the men in the living room.

After all the food was on the table, Mother announced dinner was ready. The children were called in from various areas in the house and yard, and then everyone came around the table and joined hands. Bishop prayed what seemed like an endless prayer. When he finally finished, everyone claimed a seat at one of the tables in the room. The mothers made sure all the children were fed, and then they made sure their husband's plates were overflowing with food. Gwen sat next to Shante. She saw Max holding his plate and looking for a place to sit.

"Max, you can have this seat. I'm going to sit with the kids. They're already throwing food." Gwen picked up her plate and headed for the children's table.

Shante shook her head. They were all being entirely too obvious, trying too hard to get her and Max together. He squeezed past some of the guests and took Gwen's vacated seat. She thought he looked so sexy. Her body tingled when his arm slightly brushed hers. She heard him laugh and almost turned to look at him so she could see his beautiful smile. She tried hard not to pay him any attention. This was the closet she had been to him in a long time. She hadn't realized how much she had missed him.

"Shante," Bishop said, ending her reverie, "what time is the church meeting next Saturday."

"Ten."

"Make sure you remind me. I want to be there bright and early."

"I will, Bishop."

She tried to pretend she was deeply involved in the conversation at the table. But every chance she got, she sneaked a look at Max. She was surprisingly relaxed with him being beside her; however, she wasn't looking forward to their conversation later. This was probably the last time she would be seeing him.

After dinner, the house became quiet except for the sound of the ladies cleaning up. Everyone was full and relaxed. Shante went to the kitchen to help clean up. Max followed her.

"Tay, can we talk now?"

"Max, I'm trying to help clean up. This is too much for Mother to do by herself."

"Go ahead, Mom. We can handle this," Camille said, taking a pot from her.

Looking at Camille's smiling face, she itched to say something to her, but there were too many people around. She and Max went out to the back porch. After they closed the door, the kitchen got quiet. Max walked down the steps and faced her as she leaned on the porch railing.

"Are they looking out of the window?" she asked, feeling the people staring at them.

"Yeah."

"Let's walk around the house."

They headed to the front driveway. The air was crisp, and autumn leaves were drifting to the ground. Trying to keep warm, she folded her arms and leaned against one of the cars.

"Would you like to go to the movies? There are a lot of good movies out now. I'll let you pick. Gwen and Ron said they'll take the boys until we come back."

"Max, I don't think that's a good idea."

"We don't have to go to the movies. Do you want to do something else? Some of the stores are open. Maybe you can help me pick out some Christmas gifts for the boys."

"Max, we really shouldn't see each other right now. I don't think it's a good idea. I can't handle it, not with all that's going on."

"I know you've got a lot on your plate. I've been praying for you."

"Thanks. I need all the prayer I can get. I don't even know if I'll have a job after next week. The board has called a full church meeting, and charges will be formally presented. The membership will then vote to keep me or fire me. They may even have me arrested. I don't understand why they would do such thing. I have done nothing wrong. And I can't believe they are doing this right before Christmas. I simply cannot fathom why I've become a target. Sometimes the whole thing seems surreal, as though it were happening to someone else."

"That's the way the enemy operates. He wants to discourage you; he wants you to give up. And he comes in all guises and forms."

"They claim they have evidence. Well, if they do, someone had to have manufactured it. I have not taken a penny from them. I haven't used or authorized the use of the credit cards. Tank took those from me. I am under a lot of pressure. I also have to preach twice this weekend."

"Really? Where?"

"Pastor Kay is having a family conference at Shiloh. I don't know why she is having it during the holidays, but I imagine she feels it's a good time because a lot of people will have time off. She is not charging admission, and that is one reason I'm doing it. She's a good person; I enjoy talking with her."

"I'm glad you are staying busy. Would you mind if I came to one of the services?"

"I can't stop you from coming to church. Almost everyone here today is coming," Shante said, trying to pretend she didn't care one way or the other. But she did care, and was glad he wanted to come out and support her.

"Well, I just may drop in," Max said, edging closer to her. She backed away. "Tay, you look beautiful. When I saw you, I wanted so much to hug you, but I knew it would make you uncomfortable."

"Max, don't." She wasn't about to admit she felt the same way when she saw him.

"Listen to me, Tay. I know you need time; I understand that. I won't put any pressure on you. You have enough to cope with right now. I only want to know one thing."

"What's that?"

"Look me in the eye and tell me you don't love me."

"Max, please," she protested nervously.

"Tay, I need to hear it. Tell me you don't love me. Tell me that and I'll walk away."

"Max, remember that day I met you in Greensboro for dinner and Sister Turner saw us dancing at the restaurant?"

"How can I forget?"

"Well, later that night I was up praying. I was really upset about what happened that day. I called Gwen. She didn't really help much, but she did pray that God reveal to me what he was trying to change in me."

"Was the prayer answered?"

"I believe so. After speaking to Gwen, I got involved in an old vampire movie on television. God really spoke to me about living a secret life."

"A secret life? What do you mean?"

"Well, you see, the vampire looked alive but he was really dead. Because of his evil desires, he drew others into a secret relationship that drained the life out of people who were alive. I knew right then I could no longer be in any secret relationships. Pastor Kay helped me realize there is a difference between secret and private. I've learned that secrets are born out of a deep-seated feeling that a particular action is wrong and should be covered up. On the other hand, privacy simply means something that is personal and not necessarily wrong."

"I never wanted our relationship to be a secret."

"I know, Max. It was me. God even revealed to me why I always wanted my relationships to be secret, and it had nothing to do with the church or you."

"What was it?"

"Well, all the things Kevin did to me—the abuse, I mean—put me in a state of secrecy. I didn't want anyone to know what was going on in my house. Therefore, I covered everything up. I kept everything a secret. I didn't tell anyone. With my designer clothes, fancy car and good job, I would leave the house, looking as if my life was perfect. However, I was really dead on the inside. My marriage was dead. My job was dead. My self-esteem was dead. Everything was dead. To everyone on the outside I appeared full of life, but I really wasn't. I was spiritually and emotionally dead."

"You could have talked to me."

"I know, Max, but I really needed direction from God. He revealed to me that people who have been in abusive relationships and have kept them secret grow accustomed to living a secret life. That's the only way they know how to have a relationship with someone. Abused people feel uncomfortable with attention being focused on their relationships, and they don't want their secrets revealed. I believe Kevin was counting on this. It was the only way he could control me. Everyone who is allowed to know the secret becomes lifeless also. They try to help you cover up the secret, and it drains the life out of them."

"Tay, what are you trying to say?"

"I'm saying I can't be in any more secret relationships. I've looked back at all my relationships since Kevin, and they all have been secretive. I used so many excuses, but the truth is they were all wrong. The first clue that I was in the wrong relationship was when I had to keep it a secret. I should have known that. I don't want that anymore. I want to live. I want to feel alive. Being in a secret relationship is being in bondage. I no longer want to be in bondage. I can't do it. No more secrets."

"I understand. Where does this leave us?" Max asked.

"Max, I need some time. I need to heal. I'll never be good to anyone if I'm not healed myself. I never allowed myself to heal after leaving Kevin. I thought I had. I realize I was still a victim of his abuse. I don't want to live like that anymore. I need some time."

"I understand, Tay. I'll give you the time you need, but you didn't answer my question."

"What question was that?"

"Do you love me? I want to hear you say yes or no."

"I can't," she said, looking at the ground. She loved him, but she couldn't bring herself to tell him.

"Thank you, Tay. That's all I need. I think I know the answer. Before I go back into the house, I would like to do one thing." She began backing away. She glanced at the house and could see people peeping out the window. She thought he was going to kiss her. She couldn't let that happen, especially with everyone looking out the window at them. "Come here. I want to pray for you. You need prayer for this situation at your church. The enemy is fighting so hard to hurt you. I can't stand by and let that happen. I used to pray with you all the time. This may be the only time I have to pray with you about this situation, and I want to do it."

"Max, I don't . . ."

"Come on, Tay, let's pray." He held out his hands to her. She reluctantly took them and moved closer to him. She bowed her head and listened to Max pray. His hands were soft yet strong. Through their touch she could feel every part of his being. She could feel the power of God moving. She tried hard not to cry. She begged God to help her be strong. She wanted so much to hold him, but was afraid she would not want to let him go if she did.

After the prayer, Max pulled her close and kissed her before she could resist. She allowed it, wanting to be kissed, to be held by him. A loud cheer came from the house, and it wasn't for the football game. He left her standing by the car and went back to the house. She stood there dazed, but happy about the kiss. She felt Max was not giving up on her.

She debated whether to go back inside, especially since they all had seen them kissing. She did not want to endure the light-hearted ribbing she was sure to get when she went back in. She wanted to leave, but her car keys and purse were inside the house. She decided to just go into the house and act as if nothing had happened. She took a deep breath and went inside.

⚉

The day had started early for Shante. First, there was the early-bird after Thanksgiving shopping with Camille, Gwen, and Patrice and her daughter. She had planned to quit around noon and go home to rest and meditate on the Word before service that evening, but she didn't get home until after three. She took a short nap and began to study. She still didn't have a sermon for the conference. This was unusual, as she always had her sermons days ahead. This time was different. She thought it was because of all the stress from the church and the Thanksgiving food drive. She began dressing for the service and prayed for God to give her a sermon.

After she was dressed, she picked up a book of her old sermons, thinking God may give her a new twist on one of them. She asked Camille to drive while she revisited them. She was looking for one to jump out and grab her. None of them did. She prayed for God to give her a word.

They reached the church an hour before the service was to start. A number of people were already there. The main parking lot was already filled, and the parking attendants were directing people to an overflow lot across the street. Camille pulled into the main parking lot and was directed to a reserved space. They went into the church, and an usher escorted them to a private room marked VISITING MINISTER'S LOUNGE—PRIVATE.

Beautifully decorated in restful shades of lavender and purple, the lounge had a flowered sofa, a Queen Anne chair, and a small table and chair across from the sofa. It also had a minibar with a sink, a small refrigerator containing various juices and water, and a coffeemaker and plastic utensils. And it had a private bath with shower. A small television set was mounted on the wall and programmed to give the minister a view of the sanctuary. The usher showed them how to turn on the television and then left Shante and Camille alone.

A short time later, Pastor Kay stopped by to greet her and offer a word of encouragement. After she left, Shante asked Camille to give her some private time. Camille left and she began praying for God to give her a sermon. She turned on the television and saw the sanctuary filling up. She looked at her watch. *Ten more minutes before service starts. God, please give me something.* She sat nervously on the sofa, at a loss as to why a sermon had not come to her. Her anxiety grew as the minutes ticked by. Hearing a knock on the door, she said, "Come in."

The door opened. It was Shelby Bryson, Kevin's current wife. She had met her when she preached at Kevin's church. She was surprised to see her there. "Shelby? What are you doing here? I'm getting ready for service; I don't have time to talk."

"I'm sorry to bother you, Pastor Dogan. I'll only be a minute," Shelby said. She was carrying a large envelope, and her arm was in a cast. Shante saw the hurt in Shelby's eyes. She looked closely at her face and could tell she had tried to cover up facial bruising with makeup. She felt sorry for her. She knew how it felt to be Mrs. Kevin Bryson, and it wasn't a good feeling. "Shelby, have a seat. How can I help you?"

"I wanted to give you this," she said, handing her the envelope. Shante started to open the package, but Shelby stopped her, saying, "No. Don't open it here. Wait until you get home. I wanted to make sure you got it, and that's why I brought it myself."

"Shelby, is everything all right with you?"

"I'm fine now. I tripped down the stairs and broke my arm." She tried to give a slight smile.

Shante knew she was lying. Kevin loved hitting women in the face. "I was married to him once. I know what you're going through. You don't have to lie to me. When did he do this? I want to help you."

"Really, I'm all right now. I tripped. Service is about to start. I'd better let you go."

And with that, she started for the door. Shante stopped her. "Shelby, don't go. I mean, don't go back to that house, to that man. It only gets worse. I know. He almost killed me, and he threatened to kill my daughter. That was the final straw that sent me running. Stay with me tonight. On Monday, I can help you find a new place and get you set up. You don't have to take this. There are people who can help you. I'll help you."

"Pastor Dogan, I'm fine. Don't worry about me. God is keeping me."

Before she could further plead with the battered and clearly frightened woman, there was a knock at the door. It was Gwen and an usher. Gwen looked at the two of them and could tell they were having a serious conversation.

"I can come back."

"No, I was leaving. Thank you for speaking with me, Pastor Dogan," Shelby said and then left. "Who was that?" Gwen asked.

"Shelby, Kevin's wife. She looks bad. Kevin broke her arm. Did you see her face?"

"Yeah. That's a shame."

"I offered to help her but she refused. I hope she gets away from him soon. Anyway, service is starting, and I need to pray."

"Okay, Shante, I'll leave you alone. I only wanted to say hello before the service. I'm going to pray with you and head for the sanctuary."

They joined hands and prayed. Gwen left and Shante went into the bathroom and turned on the light. Seeing her reflection in a full-length mirror mounted on the wall startled her. She walked closer to the mirror and studied her face. She looked at the half-moon shaped scar under her right eye. She touched the long scar that ran from her left ear to her top lip. She looked at the small keloid on her chin. Then it hit her. Kevin still had a hold on her as long as she was keeping his abuse a secret. She went to the sink and began washing her face.

"Pastor Dogan, Pastor Kay's ready to escort you to the sanctuary," an usher said after tapping on the door.

"I'll be right out."

Shante stepped through the door. At first, Pastor Kay was taken aback by the scarring she was seeing for the first time. Then she smiled brightly. "Are you ready?"

"Yes."

Shante, Pastor Kay and the usher joined hands and prayed and then entered the large traditional sanctuary and walked onto the pulpit directly in front of the choir stand. In the pulpit, Shante sat in the middle seat, while Max sat on the left side of the choir stand with the other ministers. Gwen, Patrice, and Camille were sitting on the front row with Bishop and Mother Thompson. She saw other friends scattered throughout the sanctuary.

After briefly describing the purpose of the conference, Pastor Kay asked members of New Pilgrim to stand and be recognized. Shante was pleasantly surprised that several hundred of her members had shown up to support her. She looked at Camille and smiled.

Pastor Kay then introduced Shante, describing her ministry and community involvement and praising the work she had done. She also introduced Camille, who stood and greeted the congregation with a nod and a smile.

After a selection from the choir, Shante went up to the podium. She thanked Pastor Kay for the invitation and her introduction, and then she thanked her friends, family, and members of New Pilgrim for coming to support her. She appeared somewhat reserved and a little nervous.

"Please stand and turn with me to Revelation 12:10–11. Now the reading of the Word:

Then I heard a loud voice from heaven say: 'Now have come the salvation and the power and the kingdom of our God, and the authority of his Christ. For the accuser of our brothers, who accuses them before our God day and night, has been hurled down. They overcame him by the blood of the Lamb and by the word of their testimony; they did not love their lives so much as to shrink from death. Thank you. You may be seated.

"I want to highlight a section of this passage: 'They overcame him by the blood of the Lamb and by the word of their testimony.' I struggled with the message I'm bringing you tonight. Up until about thirty minutes ago, I had nothing to give you. Then, right before I came out here, the spirit of the Lord directed me to this scripture and told me to testify. So if you don't mind, I'm going to testify before you tonight. Tomorrow I'll preach, but tonight, I want to testify. Is that all right?" She looked around the large congregation.

"Testify," someone urged.

"That's all right," someone else shouted.

"Look at my face. Look at every line, every wrinkle, every cut, and every scar. Each one has a story to tell. Look at them. The story of my life is etched on my face. You on the cameras, get a close-up of my face. I want everyone in here, including those in the balcony, to get a good look at it."

The camera crew closed in on her face. The room was silent.

"Now look around you. Look at the faces of everyone in here. Each line, each wrinkle, each spot, mole, or scar has a story to tell."

"Amen," the audience responded.

"I want every woman or little girl to stand in this room." Once every female in the audience was standing, Shante resumed talking. "Look at these ladies. Look at the woman to your left. Now look at the woman to your right. Look at the woman in the front and back of you. Statistics show that at least one of the women you looked at has been abused. It doesn't make a difference if the woman was sexually, physically, mentally, or emotionally abused—abuse is abuse. Thank you, ladies, you may be seated."

As Shante began telling the story of how she had met Kevin and all that she had gone through in their marriage, the congregation was hanging on her every word. Max leaned forward in his seat attentively. Gwen and

Patrice held Camille's hands. She talked about how he continued to abuse and harass her despite a divorce and a restraining order. She described feelings of helplessness and hopelessness. And then she began talking about salvation and how it strengthens you to face and overcome any adversity. The congregation was on its feet. She began to allow the Holy Spirit to speak through her, breaking down each segment of the verses she had read. Satan, she declared, is the father of lies and was always accusing the children of the most high God. She gave steps to overcome any adversity and encouraged them that with God's help they, too, could overcome.

Toward the end of her sermon, the musicians began to play. The congregation was responding to every word. One lady in the pulpit walked over and hit her with a handkerchief. Max's hands were lifted in worship. People began dancing in the Holy Ghost. Shante looked around the room. Her clothing and hair were soaked in sweat, and she was breathing hard, but it didn't matter. She could feel in her spirit that God had released her from all the past hurt, pain, embarrassment, and insecurities. She knew she was now free.

CHAPTER 26

The week leading up to the meeting went by quickly. Shante spent it fasting and praying. She had come to feel whatever happened would be the will of God. She was prepared to humbly accept whatever decision God made for her life. Still, it was hard to let old habits go, so she found herself cleaning up and rearranging the furniture in her bedroom to relieve the stress of thinking about the meeting. She knew she would have a lot of support whatever happened. Gary was going with her as her attorney. Even though it wasn't a trial, he wanted to be there to defend her.

When she moved the chaise lounge to the window, the envelope Shelby had given her fell from under one of the pillows. She had forgotten about it. She had tossed it onto the lounge after the service Friday night and it must have fallen behind a pillow. She opened it and removed some pictures, a DVD, and various documents.

She spread the pictures and papers on her bed and put the DVD in her player and turned it on. What she saw was shocking. She hurriedly picked up the phone.

"Gary, this is Shante. I need to see you today. It's important."

Shante looked around her office. It looked so big, yet seemed small. She should be nervous, but she wasn't, for she had peace. *God, whatever your will, let it be done.* Bishop was talking to Ron as Mother and Gwen sat quietly listening. Shante had separated herself as she was wondering if Gary was able to get everything he needed on short notice. She responded to a knock at the door and was surprised to see Patrice and Camille.

"Camille, Patrice, I wasn't expecting you here. Camille, don't you have exams coming up? You need to be back at school studying."

"Mom, we thought it would be best if we came here to support you. I can study when I get back. This is more important."

"Yeah, we couldn't miss this for anything. We wanted you to know we have your back," Patrice added, hugging her.

"I'm so glad you're here."

"Is Gary here yet?" Camille asked.

"No, but he should be here soon."

Minutes later, Pastor Kay and her husband joined the growing gathering of well-wishers. Shante insisted they stay until time for the meeting. Shortly thereafter, Gary and Max arrived.

"Max? You're here? I didn't think you were coming." Shante was so happy to see him she couldn't hide her excitement.

"You knew I would be here to support you," Max said embracing her.

Gail came in and asked if she could get them anything. "No, Gail, we have all we need. Could you leave us alone? Thank you."

Shante closed and locked the door and then they joined hands and prayed. Afterward, Gary pulled Shante to the side.

"I found him; he'll be here this morning. I knew this would work out."

"Gary, I appreciate everything you've done for me. I don't know how to repay you."

Tank came to the door to let her know it was time for the meeting. His expression was somber and he could not look her in the eye. She touched his shoulder and whispered that everything would be fine. He shook his head and left.

Shante and her supporters walked into the sanctuary and she, Camille, Gary, and Max took seats in the first row. The sanctuary was filled to capacity; however, since it was a public meeting, the media was there. To Shante's surprise, police officers were standing along the wall.

Tank opened the meeting with a prayer and then introduced Deacon Curry as the board's spokesman. Curry explained what had led to the investigation and began to lay out the evidence. The ushers handed out a budget sheet showing the amount of money missing—more than twenty thousand dollars. Shante didn't look at her sheet; instead, she folded it and tucked it into her Bible. Deacon Curry explained each figure. He had copies of credit card receipts and statements that showed numerous hotels, department stores, restaurants, and travel charges that had not been authorized by the board. He completed his report and sat down.

Tank then introduced Sarah Turner. She opened with a reminder that Christians are expected to live a moral and righteous life. She read the minutes of the board meeting at which they had asked Shante to walk in a way that would glorify God. She went on to relate that she and her husband had seen Shante and Max at a restaurant in Greensboro. She over exaggerated how Shante had been dressed. She showed a credit-card receipt for a hotel on that same day in Greensboro. The crowd gasped. She then turned to her most damaging piece of evidence, and motioned to the men in the media booth. Pictures of Max and Shante dancing on the beach at Hilton Head came onscreen. And although quite fuzzy, pictures of two lovers having sex on the beach were shown. Shante heard Gwen gasp.

"Oh, my God," Gwen said to herself.

Sister Turner looked at Shante as the pictures were shown, a slight smirk on her face. She concluded her presentation with a direct attack on Shante's character. She urged the congregation to vote to dismiss Shante and proceed to find a new pastor of high moral character. As she returned to her seat, the room was totally silent. Everyone seemed in shock. Tank went to the podium; he appeared to be holding back tears. Clearing his throat, he asked Shante if she wanted to defend herself. Shante stood and asked if it was okay for her attorney to speak for her. Tank approved, and Gary got up and faced the crowd.

"I know this isn't a court of law; however, the Bible says if you have something against your brother, you are to go to that brother and try to work things out. If this doesn't accomplish its purpose, then you are to bring in witnesses to try to set the brother on the right path. Today, I would like to bring a witness who can clarify many of the issues that have been brought forth this day. May I be permitted to do so?" he asked Tank.

Tank nodded his approval, and Gary motioned to Max, who then went to the media booth in the balcony and handed the video operator an envelope.

"I would like to call Mr. Anthony Panzenetti to the front." A tall, burly white man stood up and walked down the aisle and stood next to Gary. There was a quiet tenseness in the room. A baby started crying, breaking the silence. "Would someone please give me a chair?"

A man placed a chair near Gary and gestured to Panzenetti to sit. Another man put a microphone stand near him so everyone could hear what he had to say. After looking toward the sound booth to make sure Max was there, Gary began his questioning of the man.

"Sir, please let everyone know who you are."

"I'm Anthony Panzenetti. I'm a licensed private investigator. I own Panzenetti Investigations here in Charlotte. I've been in business twelve years. I have several investigators on my staff."

"Mr. Panzenetti, can you tell me if you've been following my client, Miss Shante Dogan."

"I was hired to investigate another minister in the area. Ms. Dogan became part of that investigation by default."

"Can you tell us who hired you and for what reason? Also, tell us how this separate investigation was linked to Ms. Dogan."

"I received permission from my client, Mrs. Shelby Bryson, to appear at this meeting and give you whatever evidence I have found that may be relevant to this case."

"Please proceed."

"I was engaged by Mrs. Bryson to investigate her husband, Reverend Kevin Bryson, because she thought he was having an affair."

"Was he having an affair?"

"Yes, he was having several. Anyway, it turned out he is the ex-husband of Ms. Dogan. My investigation revealed they were divorced due to physical cruelty. He began coming to this church pretty regularly. I thought he was having an affair with Ms. Dogan; however, he wasn't seeing her. There was someone else."

"Who was that?"

"A Miss Gail Jennings," he answered, flipping through the pages of his notebook. The congregation gasped. Gail jumped up.

"I don't know a Kevin Bryson. I never heard of him. Why are you putting my name in this mess?"

"Miss Jennings, please sit down. Let us continue," Gary said, signaling Max. A picture of Gail and Kevin came up on the large-screen monitor at the front of the church.

Gail sat there shocked. Deacon Curry leaned forward to get a better look at the picture and began coughing. An usher gave him some water.

"That's not a Kevin; that is David. He told me his name was David Templeton," Gail said, jumping up again and pointing at the picture on the screen.

Tank asked Gail to sit down, and Gary continued his line of questioning. "Mr. Panzenetti, can you tell me who these people are in this picture?"

"That's a picture I took of Mr. Bryson and Miss Jennings here at the church. Apparently he always knew when Ms. Dogan would not be here. The other picture is of them having dinner at a local restaurant."

Gary went through a number of pictures of Kevin and Gail in various restaurants, stores, and hotels. Shante resisted turning around to look into Gail's face. She was sorely disappointed Gail had done this to her. She considered Gail a friend and had never remotely imagined she would betray her trust. She realized Gail did not know anything about Kevin because she hadn't told her, but she nonetheless betrayed her by using her credit cards and taking money from the church to finance her relationship with a man. She hadn't thought Gail was that vulnerable, that gullible. But she knew Kevin could be very manipulative, and for a moment, Shante felt sorry for her.

"Did you ever see Mr. Bryson with Ms. Dogan?"

"There were times when he would follow her. He wouldn't do it a lot—I guess whenever the opportunity arose. He followed her to the beach at Hilton Head last March, according to my notes."

"He was at Hilton Head?"

"Yes, he was with a Mrs. Sarah Turner, the lady who addressed the audience earlier. They were attending a conference of ministers there. They shared a room at the same hotel where Ms. Dogan was staying."

There was a loud gasp. The congregation was paying rapt attention to everything being said and shown. It was as if they were watching a racy motion picture. Shante had no qualms about staring at Sister Turner to see her reaction to the pictures. She wanted to see if Sister Turner would have a reaction similar to hers when she had seen the pictures for the first time the night before. Gary began to show pictures of Kevin and Sister Turner in compromising positions. Sister Turner passed out and was taken from the room. Shante could not feel sorry for her. For months Sister Turner had called her all kinds of names and had labeled her a tramp. On this day, God had uncovered Sister Turner's own secret sins and revealed them to everyone at once. She wondered if Sister Turner knew about her and Kevin. And was that knowledge the reason she had fought so hard to get rid of her? She glanced up and saw Brother Turner walking out of the sanctuary. Her heart went out to him, and she prayed silently for him.

"Can you tell me what happened on the night the pictures were taken of Ms. Dogan and Mr. Patrick on the beach?"

"I was following Mr. Bryson. Apparently, he had spotted Ms. Dogan and Mr. Patrick and was following them. So I followed him following them. I guess he saw them dancing and he went to his car and took a camera out of his trunk and began taking pictures."

"You saw them dancing?"

"Yes. It looked innocent. They seemed to be acting silly, curtseying and stuff. Nothing too romantic—none of that bumping and grinding stuff."

"So are you saying the pictures allegedly of them in a compromising position didn't happen or were not them?"

"I can't say that. I can say I didn't see them do anything. They left walking back toward the street. Mr. Bryson stayed behind and started taking pictures of a couple making out on the beach. There was a party nearby. I figured it was someone from the party, and Mr. Bryson wanted some freaky pictures. I stayed on him until he returned to his room."

"So you did not see Ms. Dogan and Mr. Patrick in a compromising position on the beach that night?"

"No."

"Can you tell me about other times you saw Mr. Bryson near or around Ms. Dogan?"

"There were a few more times. Once he came to the church and threatened her."

"Threatened her? How do you know?"

"I'm a private investigator. I have my ways."

"Any other time?"

"Yes, at her house. My investigator said he forced his way through her door, and she heard loud screaming. She contacted me and I alerted the police. I didn't want my investigator to get involved; I need to protect my employees. Mr. Bryson was arrested that day, and Mrs. Turner posted bail for him. Here's a copy of the bondsman's paperwork. It shows Mrs. Turner's signature."

Somebody in the crowd cried out, "Lord, have mercy."

"Now you said earlier you followed Mr. Bryson to hotels, stores, and restaurants. How did he pay for all of this? Surely Mr. Bryson was not rich enough to have a wife and carry on several affairs, too."

"No, he isn't rich. His church is small, and so his salary is very limited. However, he would get the money from the women he was seeing. The two I named here were not the only ones. The others are not relevant to this meeting. Many of his hotel stays were paid using this church's credit card or with money withdrawn from this church's bank account."

"What!" somebody said loudly.

Gail tried to run out of the sanctuary, but was stopped by a police officer. Turning to see what the commotion was about, Shante saw the police officer escorting Gail back to her seat. She was crying. Shante watched as she sat down; their eyes met briefly. Shante turned around. She couldn't look at her anymore.

"Can you explain that, Mr. Panzenetti?"

"My report shows that Miss Jennings took money from the church petty-cash account. She would forge Ms. Dogan's signature. I followed Miss Jennings and Mr. Bryson to the bank on several occasions. Once, they dropped the withdrawal slip and my investigator picked it up. We traced the number and found that money had been withdrawn from the church's account. The copies of the checks shown earlier look like the same ones we have. At first they were small amounts, but then the withdrawals were in the thousands from the various church accounts at the bank."

"In particular, one for two thousand dollars—did Ms. Dogan authorize this withdrawal?"

"No. Miss Jennings and Mr. Bryson went to the bank and withdrew the money. I followed them to Atlanta, where he met with his and Ms. Dogan's daughter, Camille, and gave her the money. I believe you have pictures of that."

Camille began to cry when her picture came on the screen. Shante hugged her. Patrice leaned over and rubbed her back. "Mom, I didn't know. I'm sorry. I didn't know."

"Don't blame yourself. I know you didn't know. It's all right," Shante said reassuringly.

"I hate him. He's so evil."

"Camille, don't say that. You need to pray for your father."

"I can't. How could he do that to you, to us?" She began to weep harder. An usher gave her a tissue.

"Is there anyone else in the church who became a part of your investigation?" Gary continued. Deacon Curry began coughing loudly, and Gary paused. Tank went to him and asked if he was okay. He said he was and drank some water. After he settled down, Gary repeated his question. "Is there anyone else in this church who played a part in your investigation?"

"Yes, a Curry—William Curry." A low rumble of voices filled the sanctuary at the mention of Deacon Curry's name. "Mr. Bryson met with Mr. Curry several times at a bar called Juices off 85. I have pictures of those meetings."

Shante looked at Deacon Curry sitting in the pulpit with Tank. Tank gave him a pained look. She thought about all the things she had done for Deacon Curry over the years. She thought how she invited him and his family to live with her temporarily when their house burned down. She thought about the many nights she had spent counseling his family about the problems that were besetting them due to his son's drug abuse. She thought about the times she had paid for his children to go on church trips when they couldn't afford it. She was deeply disappointed that this was how he showed his gratitude.

"On one occasion, Mr. Bryson gave Mr. Curry a package. He put the package into his car, and they went into the bar. My investigator managed to retrieve the package. It contained the pictures shown here today. We photographed the contents of the envelope and returned it to the car. We watched them until they left."

"You are telling me that Ms. Dogan's ex-husband had been meeting with the chairman deacon of her church?"

"Yes. I guess that's why we're here."

"Thank you for your information. I don't have any more questions. I appreciate your cooperation with this investigation."

"No problem," Panzenetti said, getting up and returning to his seat.

Gary began summing up all the PI had revealed. The videos of Kevin's meetings with Sister Turner, Gail, and Deacon Curry were shown again. He said all the evidence pointed to a plot to get rid of Shante as pastor after the county council stopped Kevin's club. He said there was no evidence showing any wrongdoing by her or on her behalf. But there was, he charged, ample evidence of misconduct by Gail, Sister Turner, and Deacon Curry. Speaking as her attorney, he called for their immediate resignation from their positions in the church. He also asked that the church vote to keep Shante as pastor, stressing her innocence and reciting a long list of things she had done for the church, particularly how it had grown during her pastorate. After he concluded, a grateful congregation rose as if cued and applauded clamorously.

After a celebration lunch, everybody went their separate ways—except for Gwen and Patrice, who elected to continue celebrating at Shante's home. Her phone had not stopped ringing since the church vote. She was gratified and delighted that the overwhelming majority of her church members still had confidence in her and had voted to keep her as pastor. She couldn't wait to get into the pulpit Sunday morning. She imagined the celebration they were going to have. She felt it was going to be one of those mornings when the Spirit would be so high she would not have to preach. She could feel a praise coming in her spirit at the thought of the good time they were going to have the next day.

Camille went straight to her room when they got home. She had very little to say during the meal. Shante could see she was still upset about Kevin having used her.

She waited a while to see if she would reappear and join her and the others as they laughed and talked about what they had seen and heard that day. Shante finally went to see what was going on. Camille was lying across the bed holding onto a pillow.

"Camille, honey, it's all right. It wasn't your fault."

"He used me. How could he do that to me? I wanted to believe he had changed. He apologized for not being there for me. He said he was going to do better. He asked me to forgive him and told me he hoped we could get to know each other. I knew I shouldn't have trusted him."

Shante hugged her shattered daughter and prayed for her. She was angry with Kevin for using Camille to hurt her, vowing to call him and let him know exactly how she felt. She wasn't afraid of him anymore. This time he had hurt her daughter, and her maternal instinct wanted to protect her. That could wait. Right now, she was mainly focused on helping her daughter heal.

"Honey, I don't know how I can help you right now. All I can say is God knows you are hurting. He can heal your hurt. Aren't you the one who told me that you could be in a situation but not allow the situation to have you? Well, don't allow what your father did kill your joy. I can't say why he did what he did, only God knows. I do know he missed out on eighteen years of the beautiful young woman you are, and one day he will regret it all. But you can choose to love your dad without being a part of his life. I have always taught you that. Accept who your father is and pray for him. I know it's hard now. But soon you will realize that it is not good for you to hold on to anger and unforgiveness and you will look at your dad and feel sorry for him."

"I can't stand that man," Camille said.

"Camille, it's okay to get angry, but don't stay there. In a couple of days, you will be able to see that what he did to us did not stop God from blessing us. You will thank God for showing you a side of your dad you never knew and making you wiser in case he tries something like that again."

"I guess you're right."

"Am I always?" Shante asked. Camille managed a slight smile. "Now take a minute and get yourself together and join us. I'm going in the kitchen to see what Gwen and Patrice are doing."

Shante returned to the kitchen where Gwen and Patrice were sitting on barstools at the island. Patrice looked at her. "Is she okay?"

"She'll be fine." Shante pulled a pint of Ben and Jerry's chocolate fudge brownie ice cream from the freezer and passed spoons to Patrice and Gwen. "I can't believe Kevin would stoop so low as to put Camille in the middle of one of his schemes."

"I don't know what you saw in him in the first place," Patrice said, shoving a large spoonful of ice cream into her mouth.

"That's because you never saw what I saw or how he used it."

"Shante!" Gwen screeched.

"Well, it's true. We had a lot of sex before we got married, but we could not have a decent conversation. He was cute. With everything that has happened over the years, I don't even remember what I originally saw in him. I was so naïve. I thought his passion for ministry would help us have the perfect marriage, even though I wasn't saved at the time. But I was wrong."

"That was horrible. He didn't have to include Camille. Some people are going to bust hell wide open."

"Don't say that, Patrice. I know you are new in the faith. You've got to learn to pray for your enemies."

"You pray. God is still working on me." The three of them laughed.

"We are going to have a good time in church tomorrow," she said, going to answer the phone. "Let me see who is calling to congratulate me now." It was the sheriff's department. She expected the call, but not this soon. She hesitated before picking up. She didn't want to talk about Gail, Sister Turner, or Deacon Curry. She especially did not want to talk about Kevin. She wanted to bask in her victory a while longer.

"This is Shante."

"This is the Mecklenburg County Sheriff's Department. We would like for you to come down to the station to give a statement," the officer said.

"Do I have to do it today? I would like to have my attorney present."

"We can do it next week. However, we will be issuing warrants for the arrest of Gail Jennings and Kevin Bryson on several felony charges related to the theft of money from your church."

Shante was sad to hear Gail and Kevin would be arrested, especially Gail. She considered her a friend, and was trying to forgive her, but she knew it would take time. "Who was that?" Patrice asked as she hung up the phone.

"That was the police. They are going to arrest Gail and Kevin."

The phone rang again, but the number did not register on the caller ID. Shante answered anyway. "Shante, this is me, Kevin. Don't hang up." Shante sat on a barstool, in disbelief that he had the nerve to call her. "I guess now you know about some things. I had to do what I had to do. Don't blame Gail; she's a good person. I needed the money."

"So you decided to steal it from my church and hurt your daughter?"

"I didn't mean to hurt Camille. I wanted to do something for her. I finally had the chance, and I took advantage of it. I haven't been the best example of a father for her. I'm really proud of her. I wanted to tell her that at her graduation from high school, but the two of you and your family and friends looked so happy. I didn't want to rain on her day. So I walked away."

"You were at her graduation?" Shante stood and began pacing.

"Yeah. I was proud of the speech she gave. Do me a favor. She probably doesn't want to talk to me right now. Tell her I love her and I'm sorry. I didn't want to hurt her. I better go. I think the police will be looking for me soon."

"Kevin. Why did you do it?"

"I thought I could pay it back before anyone noticed it was gone. It didn't work out that way. Anyway, I better go."

"Kevin . . . Kevin," Shante yelled into the phone. But he'd already hung up.

"No, he didn't have the nerve to call you," Patrice said as she stood and walked over to Shante.

"What did he want?" Gwen asked.

"He wanted me to apologize to Camille. He said he loved her and hadn't meant to hurt her. He said he wanted to finally do something for her."

"And he did it by stealing money from your church?" Patrice asked.

"He manipulated Gail. She's young. It was easy for him to do. He said he was going to pay it back."

"Yeah, right," Patrice said. "I hope they arrest him soon."

Gwen and Patrice began speculating as to the real reason Kevin had called. Shante could not join in. For the first time, she truly felt sorry for him. She thought about all that he had lost and was apparently willing to give up, all because he was unwilling to change. She knew she would eventually have to tell Camille what he had said. But she couldn't right now. The phone call had only made her angrier. She herself would have to find a way to forgive him in order to minister to her daughter about forgiveness.

CHAPTER 27

Shante sat on the balcony of her hotel room listening to the sound of the ocean. If they had held this conference anywhere other than Hilton Head, she would not have attended. A year had passed since she was last here. It had been a life-changing and transforming year. She had no way of knowing that she would be so different today from what she had been the same time last year. She no longer cared what the other ministers thought of her or her ministry. She didn't feel the urge to socialize or network with the other attendees.

At this conference last year, she had been the golden girl. This year, people treated her as if she had the plague. She wished Gwen and Ron or Bishop had attended this year. She would have them to talk to and attend the functions with. They had decided not to attend, and Shante felt alone.

Shante's mind started traveling back to all the things she had gone through. Kevin was in jail awaiting trial, and she still could hardly believe that whole scenario. She recalled how difficult it had been to tell Camille about her father's phone call. Thinking about Camille's indifference to her father's incarceration, Shante sighed. Camille was hurting, but she couldn't get her to talk about it. She figured in time Camille would come to terms with

Kevin's failures. Until then, all she could do was minister to her the best way she knew how.

She decided to do one of her favorite things, go for a walk along the beach. She went to her room and changed into jeans and a sweatshirt. She then went down to the lobby, passing groups of ministers mingling outside the conference room where the welcome reception was being held. She kept walking and headed for the beach. The sun was beginning to set. She walked until she could no longer hear the sounds of the activities coming from the hotel and sat down in the sand. Closing her eyes, she took a deep breath and began thanking God for bringing her through the past year.

"You really shouldn't be out here by yourself," a familiar voice warned.

It was Max. She stood and wiped the sand off her jeans, saying, "Hey, I didn't think you were coming to the conference this year."

"I saw you heading to the beach. I hope you don't mind my being here. I wanted to be here to support you when you spoke. I looked at the schedule, but I didn't see your name. When are you preaching?"

Shante was happy to see him. She felt like hugging him and never letting go, but she did not know how he would react. They had not seen each other in a while. They had barely spoken to one another since the church meeting. Yet, Max continued sending her inspirational text messages and e-mail; sometimes jokes at just the right time. She had been extremely busy at the church. In addition, she was receiving more invitations to preach outside Charlotte. She also started writing her first book on salvation. She truly hadn't had much time for anything else.

"I met with the association's board this morning. They felt it was best for the organization if I didn't preach, considering the circumstances."

"Considering the circumstances?"

"That's what they told me. They felt it might hurt the image of the members of this organization if I preached. They said they had received some concerns about my integrity and being involved in questionable acts in my ministry. They took me off the program before Christmas, but they waited until this morning to tell me. I wish they had told me earlier. I wouldn't have come."

"That's probably why they didn't tell you. They still need you here. A lot of people here were waiting to hear you preach, and if you hadn't come, they weren't coming, either. I think a lot of people are getting tired of this conference. It's the same thing every year. I heard attendance is down this year. Enough about the conference. How are you doing?"

"I'm blessed. I can't complain."

"We haven't talked much lately."

"I'm sorry about that, Max. Since the church meeting and Kevin's arrest, I've been so busy."

"I can imagine."

"After the meeting, all but two of my board members resigned. Tank stayed on because I asked him to. When the board is completely replaced, he's going to resign. It's been difficult selecting deacons and trustees. I basically had to replace the entire leadership of the church and hire a new secretary."

"I know it's been rough."

"I'm sorry. I haven't been trying to ignore you. It's just that when I get home, I'm so wasted I fall into the bed—if I don't have any work to do. It takes all my willpower to get up and exercise in the morning. It's been very hard."

"I know it's been a lot of work. How are *you* doing, Shante?"

"I'm tired, very tired. I don't have any energy. I saw my doctor about it. He said I needed to take a vacation, so here I am, on vacation." She whirled around in the sand, forcing a meager smile. "My work at the church doesn't feel the same. I feel my work there is complete. I've taken New Pilgrim as far as I can. It may be time for me to step down. I don't know. I've been praying about it. It's in my spirit. I have to make sure that it's the spirit of the Lord telling me and not me telling myself. Considering all that has happened, I have to be very careful. But you don't want to hear my problems. I'm really blessed. I'm doing much better. I don't have to look over my shoulder for Kevin anymore. I don't walk in fear."

"That's good to hear. It has been a rough year, but continue praying about stepping down. That's a big decision. You have to be led by the Holy Spirit. You don't want to make matters worse."

"Yeah, and it can only get better."

"Amen."

The incoming tide was hitting her feet, so they walked away from the ocean. Her hair swayed with the cool breeze from the ocean, and she had to keep brushing it back from her face. "So, Max, how've you been? You look good."

"Thank you, Tay. I'm well."

"And the boys? How are they doing?"

"They're doing great."

"That's good. Tell them . . ." She stopped talking and turned her back to him. She bent down to pick up a shell she spotted in the sand.

"Tell them what?"

"Huh?"

"You said tell the boys and you stopped. Tell them what?"

"Max, there's something I have to tell you."

"I'm listening."

"I . . . well, I . . ." She started walking back toward the hotel.

"What is it?"

"I don't want you to get angry. I've been seeing the boys. I know you didn't want me involved with them since we weren't together, but it broke my heart not to see them. Someone has been bringing them to see me. I'm sorry I went behind your back. I had to. Seeing them relaxed me. It made me happy. With all the things that were going on in my life, they were the sunshine I needed. I made sure I scheduled time to see them. Please forgive me. If you don't mind, I would like to continue seeing them. I love them like they're my own sons. I don't like sneaking around. I don't want any more secrets. You're their father; I thought you should know."

Max walked closer to her. He lifted her chin and wiped a tear. "I already know."

"You knew?"

"Yeah, I've known for a long time, almost from the beginning. You know Josh can't keep a secret. I saw you at Jon's basketball games and at Jake's recital. I was glad you were there to support them. I asked Gwen and Gary to make sure you saw them anytime you wanted. Bishop and Mother volunteered to be a drop-off spot for you to visit them. You ever wondered why the boys were there when you visited them? That's because they would call me and let me know when you planned to visit, and I would drop them off. They wanted to be with you. I couldn't break their hearts. I know you love them, and they love you."

"Thank you so much, Max." She pulled him to her and hugged him. It felt so natural to her, but she pulled away. "I'm sorry. I shouldn't have done that."

"That's all right."

She turned her back to him and looked out at the ocean. "Max?"

"Yes."

"I was wrong."

"Wrong? About what?"

"I was wrong about the way I treated you. I was wrong about everything. I shouldn't have acted that way. I shouldn't have cut you off. I shouldn't have led you on. I shouldn't have talked to you the way I did. I was wrong." She turned to him. "I'm sorry. I apologize. Please forgive me. Forgive me for everything."

"You don't have to apologize."

"Yes, I do. I treated you really bad. You didn't deserve it. You're a great guy. I was afraid."

"Afraid of what?"

"Afraid to be loved, afraid of being in love. I knew you loved me. You didn't hesitate to tell me. It scared me. I tried so hard to live a righteous life. I was afraid Kevin would do something to harm you or the boys. When you told me he had been at your office, it scared me even more. I wanted to be with you. I knew I had crossed the line after Josh's accident. I let you get too close when I knew I didn't want to get married then. Everything in me wanted to be with you more and more each day. I think I used Josh's accident as an excuse to be with you. That was very selfish of me. I'm sorry."

"Tay—"

"No, Max. Please let me finish. This might be the only time I get to talk with you. I want to make sure I say what I need to."

"I'm listening."

"I enjoyed getting together with you for First Friday. In the beginning it was all about helping you get through Meko's death, but then it changed. It became something more. I looked forward to spending time with you. I loved being with you. I loved our adventures. I loved the conversations we had. I loved the way you made me feel when I was with you. I miss First Friday. There have been times when I've wanted to call you and ask you to meet me for First Friday. I was embarrassed by the way I treated you, and I felt I didn't deserve to be with you."

"I miss First Friday, too."

"With all that has happened, I didn't think you wanted to be with me. I wanted so badly to be with you. I missed your smile, your corny jokes, your intelligence, and your praise. I loved to hear you pray. I loved the way you interacted with your sons. There is so much I loved about you. I let what other people thought of our relationship interfere with what God was doing in my life— in our lives. To get my mind off you, I dove deeply into my work. Yes, there are a lot of things going on at the church, but some of that stuff can wait. I was trying to do things to keep my mind off you."

Max stood on the beach listening to her. "I've been talking to Pastor Kay. She made me realize I was using the boys to keep you in my life. In a way, she was right. When I went to the games or recitals, I would look for you. There were times when I couldn't keep my eyes off you. I wanted so much to go to you and say something or hold you. This realization didn't help anything, especially since I accused you of using the boys to pressure me. I had to repent. I took some time to fast and pray." She wiped her face.

"I never told you that I loved you. The truth is I did love you. I think I still do—no, I know I'm in love with you. I secretly wished you were here. I wanted so much to be with you. I remembered dancing with you this time last year. I remembered how it felt to hold you, to be held by you. I remembered your smell, your smile, and your kiss. All these memories came rushing back. It was more than I could take." Shante couldn't stop the tears. She could feel the salty taste as they flowed down her face into her mouth.

"I wish there was something I could do to change everything that happened. I know I can't change the past. I felt you needed to know. I'll understand if you don't forgive me. I wanted you to know." She wiped her nose on the sleeve of her sweatshirt.

Max walked up to her and placed his hands on her shoulders. She turned around and gripped his sides. She squeezed him tightly. "Tay, someone might see us." He pulled away from her.

"I don't care. I don't care."

He pulled her close to him and held her tightly. She squeezed him. She took a deep breath. Her tears kept flowing. She didn't realize that Max was also crying. "Max, I love you. I always have. I love you."

"I love you, too."

"Please forgive me."

"I forgive you. I understand. I love you."

He pulled away and wiped the tears from his eyes. "Tay, there's something I have to tell you."

"What is it?" A sense of dread came over her.

"I'm selling my share of the practice to Gary."

"Really? Why?"

"I believe God is calling me to full-time ministry. I can't do both."

"I know this is a big decision. I've had to make the same decision myself. You have to do what God is telling you."

"You don't understand, Tay. I'm leaving Earle Street."

"Leaving? Where are you going? I thought everything was fine there."

"It is. I feel God is moving me to leave Charlotte and start a church in another state."

"What?"

"Tay, I'm leaving Charlotte. At the end of the school year, I'm leaving and moving to South Carolina to start a church there."

"You're leaving? You're moving to South Carolina? You're taking the boys? Oh, no. Not now. Max, you're leaving?" She sat down on the sand, put her head in her hands, and wept loudly.

Max sat next to her. He, too, was crying. "Tay, I have to go. God has given me a vision for this ministry. I took a trip there. I talked to a pastor I met at the conference last year, Jarrod Fuller. He pastors a church in South Carolina. He introduced me to a lot of other ministers in the area. I walked the community. I talked with community leaders. I've prayed and prayed. I know this is what God wants me to do. I have to go."

She looked up and wiped her nose again on the sleeve of her sweatshirt. "I know you have to go. You have to be obedient to what God is telling you." She couldn't stop the tears.

Max put his arm around her and pulled her close. She rested her head on his shoulder, and they sat silently on the beach watching the moon and the waves and listening to the sound of the ocean.

CHAPTER 28

Shante sat in her office daydreaming about the conference at Hilton Head. It was so different than last year. She enjoyed this conference more than any of the previous ones. She was thankful she did not preach. It gave her and Max an opportunity to reconnect.

Max revealed his vision for his ministry in South Carolina. He wanted to work with fathers who are single parents and their children. To Shante's delight he was only moving to Columbia, an hour's drive from Charlotte. He promised her they would go there together before he moved.

She thought about Max wanting to make up for the missed First Fridays. During the week they were at the conference, they slipped away and traveled to Charleston for a day. They toured the plantations and slave cabins. They purchased handmade baskets and toured museums. Max surprised her with a romantic dinner cruise where they again pronounced their love for each other. For the past four weeks since the conference, they celebrated First Friday every Monday—their day off.

More importantly, they attended the conference together. Once they returned from Charleston, they did not care who saw them holding each other closely or whether anyone was looking at them holding hands.

They attended the meetings and evening worship services together. They enjoyed each other's company as if no other people were in attendance.

When they returned to Charlotte, Shante and Max had to field inquiries about their relationship. Neither denied anything—that was true. Shante realized other people knowing about her relationship actually made it better. Gone was the stress of sneaking around and hiding. Gone was the fear of getting caught. They could relax and enjoy each other. They openly flirted and kissed.

The boys seemed happier. Although they did not want to move, they enjoyed hanging out with Shante and Max. Each week, Max or Shante planned a day for the five of them to share. And to make up for the missed First Fridays, Max planned something special each week just for Shante and him. Shante smiled as she thought about their time together.

"Pastor." Kendra, her new secretary, came into her office. Noticing the smile on Shante's face she said, "Wow, you look happy."

"I am." Nothing could ruin her day. Her ministry was growing and she had received more invitations to preach than this time last year. Her calendar was filling up quickly. She had finally found peace in her ministry. Tonight Max was cooking dinner and she anxiously anticipated being with him and the boys.

"Well, I hope it lasts after I tell you this."

"What is it?"

"Pastor Griffin called and she will not be able to do the spring revival. She said she has a family emergency.

Where can we find a minister at such short notice? It's Thursday. The revival starts Sunday. That's only three days away."

Shante thought nothing could ruin her day. She called Pastor Griffin, who confirmed Kendra's report. As she began to go through her files to find another minister, her phone rang. It was Max.

"Hey, baby. I was thinking about you," Max said.

"Hi," Shante said, leaning back in her chair. "I hope you are praying for me."

"Always. Can you come over earlier—before the boys get out of school?"

"That's tempting, but I can't. Pastor Griffin just canceled on us. I've got to find someone else to preach our revival. So it looks like I'm going to be here unless I can find someone quick."

"Two heads are better than one."

"Come on, Max. I've got to work."

"Okay. I'll look through my Rolodex and see if someone comes to mind and let you know. I love you."

"I love you back," Shante said, hanging up the phone. Where could she find someone on such short notice? The announcement had already been made. It was too late to cancel the revival. They may have to. Shante continued to hope as she flipped through her files.

The sanctuary was filled for the first night of the revival. Shante had told her parishioners in the two morning worship services about the new speaker for the revival. It seemed people showed up to see what would happen. The pastor she found was well known and liked in the Charlotte area.

From her seat in the pulpit, she could see Bishop and Mother Thompson, along with Gwen and Ron, sitting on the right front row. Jonathan, Jacob, and Joshua were seated between Bishop and Mother. She wished Camille could have been there, but she was studying for her senior exams and Shante felt it was more important for her to stay in Atlanta. There would be other events at the church she could attend. Camille was grown now and after graduation, she was moving to New York. She had accepted a position with Bad Boy Entertainment.

As she stood at the podium to introduce the speaker, she saw familiar faces and some new ones too. She felt good. Her spirit was high. She had wanted this minister to preach at her church for a long time, but was always afraid to ask. She was thankful he was able to preach on short notice.

"How are you, New Pilgrim?" she shouted. "Bless the Lord. I am peacock proud and honeymoon happy to have such a great speaker tonight. God rearranged his schedule to be here with us." She continued the glowing introduction of him by listing his accomplishments and introducing members of his church that were in attendance.

"His sons are worshipping with us tonight. Stand up Jonathan, Jacob, and Joshua."

The audience applauded as they stood. Then, laughed when Joshua took a bow—always the entertainer.

Trying to hold back her laugh, Shante continued, "I have known this man of God for many years. We were in college together—he was at Morehouse, while I was at Spelman. We quickly became and have remained friends to this day. I know he is a man of integrity and great wisdom. We are in for a treat this week." She turned to face Max sitting in the large chair behind her. "Matter of fact, Pastor Patrick, why don't you stand and let everybody see you."

Max obliged. The congregation applauded. "Turn around. Let them see you." Max looked at her as if to see if she was serious. She motioned for him to turn around and he did. "Lord have mercy," Shante said, jokingly. "Tall, dark, and handsome. If I wasn't saved . . ." She couldn't help herself. She laughed harder. Max sat in the chair, laughing at Shante's antics. The congregation found the scene entertaining also. "Wait a minute. Wait a minute," she told the laughing crowd. "He's not married—yet."

"Not yet," Max said.

Shante looked at him and smiled. This was her opportunity to say what she had wanted to say for years. She continued addressing the crowd. "Now just because he's single, doesn't mean he's available." She paused, and then said, "Him mine. Oh yes, him mine."

ABOUT THE AUTHOR

K. T. Richey is a minister who resides in South Carolina. After earning degrees in social studies and counseling, she went on to practice social work for almost twenty years. *Lady Preacher* is the first in a series of novels that will explore the lives of women in ministry and their efforts to find balance in life, love and the church.

2008 Reprint Mass Market Titles

January

Cautious Heart
Cheris F. Hodges
ISBN-13: 978-1-58571-301-1
ISBN-10: 1-58571-301-5
$6.99

Suddenly You
Crystal Hubbard
ISBN-13: 978-1-58571-302-8
ISBN-10: 1-58571-302-3
$6.99

February

Passion
T. T. Henderson
ISBN-13: 978-1-58571-303-5
ISBN-10: 1-58571-303-1
$6.99

Whispers in the Sand
LaFlorya Gauthier
ISBN-13: 978-1-58571-304-2
ISBN-10: 1-58571-304-x
$6.99

March

Life Is Never As It Seems
J. J. Michael
ISBN-13: 978-1-58571-305-9
ISBN-10: 1-58571-305-8
$6.99

Beyond the Rapture
Beverly Clark
ISBN-13: 978-1-58571-306-6
ISBN-10: 1-58571-306-6
$6.99

April

A Heart's Awakening
Veronica Parker
ISBN-13: 978-1-58571-307-3
ISBN-10: 1-58571-307-4
$6.99

Breeze
Robin Lynette Hampton
ISBN-13: 978-1-58571-308-0
ISBN-10: 1-58571-308-2
$6.99

May

I'll Be Your Shelter
Giselle Carmichael
ISBN-13: 978-1-58571-309-7
ISBN-10: 1-58571-309-0
$6.99

Careless Whispers
Rochelle Alers
ISBN-13: 978-1-58571-310-3
ISBN-10: 1-58571-310-4
$6.99

June

Sin
Crystal Rhodes
ISBN-13: 978-1-58571-311-0
ISBN-10: 1-58571-311-2
$6.99

Dark Storm Rising
Chinelu Moore
ISBN-13: 978-1-58571-312-7
ISBN-10: 1-58571-312-0
$6.99

2008 Reprint Mass Market Titles (continued)

July

Object of His Desire
A.C. Arthur
ISBN-13: 978-1-58571-313-4
ISBN-10: 1-58571-313-9
$6.99

Angel's Paradise
Janice Angelique
ISBN-13: 978-1-58571-314-1
ISBN-10: 1-58571-314-7
$6.99

August

Unbreak My Heart
Dar Tomlinson
ISBN-13: 978-1-58571-315-8
ISBN-10: 1-58571-315-5
$6.99

All I Ask
Barbara Keaton
ISBN-13: 978-1-58571-316-5
ISBN-10: 1-58571-316-3
$6.99

September

Icie
Pamela Leigh Starr
ISBN-13: 978-1-58571-275-5
ISBN-10: 1-58571-275-2
$6.99

At Last
Lisa Riley
ISBN-13: 978-1-58571-276-2
ISBN-10: 1-58571-276-0
$6.99

October

Everlastin' Love
Gay G. Gunn
ISBN-13: 978-1-58571-277-9
ISBN-10: 1-58571-277-9
$6.99

Three Wishes
Seressia Glass
ISBN-13: 978-1-58571-278-6
ISBN-10: 1-58571-278-7
$6.99

November

Yesterday Is Gone
Beverly Clark
ISBN-13: 978-1-58571-279-3
ISBN-10: 1-58571-279-5
$6.99

Again My Love
Kayla Perrin
ISBN-13: 978-1-58571-280-9
ISBN-10: 1-58571-280-9
$6.99

December

Office Policy
A.C. Arthur
ISBN-13: 978-1-58571-281-6
ISBN-10: 1-58571-281-7
$6.99

Rendezvous With Fate
Jeanne Sumerix
ISBN-13: 978-1-58571-283-3
ISBN-10: 1-58571-283-3
$6.99

2008 New Mass Market Titles

January

Where I Want To Be
Maryam Diaab
ISBN-13: 978-1-58571-268-7
ISBN-10: 1-58571-268-X
$6.99

Never Say Never
Michele Cameron
ISBN-13: 978-1-58571-269-4
ISBN-10: 1-58571-269-8
$6.99

February

Stolen Memories
Michele Sudler
ISBN-13: 978-1-58571-270-0
ISBN-10: 1-58571-270-1
$6.99

Dawn's Harbor
Kymberly Hunt
ISBN-13: 978-1-58571-271-7
ISBN-10: 1-58571-271-X
$6.99

March

Undying Love
Renee Alexis
ISBN-13: 978-1-58571-272-4
ISBN-10: 1-58571-272-8
$6.99

Blame It On Paradise
Crystal Hubbard
ISBN-13: 978-1-58571-273-1
ISBN-10: 1-58571-273-6
$6.99

April

When A Man Loves A Woman
La Connie Taylor-Jones
ISBN-13: 978-1-58571-274-8
ISBN-10: 1-58571-274-4
$6.99

Choices
Tammy Williams
ISBN-13: 978-1-58571-300-4
ISBN-10: 1-58571-300-7
$6.99

May

Dream Runner
Gail McFarland
ISBN-13: 978-1-58571-317-2
ISBN-10: 1-58571-317-1
$6.99

Southern Fried Standards
S.R. Maddox
ISBN-13: 978-1-58571-318-9
ISBN-10: 1-58571-318-X
$6.99

June

Looking for Lily
Africa Fine
ISBN-13: 978-1-58571-319-6
ISBN-10: 1-58571-319-8
$6.99

Bliss, Inc.
Chamein Canton
ISBN-13: 978-1-58571-325-7
ISBN-10: 1-58571-325-2
$6.99

2008 New Mass Market Titles (continued)

July

Love's Secrets
Yolanda McVey
ISBN-13: 978-1-58571-321-9
ISBN-10: 1-58571-321-X
$6.99

Things Forbidden
Maryam Diaab
ISBN-13: 978-1-58571-327-1
ISBN-10: 1-58571-327-9
$6.99

August

Storm
Pamela Leigh Starr
ISBN-13: 978-1-58571-323-3
ISBN-10: 1-58571-323-6
$6.99

Passion's Furies
AlTonya Washington
ISBN-13: 978-1-58571-324-0
ISBN-10: 1-58571-324-4
$6.99

September

Three Doors Down
Michele Sudler
ISBN-13: 978-1-58571-332-5
ISBN-10: 1-58571-332-5
$6.99

Mr Fix-It
Crystal Hubbard
ISBN-13: 978-1-58571-326-4
ISBN-10: 1-58571-326-0
$6.99

October

Moments of Clarity
Michele Cameron
ISBN-13: 978-1-58571-330-1
ISBN-10: 1-58571-330-9
$6.99

Lady Preacher
K.T. Richey
ISBN-13: 978-1-58571-333-2
ISBN-10: 1-58571-333-3
$6.99

November

This Life Isn't Perfect Holla
Sandra Foy
ISBN: 978-1-58571-331-8
ISBN-10: 1-58571-331-7
$6.99

Promises Made
Bernice Layton
ISBN-13: 978-1-58571-334-9
ISBN-10: 1-58571-334-1
$6.99

December

A Voice Behind Thunder
Carrie Elizabeth Greene
ISBN-13: 978-1-58571-329-5
ISBN-10: 1-58571-329-5
$6.99

The More Things Change
Chamein Canton
ISBN-13: 978-1-58571-328-8
ISBN-10: 1-58571-328-7
$6.99

Other Genesis Press, Inc. Titles

A Dangerous Deception	J.M. Jeffries	$8.95
A Dangerous Love	J.M. Jeffries	$8.95
A Dangerous Obsession	J.M. Jeffries	$8.95
A Drummer's Beat to Mend	Kei Swanson	$9.95
A Happy Life	Charlotte Harris	$9.95
A Heart's Awakening	Veronica Parker	$9.95
A Lark on the Wing	Phyliss Hamilton	$9.95
A Love of Her Own	Cheris F. Hodges	$9.95
A Love to Cherish	Beverly Clark	$8.95
A Risk of Rain	Dar Tomlinson	$8.95
A Taste of Temptation	Reneé Alexis	$9.95
A Twist of Fate	Beverly Clark	$8.95
A Will to Love	Angie Daniels	$9.95
Acquisitions	Kimberley White	$8.95
Across	Carol Payne	$12.95
After the Vows	Leslie Esdaile	$10.95
(Summer Anthology)	T.T. Henderson	
	Jacqueline Thomas	
Again My Love	Kayla Perrin	$10.95
Against the Wind	Gwynne Forster	$8.95
All I Ask	Barbara Keaton	$8.95
Always You	Crystal Hubbard	$6.99
Ambrosia	T.T. Henderson	$8.95
An Unfinished Love Affair	Barbara Keaton	$8.95
And Then Came You	Dorothy Elizabeth Love	$8.95
Angel's Paradise	Janice Angelique	$9.95
At Last	Lisa G. Riley	$8.95
Best of Friends	Natalie Dunbar	$8.95
Beyond the Rapture	Beverly Clark	$9.95

Other Genesis Press, Inc. Titles (continued)

Other Genesis Press, Inc. Titles (continued)

Daughter of the Wind	Joan Xian	$8.95
Deadly Sacrifice	Jack Kean	$22.95
Designer Passion	Dar Tomlinson	$8.95
	Diana Richeaux	
Do Over	Celya Bowers	$9.95
Dreamtective	Liz Swados	$5.95
Ebony Angel	Deatri King-Bey	$9.95
Ebony Butterfly II	Delilah Dawson	$14.95
Echoes of Yesterday	Beverly Clark	$9.95
Eden's Garden	Elizabeth Rose	$8.95
Eve's Prescription	Edwina Martin Arnold	$8.95
Everlastin' Love	Gay G. Gunn	$8.95
Everlasting Moments	Dorothy Elizabeth Love	$8.95
Everything and More	Sinclair Lebeau	$8.95
Everything but Love	Natalie Dunbar	$8.95
Falling	Natalie Dunbar	$9.95
Fate	Pamela Leigh Starr	$8.95
Finding Isabella	A.J. Garrotto	$8.95
Forbidden Quest	Dar Tomlinson	$10.95
Forever Love	Wanda Y. Thomas	$8.95
From the Ashes	Kathleen Suzanne	$8.95
	Jeanne Sumerix	
Gentle Yearning	Rochelle Alers	$10.95
Glory of Love	Sinclair LeBeau	$10.95
Go Gentle into that Good Night	Malcom Boyd	$12.95
Goldengroove	Mary Beth Craft	$16.95
Groove, Bang, and Jive	Steve Cannon	$8.99
Hand in Glove	Andrea Jackson	$9.95

Other Genesis Press, Inc. Titles (continued)

Hard to Love	Kimberley White	$9.95
Hart & Soul	Angie Daniels	$8.95
Heart of the Phoenix	A.C. Arthur	$9.95
Heartbeat	Stephanie Bedwell-Grime	$8.95
Hearts Remember	M. Loui Quezada	$8.95
Hidden Memories	Robin Allen	$10.95
Higher Ground	Leah Latimer	$19.95
Hitler, the War, and the Pope	Ronald Rychiak	$26.95
How to Write a Romance	Kathryn Falk	$18.95
I Married a Reclining Chair	Lisa M. Fuhs	$8.95
I'll Be Your Shelter	Giselle Carmichael	$8.95
I'll Paint a Sun	A.J. Garrotto	$9.95
Icie	Pamela Leigh Starr	$8.95
Illusions	Pamela Leigh Starr	$8.95
Indigo After Dark Vol. I	Nia Dixon/Angelique	$10.95
Indigo After Dark Vol. II	Dolores Bundy/ Cole Riley	$10.95
Indigo After Dark Vol. III	Montana Blue/ Coco Morena	$10.95
Indigo After Dark Vol. IV	Cassandra Colt/	$14.95
Indigo After Dark Vol. V	Delilah Dawson	$14.95
Indiscretions	Donna Hill	$8.95
Intentional Mistakes	Michele Sudler	$9.95
Interlude	Donna Hill	$8.95
Intimate Intentions	Angie Daniels	$8.95
It's Not Over Yet	J.J. Michael	$9.95
Jolie's Surrender	Edwina Martin-Arnold	$8.95
Kiss or Keep	Debra Phillips	$8.95
Lace	Giselle Carmichael	$9.95

Other Genesis Press, Inc. Titles (continued)

Last Train to Memphis	Elsa Cook	$12.95
Lasting Valor	Ken Olsen	$24.95
Let Us Prey	Hunter Lundy	$25.95
Lies Too Long	Pamela Ridley	$13.95
Life Is Never As It Seems	J.J. Michael	$12.95
Lighter Shade of Brown	Vicki Andrews	$8.95
Love Always	Mildred E. Riley	$10.95
Love Doesn't Come Easy	Charlyne Dickerson	$8.95
Love Unveiled	Gloria Greene	$10.95
Love's Deception	Charlene Berry	$10.95
Love's Destiny	M. Loui Quezada	$8.95
Mae's Promise	Melody Walcott	$8.95
Magnolia Sunset	Giselle Carmichael	$8.95
Many Shades of Gray	Dyanne Davis	$6.99
Matters of Life and Death	Lesego Malepe, Ph.D.	$15.95
Meant to Be	Jeanne Sumerix	$8.95
Midnight Clear (Anthology)	Leslie Esdaile Gwynne Forster Carmen Green Monica Jackson	$10.95
Midnight Magic	Gwynne Forster	$8.95
Midnight Peril	Vicki Andrews	$10.95
Misconceptions	Pamela Leigh Starr	$9.95
Montgomery's Children	Richard Perry	$14.95
My Buffalo Soldier	Barbara B. K. Reeves	$8.95
Naked Soul	Gwynne Forster	$8.95
Next to Last Chance	Louisa Dixon	$24.95
No Apologies	Seressia Glass	$8.95
No Commitment Required	Seressia Glass	$8.95

Other Genesis Press, Inc. Titles (continued)

No Regrets	Mildred E. Riley	$8.95
Not His Type	Chamein Canton	$6.99
Nowhere to Run	Gay G. Gunn	$10.95
O Bed! O Breakfast!	Rob Kuehnle	$14.95
Object of His Desire	A. C. Arthur	$8.95
Office Policy	A. C. Arthur	$9.95
Once in a Blue Moon	Dorianne Cole	$9.95
One Day at a Time	Bella McFarland	$8.95
One in A Million	Barbara Keaton	$6.99
One of These Days	Michele Sudler	$9.95
Outside Chance	Louisa Dixon	$24.95
Passion	T.T. Henderson	$10.95
Passion's Blood	Cherif Fortin	$22.95
Passion's Journey	Wanda Y. Thomas	$8.95
Past Promises	Jahmel West	$8.95
Path of Fire	T.T. Henderson	$8.95
Path of Thorns	Annetta P. Lee	$9.95
Peace Be Still	Colette Haywood	$12.95
Picture Perfect	Reon Carter	$8.95
Playing for Keeps	Stephanie Salinas	$8.95
Pride & Joi	Gay G. Gunn	$15.95
Pride & Joi	Gay G. Gunn	$8.95
Promises to Keep	Alicia Wiggins	$8.95
Quiet Storm	Donna Hill	$10.95
Reckless Surrender	Rochelle Alers	$6.95
Red Polka Dot in a World of Plaid	Varian Johnson	$12.95
Reluctant Captive	Joyce Jackson	$8.95
Rendezvous with Fate	Jeanne Sumerix	$8.95

Other Genesis Press, Inc. Titles (continued)

Revelations	Cheris F. Hodges	$8.95
Rivers of the Soul	Leslie Esdaile	$8.95
Rocky Mountain Romance	Kathleen Suzanne	$8.95
Rooms of the Heart	Donna Hill	$8.95
Rough on Rats and Tough on Cats	Chris Parker	$12.95
Secret Library Vol. 1	Nina Sheridan	$18.95
Secret Library Vol. 2	Cassandra Colt	$8.95
Secret Thunder	Annetta P. Lee	$9.95
Shades of Brown	Denise Becker	$8.95
Shades of Desire	Monica White	$8.95
Shadows in the Moonlight	Jeanne Sumerix	$8.95
Sin	Crystal Rhodes	$8.95
Small Whispers	Annetta P. Lee	$6.99
So Amazing	Sinclair LeBeau	$8.95
Somebody's Someone	Sinclair LeBeau	$8.95
Someone to Love	Alicia Wiggins	$8.95
Song in the Park	Martin Brant	$15.95
Soul Eyes	Wayne L. Wilson	$12.95
Soul to Soul	Donna Hill	$8.95
Southern Comfort	J.M. Jeffries	$8.95
Still the Storm	Sharon Robinson	$8.95
Still Waters Run Deep	Leslie Esdaile	$8.95
Stolen Kisses	Dominiqua Douglas	$9.95
Stories to Excite You	Anna Forrest/Divine	$14.95
Subtle Secrets	Wanda Y. Thomas	$8.95
Suddenly You	Crystal Hubbard	$9.95
Sweet Repercussions	Kimberley White	$9.95
Sweet Sensations	Gwendolyn Bolton	$9.95

Other Genesis Press, Inc. Titles (continued)

Sweet Tomorrows	Kimberly White	$8.95
Taken by You	Dorothy Elizabeth Love	$9.95
Tattooed Tears	T. T. Henderson	$8.95
The Color Line	Lizzette Grayson Carter	$9.95
The Color of Trouble	Dyanne Davis	$8.95
The Disappearance of Allison Jones	Kayla Perrin	$5.95
The Fires Within	Beverly Clark	$9.95
The Foursome	Celya Bowers	$6.99
The Honey Dipper's Legacy	Pannell-Allen	$14.95
The Joker's Love Tune	Sidney Rickman	$15.95
The Little Pretender	Barbara Cartland	$10.95
The Love We Had	Natalie Dunbar	$8.95
The Man Who Could Fly	Bob & Milana Beamon	$18.95
The Missing Link	Charlyne Dickerson	$8.95
The Mission	Pamela Leigh Starr	$6.99
The Perfect Frame	Beverly Clark	$9.95
The Price of Love	Sinclair LeBeau	$8.95
The Smoking Life	Ilene Barth	$29.95
The Words of the Pitcher	Kei Swanson	$8.95
Three Wishes	Seressia Glass	$8.95
Ties That Bind	Kathleen Suzanne	$8.95
Tiger Woods	Libby Hughes	$5.95
Time is of the Essence	Angie Daniels	$9.95
Timeless Devotion	Bella McFarland	$9.95
Tomorrow's Promise	Leslie Esdaile	$8.95
Truly Inseparable	Wanda Y. Thomas	$8.95
Two Sides to Every Story	Dyanne Davis	$9.95
Unbreak My Heart	Dar Tomlinson	$8.95

Other Genesis Press, Inc. Titles (continued)

Uncommon Prayer	Kenneth Swanson	$9.95
Unconditional Love	Alicia Wiggins	$8.95
Unconditional	A.C. Arthur	$9.95
Until Death Do Us Part	Susan Paul	$8.95
Vows of Passion	Bella McFarland	$9.95
Wedding Gown	Dyanne Davis	$8.95
What's Under Benjamin's Bed	Sandra Schaffer	$8.95
When Dreams Float	Dorothy Elizabeth Love	$8.95
When I'm With You	LaConnie Taylor-Jones	$6.99
Whispers in the Night	Dorothy Elizabeth Love	$8.95
Whispers in the Sand	LaFlorya Gauthier	$10.95
Who's That Lady?	Andrea Jackson	$9.95
Wild Ravens	Altonya Washington	$9.95
Yesterday Is Gone	Beverly Clark	$10.95
Yesterday's Dreams, Tomorrow's Promises	Reon Laudat	$8.95
Your Precious Love	Sinclair LeBeau	$8.95

Order Form

Mail to: Genesis Press, Inc.
P.O. Box 101
Columbus, MS 39703

Name _____
Address _____
City/State _____ Zip _____
Telephone _____

Ship to (if different from above)
Name _____
Address _____
City/State _____ Zip _____
Telephone _____

Credit Card Information
Credit Card # _____ ☐ Visa   ☐ Mastercard
Expiration Date (mm/yy) _____ ☐ AmEx   ☐ Discover

Qty.	Author	Title	Price	Total

Use this order

form, or call

1-888-INDIGO-1

Total for books	
Shipping and handling:	
$5 first two books,	
$1 each additional book	
Total S & H	
Total amount enclosed	

Mississippi residents add 7% sales tax